Born in Aberdeen, Scotland, of a Polish father and Scottish mother, Jennifer Bacia came to Australia as a child.

After finishing her degree at Queensland University she worked in the fields of education, public relations, and corporate management.

She has lived in Rome, London and Los Angeles and has travelled widely in the Far East and former Eastern Bloc countries. She divides her time between Europe and Australia.

As a successful candidate for the Australian Film Television and Radio School, she is also developing her skills as a screen writer.

She is the author of the international best seller *Shadows of Power*, and *Angel of Honour*.

Also by Jennifer Bacia

SHADOWS OF POWER
ANGEL OF HONOUR

WHISPER
FROM THE GODS

JENNIFER BACIA

PAN
AUSTRALIA

For my much loved sister, Suzanne, who uniquely shares the memories and the past – and who through Catherine, Christopher, and Michelle, also offers me the future.

First published 1992 by Pan Macmillan Publishers Australia

This edition published 2001 by Hinkler Books Pty. Ltd.
17-23 Redwood Drive, Dingley, Victoria 3172 Australia

National Library of Australia
cataloguing-in-publication data:

Bacia, Jennifer
Whispers from the gods.

ISBN   1865156280

I. Title.

A823.3

Printed and bound in Australia

PROLOGUE

He called it the Shrine.

It was his secret place. His place of worship. A sanctum where the dream lived on and his fantasies could still come true.

Face flushed with anticipation, the Idolator allowed his eyes to travel slowly over the walls. Her photograph was everywhere, covering every inch of space. He knew that with the flick of a switch he could hear her voice, the voice that never failed to thrill him.

He made his selection from the stack of videos as he had done so often before. He placed the cassette in the machine, then crossed to a small, locked cabinet in the corner of the room. With reverent care he removed a slim cardboard box embossed with the name of an exclusive store.

Breath quickening, the Idolator switched off the overhead light and settled himself in the comfortable low-backed chair. He was ready. Ready for an experience he knew would be almost spiritual in its intensity . . .

A tap of the remote control button and the video began to play. With a grimace of annoyance he fast forwarded, impatient for the object of his desire.

He found the place he was searching for. Sighing with pleasure, he turned up the volume and reached for the box by his side. With trembling fingers he pushed aside the tissue paper and drew out a pair of black silk panties.

The next best thing, he told himself, his eyes fixed on the screen. Not hers, but bought at the same expensive store that had once attracted her custom.

Unzipping his trousers, he drew out his swollen penis and swathed it in the black silk. Then, slowly, his gaze still transfixed by the screen, his hand began its rhythmic movement.

Spellbound as ever by the image before him, he drank in the full luscious mouth, the seductive eyes, the magnificent body. Perspiration beaded his face; his breathing became more ragged as his hand quickened.

'Elizabeth... Elizabeth...' He moaned her name again and again.

And when at last the moment of glorious gratification arrived, the Idolator felt as if he were going to die.

CHAPTER

1

It was the longest forty-eight hours of Tess Jordan's life. All she could do was wait.

In the offices of World Link Studios the tension was palpable. The staff, nervous of the outcome, were desperately trying to maintain an alliance with both camps.

By the second afternoon, Tess could bear it no longer. For the first time in years she left the office early.

As she let herself into her Laurel Canyon home, Lola Santinez appeared from the kitchen. The Mexican housekeeper couldn't hide her surprise. In the three years she had been in Tess Jordan's employ, she had never once seen the hard-working executive return home at this hour.

'So early, Miz Tess . . . ?' Suddenly the housekeeper remembered. Her hand flew to her mouth. 'Miz Tess, you have heard! It is good news, yes?'

Tess Jordan shook her dark head. 'Nothing yet, Lola. They're making me sweat it out. I decided I didn't need an audience while I sweated, that's all.'

Dropping her briefcase by the study door, Tess headed upstairs to change. 'Lola, if the phone rings I'll be in the pool.'

In the bedroom, Tess changed into a black maillot. As

she walked barefoot across the polished wooden floor-boards and handwoven rugs, she felt some of her tension slip away. The house had that effect on her. She had fallen in love with it the first moment she'd seen it almost three years ago. With its aged timbers and rough brickwork, original fireplaces and wide, vine-covered patios, the house had an aura of timelessness and serenity not found in the brash modern mansions which lined the avenues of Beverly Hills. It was exactly what Tess had been looking for, and a six figure salary meant she was able to afford it.

Now, she thought, as she walked out of the house and down the sandstone steps to the pool, the house too was on the line.

With one graceful movement she dived into the shim-mering blue water.

Everything was on the line.

It was a few minutes past nine when the telephone call she'd been waiting for finally came.

Earlier, she'd hardly been able to eat a mouthful of Lola's spicy chicken. Her stomach had been in too much turmoil.

Goddamn it, she thought, it shouldn't matter so much.

But it did. For so many reasons.

'Tess? Mike Havelock. Hope I'm not ringing too late. But I was sure you'd want to know the news as soon as possible.'

'No problem, Mike.' Her voice, thank God, was steady. 'I was just reading.' Dressed in a robe, she was curled up on her bedroom sofa, the usual pile of scripts by her side. No need to tell Mike Havelock that she had registered barely a word of the print before her eyes.

With the direct manner she had already come to appreciate, Mike Havelock got straight to the point. 'As the new owner of World Link Studios, Tess, I'm delighted to offer you the position of Executive President.'

Executive President... The words resounded in Tess's brain and she felt a sudden wonderful giddiness. She'd done it! Mike Havelock had made the decision she'd been praying for!

She started to voice her thanks, then realised her employer was still talking: 'I'll get the attorneys to nail down the details first thing tomorrow. Then perhaps you'll be free to have a celebratory dinner with me and Paula in the evening?'

'That sounds just fine, Mike,' said Tess, marvelling at her own calm. 'And thank you again for having faith in me.'

'I'm a businessman, Tess. I make decisions based on dollars. You know what it's cost me to take on WLS; it's been well documented in the trade. It's Tess Jordan I want because I think she's the one who can put WLS back in the big league again.'

Oh God. She had pulled it off, really pulled it off...

'I won't let you down, Mike.'

They said goodnight and slowly Tess replaced the receiver. Triumph set the adrenalin pumping through her veins. She was far too excited to sit still. Scripts slid to the floor as she rose to her feet, but she barely noticed. She paced the spacious room, her eyes shining.

Executive President... of one of Hollywood's oldest studios. It was the moment for which she had been striving for almost seventeen years. Her every move had been made with ruthless calculation to achieve this pinnacle.

She was well aware that to her industry peers the appointment of Tess Jordan as the first female president of a major — if ailing — studio would mean, first and foremost, status, acclaim, and a breathtaking salary.

Not one of them would believe that none of that was what mattered to Tess.

Flushed with excitement, she caught sight of herself in the ornately framed mirror that hung above the bedroom fireplace. Staring back at her was a woman whose green eyes glittered with fierce determination, whose pale oval face was filled with resolve.

She had done it. Now at last she could keep the promise she had made to herself on her twenty-first birthday — the day she had finally learned the truth.

Her eyes darkened and her hands clenched into fists. *She had climbed the final hurdle. Now nothing was going to stand in her way.*

'Good morning, Miss Jordan,' greeted her bright-eyed secretary as Tess stepped out of the executive elevator.

The formality was indicative of the relationship Tess chose to maintain with her staff. She knew she was considered aloof and distant, but that was how she preferred it. There was danger in a more relaxed approach, danger in the sort of familiarity that could lead to probing personal questions ... Tess had always had too much at risk to allow that.

For the rest of the day she hid her excitement behind the cool professional exterior that had always served her so well. The announcement of her appointment was to be kept under wraps until the end of the week. 'That way,' Mike Havelock had explained, 'we'll make all the week-end editions. So far, apart from yourself, only the Board and the head of Publicity know of my decision. And, of course,' he added, 'Joel Heneke.'

Joel Heneke.

Tess could imagine his bitterness. He had been head of WLS for the last three years — quite a feat in these volatile times. During that period he had presided over flop after flop; but somehow it had always been others who shouldered the blame for Joel Heneke's errors of judgement.

He must have realised the threat Tess represented to him as soon as the figures came in for *First Rites*. Tess had fought long and hard to get Joel Heneke's approval for the project and in the end she had only won, she felt, because he was so certain the movie would fail. No doubt Joel Heneke had reasoned that such a failure would get rid of Tess Jordan — just as he had gotten rid of all the others who might have threatened his command.

But *First Rites* hadn't flopped. It had become one of the successes of the season: not big enough to put WLS back in the black, but judged good enough by its industry peers to receive two Oscar nominations — for best screenplay and best director.

First Rites hadn't won either but its acclaim had merely increased Joel Heneke's animosity towards Tess. Try as he might he could take little credit for WLS's first box-office success in a long while. It was common knowledge in the industry that Heneke had been contemptuous of the project from the start.

'A *woman*'s story, Tess? Not a major male actor in sight? And the lead actress in her late thirties?' Joel Heneke's mouth had curved in a patronising smile. 'Hey, come on, you're having me on, right? Don't you read the surveys? Audiences want action, violence, male heroes.'

They were in his plushly appointed office and Joel Heneke shook his head in disdain as he tossed the treatment back to her.

For a moment Tess was silent as she studied the man in front of her. Joel Heneke was in his early fifties, immaculately groomed, with steel-grey hair and a matching Vandyke. Always sartorially vain, he wore three-piece hand-tailored suits expertly cut to hide his spreading paunch. But nothing could hide his smug arrogance.

Allowing no hint of the anger she felt, Tess answered coolly, 'You've got to read some of the more subtle signs that are coming through on those surveys too, Joel. Our female audiences are changing. It irritates them that only the hero pulls off the deal. They're asking, why not women as leads, as role models? Times are changing. Women want to see their new status reflected on the movie screen. So far, that hasn't happened.'

But it had taken another six months of almost daily battles with Joel Heneke to finally get budget approval for *First Rites*.

And if Tess had thought the success of the movie would make it easier to get her next project off the ground, she was quickly disillusioned. Joel Heneke had been equally disparaging of her proposal for *Public Document*.

'We all get lucky sometime, Tess,' he sneered. 'Just because you touched a chord for a bunch of aging broads with *First Rites*, don't think you've suddenly got the golden touch. Flukes don't happen two in a row, honey.'

This time it was even harder for Tess to bite back her anger at the insulting tone, his belittlement of her success.

But she did. She knew the time hadn't quite yet come for open warfare with Joel Heneke. She had heard the rumours that WLS was looking for a buyer.

Once one of Hollywood's major studios, WLS had been bought four years before by a massive Japanese consortium, whose only drawback appeared to be little knowledge of or interest in the movie-making process. Sensitive to local antagonism towards Japanese owner-ship of such a significant American icon, the new owners had maintained an all-American management team. At its head they placed Joel Heneke. Ramming his way through the executive ranks, Heneke had managed to convince his new Japanese bosses that he was the man they needed to present an acceptable local face to the American public while also understanding the demands of movie-goers. It had taken a string of losses to make the Japanese owners nervously reassess their investment — and come to the patently obvious conclusion that movie-making was not their forte. Quietly, they began to sound out the market for possible buyers.

In a town like LA, such a move could not be kept secret for long, and when Tess heard the rumours she knew she had to be patient for just a little longer. When it finally came, a change in ownership would, she felt sure, create the opportunity she had been waiting for. Then she would be perfectly placed to make a running for Joel Heneke's job. And Heneke knew that every bit as well as she did.

That was why he'd been so opposed to *Public Document*. He couldn't take the chance of allowing Tess a follow-up success.

But the moment Tess had first read the script she knew that *Public Document* was exactly what she was looking for. A courtroom drama, centring on the conflict between a radical female judge and a conservative male attorney, *Public Document* was a natural successor to *First Rites*.

As before, Tess set about the battle to get her project to the screen. Six years of crawling and manoeuvring her way ever closer to the top had honed her negotiating skills. But this time Joel Heneke was intractable. He wasn't about to take the chance that Tess Jordan might consolidate her success.

Later, when the script became a major box office winner for a rival studio, Tess's only consolation lay in the confirmation of her judgement. When the time came, she thought, she would show them all . . .

A few months later when Havelock International negotiated a breathtaking takeover of WLS, Tess knew the opportunity she had awaited so long had finally arrived.

Tess freshened up in the elegant green marble bathroom attached to her office before leaving work. She was due at the Havelocks' before seven. Tess was not one of those Californians who enjoyed the beach, and her reward, at thirty-eight, was an almost totally unlined complexion. Her frantic schedule meant that of necessity her beauty routine had to be kept fast and simple: a slick of soft peach-coloured lipstick to her generous mouth, a dusting of powder and blusher, and a sweep of dark mascara to lashes that were as long and straight as a child's. Now she ran a comb through her shoulder-length dark hair and gave herself a final appraising glance in the full-length mirror. The Azzedine Aläia two-piece cream knit suit was perfect — not too dressy for the office, yet with the addition of a twisted gold necklace and matching earrings, completely suitable for the evening ahead.

An evening, she thought with a sudden rush of adrenalin, when she would do her best to prepare the groundwork for achieving the goal she'd dreamt of for so long.

Despite access to a company limousine and driver, Tess still preferred to drive herself in the distinctive dark green E-type Jaguar which was her pride and joy. She delighted in taking the wheel of a machine built with such attention to craftsmanship.

The traffic was its usual snarl as she headed for Holmby Hills, that elite enclave of the very rich where the air was cooler and supposedly clearer, thanks to the elevation.

The Havelock mansion was in Carolwood Drive, the area's best address. Mike Havelock welcomed her at the towering portico of the Georgian-style mansion.

'Tess,' he smiled and put a hand on her elbow, 'come on in.'

This was their first meeting outside the formality of an office environment. Tess noted the change in her employer; in place of the intense, quick-talking businessman she found a relaxed and less demanding human being. On his home turf Mike Havelock could obviously 'turn off'.

Chatting easily, he led the way past a magnificent curved staircase that rose from the marble-tiled foyer, down a wide, thickly carpeted hall. The combination of wealth and taste was unmistakable — particularly in the elegantly appointed living room. Tess took in the bleached oak flooring overlaid by a stunning Aubusson carpet, the Bechstein grand piano gleaming in one corner, the mix of traditional and modern in the furnishings and the art works which adorned the silk-covered walls. It was a room that didn't appeal to Tess's personal taste but she could still appreciate its elegant grandeur. Mike Havelock, she mused, had come a long way for a man who once owned a small chain of hardware stores.

An exceedingly private individual, he had managed to avoid a high public profile as his empire grew. Even now, after his successful takeover of WLS, the press had managed to ferret out little but the most prosaic of details: a tall, lanky, native Californian of fifty-two, Mike Havelock appeared to have made his fortune through a mixture of hard-headed business acumen and a penchant for taking calculated risks. His only noteworthy feature as far as the media were concerned was his seemingly strict adherence to morality in all his business dealings. As one financial columnist observed, Havelock was 'a tough-minded businessman who appears to have made his money without compromising his ideals'.

'Take a seat, Tess. Paula will join us in a minute. What can I offer you to drink?' Without waiting for her reply, Mike smilingly suggested, 'Champagne would be fitting, don't you think? We certainly have something to celebrate.'

'That'll be fine, Mike.' Tess returned his smile as she sat down in an easy chair.

There must have been a hidden bell, for next moment a smiling manservant entered the room.

'The Bollinger, please, Dominic.'

With a small bow and a murmured response, the man left the room.

Mike Havelock took a seat in the buttercup yellow sofa opposite Tess. 'Now, I — '

He was interrupted as a petite blonde in her late

forties entered the room. Rising once more to his feet, Mike Havelock stretched out a welcoming arm to his wife. 'Honey, come and join us. I'd like you to meet Tess Jordan. Tess . . . this is my wife, Paula.'

Paula Havelock put out a well-manicured hand. 'How very nice to meet you, Ms Jordan. And may I congratulate you on your new appointment. Mike feels sure that you're the best person he could have at the helm of WLS.' Paula Havelock was quietly spoken, but Tess sensed the warmth and sincerity of her words as their hands met.

When the drinks were poured, Mike proposed a toast. 'To our new Executive President and the future of WLS. May our change of direction set the box office on fire!'

Tess felt a flutter inside her as she raised her glass. When she revealed to Mike Havelock what she had in mind, her bright new future might be destroyed before it had even begun.

CHAPTER

2

For a long time after the masseuse had left, Adelle Madigan continued to lie on the padded massage table. Her body felt wonderful, relaxed and glowing, but her mind darted restlessly from one incredible scenario to another. She couldn't remember the last time she had felt so excited — unless it was that day over twenty-five years ago when she had stood beside Tom when he was sworn in as President of the United States.

Everything about that moment was still etched with wondrous clarity in Adelle's mind: the feeling of triumph and giddy expectation, the sense of history, the first intoxicating awareness of her new power...

That night, as she had dressed for the Inaugural Ball in the bare-shouldered Givenchy gown — nothing could have made her wear some lousy American designer on *that* occasion — Adelle had laughed aloud in sheer delight. Laughed at the sheer effrontery that had helped her pull it off. At the sheer guts and hard-headed determination which had transformed poor hand-me-down Adelle Tissot into the First Lady of the United States of America.

It was never beyond my wildest dreams, she had whispered to her reflection in the mirror, her eyes shining with delight. It was exactly what she had planned from the

13

moment she met Tom Madigan and read the ruthless ambition in his handsome face.

From the start Adelle had seen that her best chance lay in charming the old man, the father. Kevin Madigan had arrived in the United States a penniless Irish immigrant, and with single-minded determination had set about making his fortune. While he was a ruthless businessman, Adelle had soon discovered that his weaknesses were women and an overwhelming desire for social acceptance.

With that in mind, Adelle had played the sweet Southern belle for all she was worth, while making reference — oh so casually — to the French Louisiana connection. Kevin Madigan had been impressed — at least with the way Adelle told the story.

In retrospect, Adelle felt sure it was old man Madigan who helped her get his son to the altar so quickly. The day they were married in New York's St Patrick's Cathedral, Adelle had been dating Tom Madigan for a mere six months. She was twenty-one years old.

Eleven years her senior, Tom Madigan had been very different from her usual escorts. With the others, she could tell at once how quickly they were smitten, how heavily they had fallen. Used to men tumbling head over heels for her, Adelle took it for granted, loved to see how far she could push and tease them, to what lengths they would go to satisfy her whims. But when at last she had managed to wangle an introduction to the handsome eligible scion of the Madigan clan, she had seen none of the obvious signs of infatuation. Nothing had happened in those cool blue eyes as she tried her usual approach.

It was then Adelle knew she was going to have to be not only patient, but very very clever ...

She had won in the end, of course, as she had been so sure she would. They made a dashing young couple: he, the handsome charismatic young Senator with a passion for liberal reform, she, the beautiful young wife from a 'well-to-do' French Louisiana family.

The press, thank God, were less intrusive then, and Adelle's vague references to her antecedents were easily accepted. Since leaving New Orleans as a self-possessed and ambitiously self-seeking eighteen year old, Adelle had worked assiduously at establishing an appropriate background. When it was inevitably assumed that she was one of *the* Tissots, the wealthy and multitudinous family whose name was synonymous with the industrial and cultural development of New Orleans, she saw no reason to correct the misconception; no reason to reveal that, to the contrary, she had grown up in a two-room cold-water tenement, raised by a mother who very early on had recognised the power of her daughter's beauty and personality and set about instilling expectations far beyond her own.

'At least the bastard who fathered you passed on his good looks, Della.' It was a rare reference by Janet Tissot to the man who had made her pregnant. 'Keep your legs crossed until the right one comes along, honey, and you ain't goin' to end up doing other folk's stinkin' laundry like I've had to. Why, with your looks, there's every chance you can land some fancy doctor, or lawyer, or somesuch.'

Later, coolly studying her perfect profile in the mottled bathroom mirror, Adelle knew she was going to set her sights higher than that. Much higher.

Arriving in Washington, she had eked out her savings until finally landing a job as a researcher on Capitol Hill. 'I wanted a *real* job,' she insisted to all those impertinent enough to wonder aloud what a Tissot was doing off her home turf. 'In this day and age a girl should do more than just lunch and shop, don't you think?'

Yet her 'job' gave her plenty of time for both — as well as catapulting her into the circles that mattered. And among all those jostling for power, it was Tom Madigan who stood out. It didn't take Adelle long to recognise that the young Californian Senator was a young man in a hurry, a young man every bit as ruthlessly ambitious as herself, who was going straight to the top, riding on his family fortune. She decided she wanted Tom Madigan.

He didn't make it easy. Tom Madigan was a magnet to women. He knew it, and made the most of his boundless opportunities. But Adelle bided her time and worked on the old man . . . and just three days after her twenty-first birthday was signing the register in St Patrick's Cathedral as Mrs Tom Madigan.

Not that the other women went away after the marriage. Adelle would have had to be blind not to see that. But she was sure Tom would never leave her, would never threaten his political future. Now, as she recalled those times, her eyes darkened. Only once had she sensed a danger. Real danger. But that too had passed.

The role of Senator's wife was one Adelle played to perfection. Yet all the while she was acutely aware of being watched and studied by those whose job it was to do such things. Twelve years later, on the day her husband won his Party's nomination as Presidential candidate, an ecstatic Adelle knew she had passed all the tests. At the same time too, she realised that the looks and charm which had got her so far would now have to be used to woo America at large.

It was the sort of challenge for which Adelle Madigan felt more than a match.

In only five short years the dream was shattered. Blown apart by the bullet that ripped through her husband's heart.

The assassination occurred just weeks into Tom Madigan's second Presidential term. In Chicago for an official two-day visit, he had been shot down by a crazed gunman on the steps of his hotel and had died instantly.

Adelle had been with her hairdresser when the shattering news reached her. Her first concern had been for her sixteen year old son.

'Who's going to tell Robbie? Who's going to tell poor Robbie?' Tonelessly, she repeated the words over and over, staring blankly at the ashen faces around her.

Breaking the news to the son she adored was the hardest thing Adelle ever had to face. She would have done anything to spare him the shock and grief. For Adelle had admitted to herself long ago that whatever feeling she might once have felt for his father had since been transferred tenfold to her beautiful loving son. Her love for her son was the only pure untainted emotion Adelle had ever known.

But she knew too the depth of Robbie's feelings for his father. At sixteen, he had lived in the White House for over four years. He understood the responsibilities his father shouldered, saw the day-to-day problems faced by a head of state, and his admiration and respect for Tom were obvious. How, Adelle wondered fearfully, would he cope with his murder?

In the end, they both survived: the son who had lost a father he worshipped, and the wife who had been robbed of her glittering future.

Her glittering future . . .

Adelle eased herself up from the padded table. Slipping on a rose-coloured robe, she entered her opulent marble bathroom with its mirrored walls and soft flattering lights.

Leaning close to the glass, the widow of Tom Madigan studied her reflection: the strong bone structure, the large luminous eyes, the aristocratic nose. With satisfaction she noted the firm, smooth complexion, the sharp jawline, and blessed again the day she had heard the name Raoul Mendhellson.

It was almost eight months since her most recent operation and as always, Doctor Mendhellson's renovations had been contrived with skill and subtlety. Adelle had had her first operation — an eye-lift — at forty-two. Now, thanks to three follow-up visits to the clinic outside Geneva — more like a five-star hotel than a hospital, with a staff guaranteed utterly discreet — Adelle could still pass for a woman in her forties. Even *she* found it hard to believe she had 'celebrated' her sixtieth birthday almost nine months before.

She had always photographed stunningly. The press had never lost their interest in her, and now with Robbie's candidature finally confirmed, the media frenzy could only gather momentum.

A thrill of delicious anticipation ran down Adelle's spine. *It'll be just like the first time*, she thought. *Everything — the fame, the glamour, the power — would be just as it had been twenty-five years ago.*

For Adelle had no doubt that the Madigan name would once more work its magic and her son would follow his father into the White House.

Nothing, and no one, could prevent that.

After a light lunch, she placed a call to her daughter-in-law.

'All OK for this evening, Sara?' There were no endearments between them. Neither felt comfortable with that.

'Sure, Adelle. Everything's under control.'

Adelle knew it would be. Sara Madigan never left anything to chance. From the start she'd had a single-minded dedication to her husband's political ambitions.

With her scrubbed plain looks and lack of style, Sara Madigan was a stark contrast to her famous mother-in-law. But from their first meeting the older woman had recognised the intelligence and political nous that would make Sara Conroy the perfect political match for her son.

As a result, Adelle had done everything she could to encourage the liaison between Robbie and the petite, auburn-haired daughter of high-profile millionaire Walter

Conroy. The fact that Conroy had spent two terms as Governor of Texas during his daughter's formative years had given Sara first-hand experience of campaigning and an understanding of the political process. Adelle felt certain her daughter-in-law would not be intimidated by the role of First Lady.

'We couldn't have a better team working for us, Adelle,' said Sara with her usual optimism. 'None of them doubts that Rob will make it into the White House.'

'Why should they?' Adelle answered with unshake-able confidence.

The atmosphere in the room was electric. The meeting of party managers, fund raisers, and aides was taking place in the spacious living room of Robert Madigan's Beverly Hills home. The group of almost a dozen men listened intently to the handsome Californian Senator who would, they believed without doubt, sweep the Democrats to power at the forthcoming Presidential elections.

Tall and dark, with a strong square jaw and intense Irish blue eyes, Robert Madigan was the image of his father. At thirty-seven, he had been a Senator for almost ten years and his credentials as his Party's nominee were first class: he carried the Madigan name, he was backed by Madigan money, and his record in the legislature was impressive.

As he addressed those gathered around him, Robert Madigan knew his listeners were absolutely certain he would be the next President of the United States. They were positive he was the man who would re-establish the strength and morale of the Democrats.

For most of his adult life, Robert Madigan had felt the pressure of other people's expectations, felt the burden of responsibility to follow in his father's footsteps. He represented a second chance for all those who had seen the dream cut tragically short. The chance of seeing the Madigan name work its old magic and return the party to its golden age.

Robert Madigan had bowed obediently to his fate. From the time of the tragedy, his every step, his every move, had led inexorably to this moment. He had realised very early on that the choice was not his. His destiny had been marked out for him by the name he carried.

Only once had he dared to voice his doubts, to suggest that what was desired by so many might not be what he, Robert Madigan, wanted for himself. For he had been old enough to understand the pressures the Presidency had placed on his father, to realise the sacrifices, the dangers . . .

Twelve years later, he still remembered vividly his mother's reaction to that singular admission of doubt. Her features had turned to stone, the flesh tightening over the bones. Two spots of colour high on her cheekbones were all that broke the whiteness of her face. When at last she spoke, it was in a voice he had never heard her use before, a voice as sharp and cold as steel.

'You're Tom Madigan's son, Robert. You have a duty. There is no choice.'

They never spoke of it again.

Sara Madigan's eyes shone as she looked at her husband and listened to his proposal for the reform of a health system that had put medical care out of the reach of hundreds of thousands of ordinary Americans. It was a topic they had discussed endlessly during the months leading up to the campaign and much of the final proposal was based on Sara's own analysis.

Masters Degrees in Political Science and Public Administration had afforded Sara Madigan the ability to grasp and articulate a wide range of issues. It was the sort of background that could easily have led to a political career of her own but Sara Madigan had chosen instead to throw her full support behind her husband's political future.

They had married almost sixteen years ago. At the

time, if she had been less thick-skinned, Sara might have been hurt by the tabloid response to her marriage; at the cruel questioning as to what the handsome only son of Tom Madigan had seen in the less than glamorous Sara Conroy.

Over the years the popular press had rarely let up, criticising Sara's short, careless curls, her perfunctory use of make-up, her lack of interest in fashion. Invariably comparisons had been drawn with her mother-in-law, but Sara had never had any desire to emulate Adelle's glamour and chic. In the beginning Adelle had made a few subtle overtures regarding her daughter-in-law's image but in the face of Sara's obvious disinterest, had soon admitted defeat. Sara knew that Adelle was clever enough to see that while her son might not have married a fashion plate, he had something much more valuable: a wife who was as determined as Adelle herself to see him take up residence in the White House.

'Now this final point,' Robert Madigan continued, 'is something I might let Sara explain as she was the primary mover of the proposal.'

With a quick smile at her husband, Sara Madigan took over, launching into a quick overview of a particular aspect of the proposed health bill. She was an effective speaker and as he saw the intensity in her animated features, the shine in her grey-blue eyes, it occurred to Rob Madigan — not for the first time — that his wife would have made an equally effective candidate as himself. Instead, Sara had chosen to support his ambitions.

The marriage was a good one. Their daughter, Jessica, was almost nine; when three other pregnancies had ended in miscarriage, it was Sara who had more easily accepted that they would be parents of an only child.

'It just means I'll have more time and energy to help you, Rob,' she had stated with her customary pragmatism.

Sara Madigan rarely let anything get her down, and her husband drew freely on her optimism and enthusiasm. While he had dated women much more attractive, Robert Madigan had never regretted his decision to make Sara Conroy his wife.

While on the surface it might seem as if his mother had little in common with her unglamorous daughter-in-law, Robert knew that Adelle had given her wholehearted approval to the match. She had been quick to recognise in Sara Conroy those qualities that would assist in fulfilling the Madigan destiny.

'At least that's the way I see it . . . And you agree, don't you, Rob?'

Robert Madigan realised his wife was looking at him expectantly. He had allowed his attention to wander.

'Yes, yes, sure, Sara. That's my view entirely. But maybe the others . . . ?' He raised an enquiring eyebrow at the dozen or so grey-suited men who were spread around the living room.

'With all respect, Rob, I think that particular aspect needs a lot more discussion before the campaign gets into top gear.' Larry Brandt just managed to keep the distaste he felt for Sara Madigan out of his voice as he ignored her to address her husband.

As the former campaign strategist for Tom Madigan, Brandt was part of the old team — men now in their fifties and early sixties who had come together again to make their long-held dream come true: to see another Madigan in the White House.

Just over average height, with a tough, wiry physique and thinning hair, Larry Brandt had been credited with engineering Tom Madigan's two terms in office. After the assassination, he had dropped out of the political game for a number of years, moving restlessly between various corporate posts. But when the invitation came to rehone his talents in an attempt to put another Madigan in the White House, Larry Brandt's ego wouldn't let him say no. He had missed his brief, shining hour of power and fame.

Sara Madigan sensed Larry Brandt's dislike — and the feeling was mutual. Brandt might be a brilliant tactician, but as far as she was concerned, he was also one of those out-of-touch men who refused to see that women no longer had 'a place' to be kept in.

Yet nothing in her manner betrayed her feelings as she stood beside her husband to farewell their visitors. The only thing that mattered, after all, was that Rob's run for the presidency was successful.

Nothing must be allowed to get in the way of that.

'*Never, never* let me see you doing that again!'

Spittle flew from Anne Conroy's lips as she screamed at the startled maid. Newly employed, the girl had been on the marble-floored patio tidying up after the luncheon party. She'd been about to toss out the bowls of half-eaten salad, when she had been confronted by the red-faced rage of her employer.

'My husband and I didn't get rich by indulging in such shameful waste! Didn't anyone inform you of my explicit instructions that leftovers are to be saved in this house?'

'No, ma'am,' the girl answered respectfully enough, although inwardly she was cursing her crazy bitch of an employer. The dumb broad, the wife of one of the richest men in Texas, was losing it over a couple of bowls of wilting lettuce.

'Well, you know now!' Breathing heavily, Anne Conroy turned on her heel and stormed back into the house. It was almost four and the luncheon had quite tired her out. She didn't entertain often. Entertaining cost money and Anne Conroy had better things to do with her money than that. Money was her power, her secret weapon . . . against the conspiracy.

Passing through the living room, she took pride in the fact that the drapes were still the originals. Like the carpet beneath her feet, they had been fitted when she and Walter had bought the mansion in Dallas's Turtle Creek Row almost ten years previously. Sure, there was a bit of wear and tear, the odd stain, but Anne Conroy didn't see that as an excuse to spend her precious dollars.

And Walter didn't care how the place looked. Her mouth twisted sourly. He barely spent enough time there to notice. The last eight months had been the worst of all. Almost every weekend she'd spent on her own.

Anne Conroy's face grew tight. It had happened before, but never like this. These days he barely bothered with excuses. That's why Anne knew it was serious.

And now she knew who it was. Thanks to some sleaze-ball private investigator whose fees had been an outrage.

Eleanor Benson. Divorcee. Blonde, pretty, thirty-two.

Anne Conroy knew it was just a matter of time. As soon as Sara was safely ensconced in the White House, as soon as there was no danger of a scandal that might in any way cost his son-in-law votes, Walter was going to leave his dumb, do-nothing wife for a younger woman.

Well, Walter was in for a surprise.

In her bedroom, she undressed and hung the floral, button-through dress carefully on a hanger. Bought at a sale almost five years ago, it still had a lot of wear in it. Then, wrapping herself in a chain-store cotton robe, the wife of one of Texas's richest men decided to grab a quick nap before she went down to supervise the preparations for the evening meal.

That's all Walter considered her good for, she thought as her head touched the pillow — an empty-headed hostess who kept the domestic wheels turning. But it was Sara he adored, Sara with her diplomas and degrees, with her sharp brain and political nous to match his own.

The sour taste of disgust filled Anne Conroy's mouth.

God, it was obscene the way those two carried on. Father and daughter . . . A relationship so close and devoted that Anne had long ago felt herself totally excluded.

Her eyes closed. They thought she was stupid, good for nothing but keeping house. Well, when the time came, they'd learn just how wrong they both were.

Walter Conroy was a frightened man.

The last time he could ever remember being frightened was when he was eleven years old and waiting for his father to come home and thrash the living daylights out of him. On that occasion he had used his father's cherished fishing rod without permission and it had ended up at the bottom of the Robinsons' dam. Walter had felt physically sick at the thought of his father's wrath.

Almost as sick as he felt now, fifty-three years later, as he read the letter lying before him on the magnificent cedar desk.

He couldn't believe it had come to this. Couldn't believe that after a lifetime of achievement and success, he could lose it all.

With a clean white handkerchief he wiped a film of sweat off his balding forehead and pushed himself to his feet. His height and powerful build added to the usual rich man's aura of confidence and command. Walter Conroy towered over normal men just as he towered over his massive business empire. But now it was all at risk. The letter he had just read could mean the end of everything. Walter knew the only thing he had going for him was time. If he could play for that then there was a way out.

With his son-in-law in the White House, Walter Conroy knew he would be safe.

Dry lips moving silently, the owner of Conroy Aircraft Corporation vowed to himself that nothing must stand in the way of Robert Madigan becoming the next President of the United States.

Nothing.

CHAPTER

3

❛... and of course my aim is to ensure WLS reclaims its position as a major player in the industry.'

Flanked by the studio's lawyers and publicity personnel, Tess faced the barrage of questions from the crowd. In a town where the male prerogative had prevailed for so long, the first female studio boss was a decidedly newsworthy item.

'Ms Jordan, will your appointment bring a particularly female focus to future WLS productions?' The question came from a ruggedly attractive male reporter in the front row. He was dressed in jeans and his thick dark hair curled over the collar of his casual shirt.

Her reply was unequivocal. 'With women providing an ever increasing proportion of the viewing public it makes sense to provide the sort of entertainment they can relate to.'

A reporter from the *LA Times* shot the next question. 'Can you give us an idea of some of the immediate projects we can expect to see from a revamped WLS?'

'We have numerous productions on the drawing board. I can promise you WLS is about to give new meaning to the word "competition".'

Tess's answers were delivered with the cool composure that was automatic now; no one watching her could have guessed at the real person under that calm exterior.

Her professional background, the steps that had taken her to the top were well documented. To all appearances, Tess Jordan was the classic career woman: thirty-eight, never married, all her energies consumed by a single-minded ambition to achieve her goals.

Only Tess knew that ambition was the least of her motivations.

Over the next six months it took all Tess's self-discipline to hide her impatience. It was important, she knew, to establish the right sort of relationship with Mike Havelock. Only when he had come to trust both her motives and her judgement would she feel the time was right to drop her bombshell.

In the meantime she was working harder than ever, relishing her new-found professional freedom. After the difficulties of being answerable to Joel Heneke — whose resignation had been a foregone conclusion — it was a heady feeling which nothing, not even her crushing work load, could diminish.

She enjoyed an easy relationship with Mike Havelock. His wide-ranging business interests meant he was happy to leave the day-to-day decisions to Tess and her team, concerning himself only with those matters where he felt his input was valid. As she got to know him better, Tess's liking and respect for her new boss grew.

Then at last she could wait no longer. It was just two days before Christmas when she decided it was time to make the move she had been planning for so long. The timing, she figured, would allow Mike Havelock the holiday break to decide what to do.

Tess took a deep breath as she reached for the phone to arrange the appointment. She was about to take the first step to ensure that the sinners paid for their sins . . .

Mike Havelock had scheduled their meeting for the end of the day. In the six months since his takeover of WLS it had been proved to him time and time again how right he had been to appoint Tess Jordan as President. Her background and experience in the industry were such that Mike rarely questioned her judgement. He vaguely recalled that her stepfather had been an attorney specialising in actors' contracts. That, no doubt, he decided, was what had wakened her interest in the industry.

As he waited for Tess to arrive he ran over the figures in front of him once again. They showed the results of recent WLS releases, projects that were too far down the line to cancel or change when Havelock International had taken over.

There was nothing in the figures to gladden Mike Havelock's heart. He knew it wasn't going to be easy; he'd never kidded himself about that. The turnaround would come when WLS found that one special project, that unique outstanding property that would send the press rushing to their PCs and have the public lining up around the block. Mike Havelock knew they had to find it quickly.

There was a tap on the door.

'Come in, Tess.' With a weary smile, the owner of WLS rose to his feet. 'If your day's been anything like mine, you could do with a coffee too.'

'Thanks, Mike. I really don't think I remembered to eat lunch, to tell you the truth.'

He looked at her more closely as his secretary brought their coffee. There were shadows of fatigue around her eyes and he didn't think he was imagining that she appeared to have lost weight: she was slim to the point of fragility.

'I hope you'll find time to relax over Christmas, Tess. You've been working yourself like a demon.' Mike Havelock's tone revealed his concern. 'Have you got anything planned?'

Tess slid her gaze away from his. 'Oh, the usual. You know.'

The usual. Empty hours to fill with the briefcase full

of work she would be taking home. No family to share the holiday with. No boyfriend. The men she met were strong, intelligent achievers, yet they were invariably threatened by her ever-increasing power and prestige. The relationships never had a chance.

But a lack of personal life was just one of the many sacrifices she'd had to make to get to the top. And now, Tess thought with a little stab of fear, she was about to find out if it had all been worth it.

She slid a thick folder across the desk. 'Mike, this is something I very much hope you'll have the time to read over the holiday. It's a project I've been interested in for a long time, something I'm quite certain will send WLS straight to the top again in this town.'

She saw the interest flicker in his face. 'Only problem is, it's going to take someone with real courage to run with it . . . '

The owner of WLS read the open challenge in those beautiful green eyes.

As the E-type Jag turned out of the studio gates, the watcher in the dark blue Lincoln quickly switched on the ignition.

The distinctive British sports car was easy to tail and the driver of the Lincoln kept it in sight in the evening traffic. He was not surprised when at last the car turned into the leafy environs of Laurel Canyon. The magazine article he'd read, the one now folded in the back section of his wallet, had given no clue to her address, but had mentioned the distinctive sports car.

She had turned off the winding road and was slowing at a pair of security gates set between the trees. The man knew this was his chance.

As the gates began to swing open, he stepped on the gas, shooting the Lincoln over the kerbing, half-blocking the E-type's access to the drive beyond.

He saw her startled expression as he threw open his

door. 'Tess! Tess, it is you, isn't it?' He tapped on the driver's window.

Tess stared transfixed into the face she had never forgotten. A face from another time, another place . . .

'Nick . . . ' she breathed.

Oh God.

CHAPTER

4

The child waited till she was sure they were asleep.

It didn't take long. Donald and Leah Franklin had come home in their usual inebriated state after an afternoon spent at the track.

After six months Tess knew the routine. Whether they won or lost, the Franklins drank — in shrill excitement or vile black temper. Quick to pick their mood, the children knew to keep out of the way when the latter was the case.

Only tonight Tess hadn't been quick enough.

Donald Franklin had lashed out at her on the flimsiest excuse. And this time the beating had been particularly vicious. For a moment, Tess had feared it wouldn't end until the flesh had been stripped from her buttocks. She had screamed an apology for her error, begged to be forgiven.

But Donald Franklin had shown no mercy. 'Ah'm gonna learn you that when ah say somethin's to be done it's done right. You hear me, Tess?' His small eyes glinted as he raised his arm above his bristly head. 'You don't know when you're well off, girl, that's your probl'm. A roof over your head, food in your belly, schoolin' . . . Ah gotta teach ya t'appreciate your good fortune, Tess. That's what ah gotta do . . . ' And with a grunt he brought the strap down on her naked flesh.

Donald Franklin weighed over ninety kilos and seemed to be permanently hungry. Tess's error was to be running late with his usual Saturday night repast of a mountainous mound of french fries and a plateful of baloney sandwiches.

But that evening the twins had been more than usually troublesome to get into the bath, and Leah Franklin had warned what would happen if the stack of ironing was still there when she got home . . .

For Tess, punishment had been inevitable that evening.

When Donald Franklin had finally vented his temper, Tess could barely crawl out of the room. Her flesh burned and the throbbing in her right eye told her it would soon turn black.

She fled to the cramped cheerless room she shared with the twins and threw herself on the bed, trying to muffle the sound of her crying against the grimy pillow.

'*It's not fair*,' she sobbed. '*It's just not fair.*'

But then nothing had been fair since the day eight years ago when her mother had walked out . . .

It had started happily enough.

From the moment she'd opened her eyes that morning, she had felt a warm sense of excitement. It had taken her a second or two to remember why.

Of course! Her mother's birthday! Throwing off the covers, Tess leapt out of bed and ran to a cupboard in the corner of the room. Pushing aside a couple of cardboard cartons, she found the gift she had wrapped so carefully. She'd thought for a long time about what her mother might like, and in the end had decided to part with one of her very favourite possessions. She just knew her mother would love it.

She raced through the house, and burst into the kitchen.

'Well, well, Tess,' her mother smiled. 'I thought you were going to sleep till noon.'

'Oh, no, Mom! Not today!' She had the gift hidden behind her back. Then she caught sight of the huge bunch of flowers arranged in a vase at the end of the table. 'Oh, Mom, what pretty flowers! Who sent them? Are they for your birthday?'

'Yes. Your Aunt Francie never forgets. Aren't they beautiful?'

Tess could barely remember Aunt Francie. She didn't visit often but always sent plenty of wonderful presents — even when it wasn't anybody's birthday.

Then she remembered her own gift and with a triumphant flourish, produced it from behind her back. 'Happy birthday, Mom! I love you a lot.'

'Why, honey, how sweet of you! Whatever could it be?' Her mother carefully untied the paper and string. 'A mink coat, perhaps? A golden crown?'

Tess giggled in excited impatience. She loved it when her mother teased. It was a game they often played together. There were just the two of them; her father had died before Tess was born so Tess had never really missed him. Sometimes however, her mother seemed sad about it, and then Tess would try her best to cheer her up. 'But we don't really need anyone else, do we, Mom?' Circling her arms around her mother's neck, she would look into her sad brown eyes. 'We have each other and I love you more than anybody else ever could.'

'Oh, Tess!' Her mother was staring down at the red plastic heart on its green ribbon and Tess heard the catch in her voice. 'Your favourite locket! Surely you don't mean it for me?'

The locket had been a giveaway in the bottom of a box of cereal and it *was* Tess's favourite. That was why it seemed the perfect gift.

Pleased by her mother's reaction, she nodded her head emphatically. 'Yes, Mom, it's for you. Because I love you, I want you to have it.'

There were tears in her mother's eyes as she hugged

Tess close and kissed her. 'Thank you, my darling, it's very very special. I'll keep it always.'

That same evening, her mother disappeared from her life.

For a long time Tess refused to believe it.

'You gotta accept what you've been told, honey.' As she stood in the sunshine watching the group of playing children, the woman in the striped uniform allowed a touch of irritation to creep into her voice. After three months she was getting tired of answering the same questions. 'Your ma's not coming back. That's why you're here.'

Here. A dreary two-storey stone building on the outskirts of town; a bedroom shared with five other strangers; and loud-voiced women who seemed to be always giving orders.

On the morning of her arrival, Tess was told that St Beatrice's was an orphanage. A place, it was explained, where children lived who had no mother or father to care for them...

'But I *have* got a mother!' Tess screamed tearfully at the grey-haired woman who sat behind the enormous polished desk. 'My mother loves me. She'd never, never leave me!'

The woman known as Matron exchanged meaningful looks with the two welfare officials who had handled the case. A pity, of course, but in time the child would forget. And that would be for the best.

But Tess never forgot. Never forgot the sense of betrayal and abandonment.

The anger burned deep inside her for the mother she had loved who had tossed her aside...

Terrible Tess they called her. Wild. A rebel. Uncontrollable.

As time passed, Tess was shunted in and out of more

than a dozen different foster homes. Part of the problem was the unquenchable pain caused by her mother's abandonment. Tess discovered that, in some strange way, hitting out at those around her helped ease her suffering. Why should other people be happy, she reasoned angrily, when she was so miserable?

But her rebellion also stemmed from a growing awareness of the motives of those who took her into their homes. The Franklins were a case in point. It hadn't taken Tess long to understand that the government welfare cheques provided the couple's main incentive for foster parenthood.

At almost fourteen, Tess was the eldest of the four children currently in their care. With the heavy domestic load she was made to bear, Tess soon realised she was also a source of unpaid labour to the scheming couple.

The brutal beating was the last straw.

As she listened through the paper-thin walls to the chorus of snores from Donald and Leah Franklin, Tess knew the moment for action had come.

Not daring to switch on the light in case she woke the twins, she slipped out of bed and dressed in the dark. Making her way carefully down the hallway, she opened the latch on the kitchen door and let herself out of the shabby clapboard house.

Thankful for the faint light of the moon, Tess picked her way across the overgrown yard. The rotting garden shed was never locked. Who would be interested in stealing the ancient rusting lawnmower or the half-empty tins of stiffening paint? In all the six months she had been with the Franklins, Tess had never seen either of them enter the place. That's why it was perfect.

Running her hand over a dusty shelf, Tess felt for the torch she had placed there. She shone its narrow beam behind the pile of crumbling bricks and found what she was looking for.

The cheap vinyl overnight bag was exactly where she

had left it. She zipped it open and checked the contents: one change of clothes — and the brown paper package bound with rubber bands.

Tess had no need to count the money it contained. She knew exactly how much was there. Sixty-eight dollars: money stolen, a few dollars at a time, when the Franklins had come home lucky from the track. Counting on the fact that in their drunken euphoria Donald and Leah Franklin would have no exact recollection of their winnings, Tess had slowly built up her cache.

Never had she felt a moment's guilt. Not when she thought of how she'd been treated by those charged with her welfare.

Her goal had been to have one hundred dollars before making her escape.

But she couldn't bear it any longer.

The coach schedule was already imprinted on her memory. She knew that at ten past midnight she could catch the Greyhound as it passed through Walkerville, three miles away.

Clutching her precious bag closely against her, Tess hurried off in the direction of the highway. She knew she hadn't a moment to lose.

Sam Howard was dreaming.

He was dreaming of the house he'd buy in Palm Springs when he won the lottery; of how he'd give Rita and the kids the life they deserved. Maids, butlers, gardeners, a swimming pool, and a tennis court for Jody who, they said, showed promise, but who'd be lucky if her pa could find the dough to pay for the next season's lessons . . .

'Jesus H. Christ!' Swearing under his breath, Sam Howard slammed on the brakes and brought the huge semi to a grinding halt. His reverie forgotten, he wound down the cabin window and called to the figure in the darkness. 'Hey! You all right out there?'

Tess stood stock-still trying to make a snap judgement. There had been nowhere to hide on the side of the highway and she'd been caught in the blinding glare of the truck's headlights like a rabbit in a spotlight.

The man was climbing out of the cabin now, walking back towards her. Tess felt her heart flop in her chest. They were all alone...

Sam Howard saw her fright. 'Hey, calm down, honey. I won't hurt you. Just wonderin' what a kid your age is doin' on the open road this time of night.' He saw the overnight bag. 'You headin' somewhere special?'

Tess nodded. 'Y-yeah.' Her tongue felt stuck to the roof of her mouth. 'I'm going to Walkerville. Can — can you give me a lift?' Something in the man's tone, the look of real concern on his unshaven face, told her she could trust him.

She sat ramrod stiff and silent in the seat beside him, hoping he wouldn't ask any questions.

But Sam Howard, father of five, was curious to know more. He gave her a sideways glance. 'You catchin' the midnight Greyhound in Walkerville?'

'Yeah.' Not too difficult to guess that, Tess figured.

'Where you headin' for?'

'Scarsdale.' Better to lie, she thought.

'You got family there?'

'An aunt.'

'So why you gotta go at this time of night? Too safe in the daytime for you?'

Tess wished he'd shut up. She didn't want to answer any more of his stupid questions. She sat in tight-lipped silence.

'You're takin' off from home, right?' When again she didn't answer, the man persisted: 'Honey, think it over. I got kids; I know how things can get outta hand sometimes. But home can't be all that bad; not compared to what can happen to a kid roamin' around in the dark by herself.'

'He molested me.'

'What did you say?' Sam Howard's grip tightened on the steering wheel.

'My stepfather molested me. I ain't goin' back.'

The lie shut him up.

They got to Walkerville just in time. As she turned to say a curt thanks, Sam Howard saw the beginning of the black eye. Jesus, that sonofabitch...

He drove away thanking the Lord he'd been the one to pick her up.

In the starkly lit depot, Tess hurriedly paid for her ticket. Fifteen of her precious dollars already gone.

Just minutes later, she was following the two other tired looking passengers out to the yard as the coach drew in.

Her heart leapt as she caught sight of the illuminated sign above the windscreen.

New York.

The words conjured up a dream city she had only heard about and seen on TV. A place where excitement and adventure were part of everyday life. A place where she could leave the past behind.

She leapt up the step and the automatic door hissed closed behind her.

CHAPTER

5

The woman raised her voice above the noise of the lunchtime diners.

'How old are ya?' Her irritation showed. Her goddamn period was killing her and that no-good scum in the kitchen had screwed up two of her orders.

'Sixteen.' Tess tried to keep her voice steady as she told the lie. She was tall for her age and hoped the chain-store cosmetics would make her appear older.

'You done this sort of work before?' The woman raised an overplucked eyebrow in Tess's direction as she clumsily stacked her tray with dirty dishes.

'Y-yes.' How difficult could it be to wait tables? 'And I'm strong and — and very reliable.'

Tess could hear the desperation in her voice. She had only eighteen dollars to her name and just that morning she'd had to relinquish her bed at the YWCA. For three days now she'd been tramping the streets looking for work. Without success.

Suddenly New York appeared more frightening than exciting.

'Take my word for it, honey, try somethin' else.' The woman threw the words over her shoulder as she headed towards the kitchen with her overflowing tray.

'But — '

Tess knew it was no use. Like everyone else she'd spoken to in New York, no one cared about her problem. Blinking back tears, she turned and pushed her way out of the crowded diner. For the first time she began to wonder if she had done the wrong thing in running away.

But no, she admonished herself fiercely, she wasn't going to think like that. She had made her decision. She would stick with it. Someone, somewhere would *have* to give her a job.

By the end of the day Tess was exhausted and totally dispirited. The story had been the same everywhere — one of two reactions: a flat knockback, or a half-hearted offer to 'take her name and number in case something came up'.

But I need something now! Today! Tess felt like screaming at the closed-off, disinterested faces, while a burning envy overcame her for those with a safe secure haven in this awesome metropolis.

By seven, hunger was gnawing at her belly. She hadn't eaten since the evening before and knew she would have to spend some of her meagre funds.

Pushing her way through the stream of evening commuters she stopped at a kerbside hot dog stand. It seemed as if hot dogs were all she'd eaten since arriving in New York. But they were tasty and, more importantly, cheap.

It happened as she opened her purse under the gleam of the streetlight.

A sharp shove in the small of her back.

Tess lost her balance and fell to her knees. Then, to her horror, she saw a hand reach down to scoop up her purse lying on the sidewalk beside her.

'NO! STOP! *No!*'

Scrambling to her feet, she caught sight of the tall thin youth shoving his way through the crowds.

Instinctively, driven by anger and despair, Tess set off in hot pursuit. How dare he! How dare he take the last of her money! Tears of rage rolled down her cheeks, as she wove a passage through the busy streets. No one was going to rob her that easily!

Gasping for breath, she managed to keep the thief in her sights. Then, just when she felt she couldn't keep up the pace a moment longer, she saw him dodge down an alley to his right.

Vaguely aware that the streets were meaner now, the crowds not as well dressed, Tess reached the entrance to the narrow lane. She saw no lights or sign of life. But nothing was going to deter her now. Stumbling in the darkness, she moved as quickly as she dared. There were high brick walls on either side of her. The youth seemed to have disappeared. As her eyes filled with frustrated tears, Tess stood stock-still, her chest heaving with the effort of the chase, striving to catch any sound that might point her in the direction of her quarry.

Then, as her eyes became accustomed to the darkness, she saw a flickering light through the crumbling wall beside her. There was a break in the bricks she had not noticed until then. Cautiously, quietly, she moved forward. She —

'OH!'

The hand came out of nowhere. Clamped around her mouth, cutting off her breath.

Squirming and struggling, she felt herself dragged over the rubbled ground. The next moment she was being thrust through a half-open door. She saw a circle of startled faces in the light cast by several oil lamps.

'Look what I found crawlin' about outside!' Her attacker released her mouth, at the same time cruelly twisting her arm behind her back.

'Whaddaya want, sister? You lookin' for trouble?' A thickset girl with greasy black hair had got to her feet and stood menacingly in front of Tess. 'Hey,' she swung round to the others, 'maybe she's a spy from the Serpents! You want me to fix her, Skipper?'

Her face twisted in pain from her attacker's grip, Tess suddenly realised to whom the question had been addressed. 'You!' She spat out the word. 'You're the one who stole my money! That was every goddamn red cent I owned! You give it to me this instant!'

The tall thin boy stood up, his fair hair drooping untidily over his face. 'Let her go, Drummer.'

'The lady wants her dough back, Skipper, you hear that?' It was the tough-faced girl talking again, a sneer twisting her plain features. 'Hey,' she snarled, grabbing Tess by her shirt-front, 'you want it gift-wrapped, sister?'

'Leave her alone, Sissy.' It was the one they called Skipper who spoke. 'I want to ask the lady a few questions.'

'I'm not here to answer your lousy questions!' Shrugging off her captor's hold, Tess faced up to the fair-haired youth. He was about seventeen and obviously the leader. 'Just give me what belongs to me and let me go! I haven't eaten today, and that goddamn money is all I have to my name.'

'How's that?'

Tess was caught off balance by the boy's tone. There was no trace of the others' belligerance. He had a languid self-possession that irritated her.

'None of your goddamn business! Just give me what's mine and let me outta here. I can't — '

Suddenly everything went black.

Tess blinked and opened her eyes. The face was the first thing she saw. It was strangely familiar . . .

Then she remembered.

'Wha-what happened?' She was lying down on some sort of pallet and her head was throbbing painfully.

The boy called Skipper looked down at her. 'You fainted. I guess you're real hungry . . . That right?'

Tess nodded. It only made her head feel worse.

The boy saw her wince. 'You hit your head before I

could catch you. I've sent Sissy and Hog out for hamburgers. They won't be long.'

Tess struggled to sit up and he held out a steadying hand. 'I'm sorry I stole your money. I didn't know . . . I just saw the open purse, and . . . ' He handed her a cracked cup of Coke. 'Here, take a sip of this.'

Parched from the chase, Tess gulped down the drink. The boy said nothing till she'd finished.

Then he asked, 'What's your name?'

Tess put down the empty cup. She stared at him for a long moment. 'Tess,' she finally replied.

There was something in his eyes that made her feel he wouldn't do her any harm.

She wasn't quite sure how it happened but she ended up staying. And in time they became the family she had never had. She loved them all. Even Sissy, who had resented her so much at first.

Now, after almost ten months, Tess felt as if she had always belonged with Hog, Drummer, Skipper and Sissy. She was a fully accepted member of the gang and they had taught her all they knew. Taught her how to survive on the cold mean streets of New York where self-preservation was the golden rule.

They stole to eat, and slept wherever they could find shelter. Their predators were the New York Police Department from whom they were always in danger of imminent arrest for vagrancy or theft; and the violent territorial gangs who roamed the city streets looking for the thrill of a kill.

It was a dangerous life but Tess adapted. She found her wits growing sharper, her instincts stronger, as she fought to survive. She was often hungry, dirty, cold, or wet, but she found that mattered little as long as she was with people who really cared. At night, when they lay huddled together like a litter of newborn pups, Tess felt a sense of belonging she hadn't experienced since her mother had left. It was a feeling she had almost forgotten.

Gradually she pieced together the stories of her new friends, the backgrounds and experiences that had eventually brought them to the streets. She learned that behind Drummer's tattoos and menacing manner was a boy who had been sexually violated by his father from the age of four.

In one terrible outpouring of grief, Sissy finally spoke of her mother's death from an overdose, and of the three sisters she had lost contact with when they'd been placed in care.

To Tess's surprise, she learned that Hog's mother had been a high school teacher. When she'd married a wealthy, upwardly-mobile attorney, it was made clear that Hog was not welcome as part of the package. His mother took him to the welfare office herself . . .

And then there was Skipper. Nicholas Lang.

The day after Nick turned thirteen, his father had packed a suitcase and walked out of his life. '*You're* old enough to look after her now,' his old man had said, and left without even a goodbye to his cancer-ridden wife.

Once over the shock and anger, Nick had been determined to do everything he could to soften the horror of his mother's final months. In the short time left to her, he wanted to do everything possible to make up for her hard and joyless life.

So Nick learned to steal. Silky negligées, French perfume, expensive cheeses, tropical fruits, glossy magazines. It was easy when you knew how and Nick wanted his mother to have the best.

When occasionally the dying woman wondered aloud how her son was able to afford such luxuries, Nick would talk enthusiastically — if vaguely — about his 'great job', about the overtime and perks. If she had her suspicions, by then his mother was too weak to care.

In turn, Tess told her new family the bare outlines of

WHISPER FROM THE GODS 45

her own story. She didn't like to talk about it; she had tried to push out of her mind the memory of the mother who had abandoned her without explanation, the years of abuse and exploitation, and the last horrific beating that had led her to the streets of New York.

'But you're a survivor, Tess, aren't you?' It was Nick who asked the question. 'Nothing's going to keep you laid out for too long. Somethin' tells me you'll get what you want out of life.'

He was looking at her with an odd expression on his face, his voice as gentle as always. There was something about Nick — only Sissy called him Skipper — that Tess found infinitely soothing and reassuring. Sometimes, when the others were asleep around her, Tess would lie and stare into Nick's thin, lovely face. And then an ache, a yearning she barely understood, would start inside her — feelings that carried over into her dreams ...

They were eating what passed for supper in the draughty cover of a disused warehouse. Nick watched as Tess shared the last of her sandwich with a couple of grimy-faced kids who'd joined them.

She played it tough, he thought, but this wasn't the first time he'd seen her deprive herself. In a strange way her behaviour had had an effect on the others; it softened the hard edges, made them more open to their feelings. He saw it especially in Sissy. She and Tess were almost as close as sisters.

The trouble was, thought Nick as he chewed on a two-day-old breadroll, as far as Tess was concerned, he was beginning to feel less and less like a brother ...

They had no warning. The horror struck out of the blue. Tess blamed herself. But it had all happened so quickly.

It was after dark, and Tess had suggested the short cut through Chinatown as she and Sissy hurried back to their latest squat. Their bulging coat pockets banged against them and they were laughing loudly at the ease with which they had lifted supper for everyone.

'That guy knew we were up to something,' Sissy giggled, referring to the deli owner, 'he just couldn't figure out what!'

'You should have seen his face when — '

Tess's laughter was cut short by the three well-built youths blocking their way.

'Having your constit-ootional, girls?' The one in the middle swaggered forward with a sneering grin on his flat face and stood with his hands on his hips. 'What say you show us what's making you bulge in all the wrong places, huh?'

'Get outta the way.' Sissy's voice was dark and threatening.

'Hey!' The same youth spoke again, calling the words over his shoulder to his companions. 'The ugly's tellin' us what to do, guys. What d'ya say to that?'

'I say, make her uglier, Spider!'

'Ya got it wrong, pals.' It was the third one speaking now as he and his companions encircled Tess and Sissy. 'It's the skinny princess who's makin' me hot.' He unzipped his jeans and pulled out his penis as he moved towards Tess.

She stood frozen in horror. What the hell were these thugs going to do to them . . ?

As the others grinned, the exposed youth made a lunge for Tess's arm. Stepping sideways, she eluded his grasp, but at that instant Sissy's fury was unleashed.

The knife appeared in her hand from nowhere.

'Run, Tess! Run!' Sissy screamed out the words as she pointed the blade at arm's length towards their would-be assailants.

Rooted to the spot, Tess heard the men's sneering laughter as they moved closer. But they had underestimated Sissy's skill and speed with her weapon.

Hand moving with lightning speed, she slashed out

savagely, slitting open the nostrils of one, splitting the cheek of another, changing the laughter to screams of pain and foul-mouthed curses.

Suddenly, as if awakening from a daze, Tess reached under her coat and began to hurl tins of food at the injured youths. The dual onslaught momentarily beat them back. Now it was Tess's turn to cry: 'Leave it Sissy! Come on!'

Together, hearts pounding, they ran off into the darkness.

It was the first time Tess had ever seen Nick angry, not a hot, fiery anger, but rather an ice-cold fury.

'You know I told everyone always to be back at the squat by dark. If we go out at night, we go as a group. It's askin' for trouble otherwise. You of all people should know that, Sissy.'

The dark-haired girl shrugged her shoulders. She resented the put-down; she'd had enough put-downs in her short life. All that mattered was that Tess was all right. Sissy knew she'd have killed if they'd harmed a hair on Tess's head.

'It's over now, Skipper,' she said tersely. 'Let's leave it, huh?'

But it wasn't over.

Three days later when Sissy hadn't returned by dark from a trip downtown, they went looking.

It didn't take long to find her.

Her body was lying face down on a stretch of wasteland just ten minutes' walk away. When Nick gently turned her over, they could see that both breasts had been cut off and her belly slashed from navel to panty line. Her own knife was stuck in the cavity.

With a low moan, Tess turned away and vomited among the rubble.

*

For weeks afterwards, she was tormented by nightmares. Trembling and sobbing, she would jolt awake, and it was Nick who would hold her close and soothe her back to sleep.

But not even the news that Sissy's murderers had been identified and caught could put Tess's mind to rest. She continued to blame herself.

'If only I hadn't suggested that short cut, Nick, she might still be here.' The tears ran down her cheeks. 'It's all my fault. I'll never be able to forgive myself.'

'Oh Tess . . . ' Nick put his arms around her as they lay together in the darkness. 'You mustn't torture yourself . . . It could have happened any time, anywhere . . . Sissy knew that, we all do. This is New York; no one is safe.'

She clung to him, the ache inside her still unassuaged. He stroked her hair, then her cheek, his breath warm against her forehead. And suddenly, to Tess's bewilderment, the hard leanness of Nick's body through his worn jeans and T-shirt made that other ache start inside her . . .

'Oh, Nick, hold me . . . hold me.' She whispered the words as she moulded her body even closer to his.

Nick caught his breath. He sensed that in an instant one need had been exchanged for another. Comfort had become desire . . .

A shiver ran through him as she turned her face up to his. For a second they looked into each other's eyes and then their lips met in an explosion of longing. The kiss seemed to last forever, and they repeated it again and again. Neither spoke a word; beside them they could hear the deep, steady breathing of Hog and Drummer.

Nick felt as if his whole body was on fire. The feelings he had suppressed for so long cried out for release. But he hadn't known, hadn't been sure . . .

Until now.

Silently they fumbled off their clothes and clung to

each other's nakedness. Breath ragged, Nick whispered: 'It might hurt, you know that ... ?'

'I don't care, Nick ... All I know is that I want you.' Her voice was a raw whisper.

And there, on the hard, littered basement floor, with the muffled sounds of the deadly urban jungle as accompaniment, Tess learned her first lesson in love.

While they didn't flaunt the change in their relationship, Tess felt sure the others could not have failed to notice the new intimacy between herself and Nick. They spent every moment together, touching, holding hands, savouring the delights of their new found happiness.

But at the same time the emotions Nick had awoken in her frightened Tess. She remembered the terrible void left by her mother's abandonment; the scars were etched deep. If she allowed herself to fall too deeply in love with Nick, she told herself, the same thing could happen again ...

Nick sensed those fears and did his best to reassure her. His own feelings were unambiguous. For the first time in his life he felt truly happy. He loved Tess and knew she was the woman he wanted by his side for the rest of his life.

The relationship also gave greater impetus to his plan to escape the dangerous, dead-end life he had led for too long. He was now just six months off his seventeenth birthday. Very soon he would be eligible to enlist in one of the branches of the military. Nick knew it was his only chance of gaining an education and making something of his life.

But when he finally confided his dream to Tess, he was not prepared for her reaction.

'The *military*!' she was outraged. 'You mean you'd *willingly* become part of the establishment, Nick? Let those bastards in Washington brainwash you and turn you into a flag-flying doughboy?'

'You don't understand, Tess, I want to marry you, give you everything you deserve,' Nick did his best to explain. 'It's the only way I can get outta this sort of life, get an education and make somethin' of myself.' His eyes lit up with a sudden shine. 'The air force is where I'd really like to make the grade. Cruisin' up above all this shit down here, lookin' at — '

Tess cut him off. 'You're crazy, baby, stoo-pid, no frills, crazy.'

But Nick knew he had to try — had to do something to try to make that dream come true. Before he'd been forced to leave school and care for his ma, his grades had been good. He knew if he was only offered the chance, he could climb his way out of this go-nowhere life and make a real future for himself and Tess.

And once he was enlisted, he told himself confidently, Tess'd accept what he had to do . . .

Then, a few weeks later, something happened which altered all their plans.

The squat seemed perfect. An empty brownstone ready for demolition — according to the sign outside — but still with carpet on the floor and even running water. With the nights becoming colder, it was a supremely lucky find.

Two of them always had to remain in the place to keep it from being taken over by others. Tess and Nick, and Drummer and Hog, took it in turns to go out and find food, and for almost three months they lived in relative comfort and security. But even the shelter of the brownstone could not save Hog from the effects of the cold. Frail and weak-chested, he was felled by a raging temperature and racking cough. Worried when his condition failed to improve, Tess stayed by his side while the others went on the endless search for food. On their return she would heat some tinned soup on a small fire lit in the cavernous, old-fashioned fireplace, and force Hog to take a little

nourishment. A larger fire would ~~.~~ ed to heat the
room as well, but they knew they coul~~...~~ed to heat the
of attracting attention to themselves. With luc~~...~~ chance
see the winter out in the shelter of the brownstone~~...~~

Their luck didn't hold.

Tess was alone with Hog when she heard footsteps
tramping up the hallway. Their glances met and Tess put
a finger to her lips. Who could it be? The police? Other
street-dwellers like themselves? Friendly or hostile?

They held their breath as the footsteps seemed to
pass, but a second later the door was thrown open.

'You see! I told you I saw smoke! Now get rid of these
vermin. Get rid of them at once!' The woman was small,
past middle age, dressed in an expensive fur coat. Her
face was flushed with anger, her accented voice high-
pitched and shrill as she addressed the two burly uniformed security guards by her side.

'You heard the lady. Get movin'.' The men advanced
threateningly into the room.

'Who the hell are you to give orders!' Tess stood up
from where she had been sitting by Hog's side, reacting
instinctively to the aggression.

'I am the owner of these premises, you filthy tramp,
and if you don't want to be arrested for illegal trespass
you'd better get yourself and this junk out of here at
once!' The woman's tone rose in pitch. 'Do you understand! *At once!*'

'You hear what Mrs Steiner said? Out! Now.'

One of the guards grabbed Tess by the arm and began
to drag her out of the room while the other hauled Hog off
his mattress of newspapers.

Hog began to cough, his grey face covered with a film
of sweat.

Struggling furiously, Tess screamed, 'Can't you see
this guy's real sick? What harm's it doin' you if we stay
here? We're not hurtin' the place! We just want — '

Held helpless in ~~~ong grip of the guard, Tess was unable to avo~~~ backhander to her right cheek. The woman ~~~ but well-built and the blow was deli-~~~ -force.

~~~m like you should be locked away!' Her face was ~~~sted with rage, and she spat out the words from her thickly lipsticked mouth. 'How dare you think you can just take over decent people's property? I pay my taxes, I shouldn't have to put up with — '

'You bitch!' Tess cut across the tirade, 'You dirty, money-hungry bitch! You'll pay for this!' Tears of anger and frustration ran down her cheeks as she watched Hog being pushed out of the door. 'I swear you'll pay for this!'

Ten minutes later when Nick and Drummer approached the house the sight of the two uniformed men standing guard at the boarded up front door stopped them in their tracks.

'Je-sus,' Nick breathed. 'What's happened to Tess and Hog?'

Tess came hurrying towards them through the darkness.

It had taken her some time to find a suitable shelter for Hog. In the end she had left him wrapped in one thin blanket and wedged in the narrow entrance of a darkened storefront. Then she had hurried back to wait close by the brownstone for Nick and Drummer's return.

As she explained to Nick what had occurred, his anger mixed with the frustration of powerlessness. It was always the same, he thought bitterly, the rich could always exploit and manipulate the poor.

But when Tess led the way to where she had left Hog, Nick's anger was overridden by concern for the obvious deterioration in his friend's condition.

'He's burnin' with heat, Tess. We gotta get someone to look at him.' Nick frowned as he knelt beside Hog and held a hand to his forehead.

'St Helen's is the closest,' on̶ ̶ ̶ ̶ ̶ ̶ ̶ ̶ ̶ ̶
time I got my eye cut open fightin' on̶ ̶ ̶mmer. 'The
they looked after me real good. Waited god̶ ̶ ̶ ̶ ̶ ̶ ̶ ̶nents
though.'

Nick was fitting Hog's arm around his shoulde̶ ̶ ̶,
lifting him to his feet. 'Yeah, well, even if he has to sit
there all night waiting for treatment it'll be better for him
than hangin' around on the freezin' streets.'

Tess knew Nick was right. She could see how much
Hog's condition had worsened in just the short time since
they'd been kicked out of their squat. Trying to hide her
fear, she said brightly, 'Come on, Hog, let's go find you a
real sassy lady in a starched white cap.'

For over four hours they sat in the overcrowded corridor
surrounded by an amazing array of New York City's sick
and injured. Some were victims of the violent streets, like
the skinny black kid who lay groaning on a trolley, blood
seeping through his rough bandages. Others, like the fat
middle-aged woman slumped on the hard plastic chair
were suffering from self-inflicted misery. Tess could
smell the alcohol from where she sat.

Finally they were ushered into a tiny curtained cubi-
cle where the overworked young medic gave a quick
glance at the card on which the admissions nurse had
recorded Hog's particulars. An equally speedy examination followed — pulse, temperature, stethoscope to chest
and back.

The woman spoke quickly too. 'This guy's real sick.
Looks like pleurisy to me. I'm going to recommend he's
found a bed for a couple of days.' She filled in a form as
she talked. She raised her head and looked at Nick. 'You
guys his pals?'

'Yeah.'

'Give the desk a call day after tomorrow. Here's the
number.'

*

'Je-sus . . . , ___ ___ver back on the hook and Tess saw
Nick put ___hite as he turned towards her and
his f___at is it, Nick? What's happened?'
He took a deep breath. 'Hog's dead.'

CHAPTER

6

Tess allowed herself no rest.

All the toughness and guile she had learned on the streets made her absolutely determined to wreak revenge on the woman she blamed for Hog's death.

Mrs Steiner...

The only clue to her whereabouts was what Tess had overheard that day as she and Hog had been herded onto the street. The cab had been waiting for the hard-faced woman. She had snapped out the address. 'Sutton Place.'

Tess remembered it.

Every day for the next three weeks she patrolled the fashionable area, drawing suspicious looks from the various doormen who ushered the rich and powerful in and out of their fortresses.

While she walked, her eyes continually combing the crowds, Tess's anger grew. She was determined that somehow that rich bitch would be made to pay for Hog's death.

Nick did his best to talk her out of her obsession. 'Leave it, Tess. There's nothin' we can do. Hog's gone and nothin's gonna bring him back.'

'That bitch is gonna get what's comin' to her, Nick.'

teeth. 'Somehow, she's gonna

Tess spoke through to Hog.'

pay for wh found her. Tess saw the woman she hated
rom a cab in front of the Mansion apartments;
white poodles wearing jewelled collars and leads were
springing around her feet. The smiling doorman accepted
the pile of department store boxes from the cab driver;
Tess heard his booming voice: 'Take these straight up to
403 for you, ma'am?'

403.

Now Tess knew the place and the number of the
apartment.

Nick couldn't help but admire her detective work. And he
felt forced to listen as she explained her plan. Maybe . . . if
they covered all the angles . . .

'Listen,' insisted Tess, at her most persuasive, 'I've
hung around there every day now; the routine's always
the same. At exactly eleven, the man from Doggie Date
arrives.' She screwed up her face at the kitschy name.
'He takes the bitch's two poodles out for half an hour
and then returns them to the apartment.' She looked
from Drummer to Nick. 'That's the only chance we've
got.'

'You really wanna go through with this, Tess?' Nick
still sounded hesitant.

Tess's green eyes darkened dangerously. 'The only
way the rich hurt, Nick, is if you unload some of their
dough. I'm gonna get into that bitch's apartment if it's
the last thing I do.'

The plan was simple, as all good plans are.

It began with a call to the offices of Doggie Date.

'Good morning,' Tess affected an accent. 'This is
Mrs Steiner's maid speaking. Mrs Steiner wishes me to
tell you that she won't be requiring your services for the

Returning to the living room she raised her arm and, stony faced, swept the array of china figurines to the floor. Then she picked up a spindly-legged chair and threw it at the gilt-framed mirror over the fireplace. It made a noise like a shotgun going off as it splintered into hundreds of pieces. Warming to her task, Tess hurried into the kitchen. Taking flour, sugar and coffee, she ran through the apartment flinging them all about with feverish abandon. She was panting with delight, completely absorbed in the exquisite moment of revenge...

'*What the fuck are you doin*'!'

Spinning round, Tess saw the outraged face of the doorman. He was standing in the doorway to the hall, blocking her escape.

'Get outta my way!' Threateningly she ran towards him, attempting to push him off his feet. He wasn't a young man and was carrying his fair share of extra weight.

'You're not goin' anywhere, you fuckin' goddamn hooligan!' Recovering his balance, the man reacted with surprising speed. Grabbing at Tess he threw her with all his strength back into the room. Winded, she hit the wall, but seconds later launched herself at him again. Again the man grabbed her but this time he held on. Tess squirmed, fought like a wildcat, but his grip was too strong.

Then suddenly from the open doorway there came a plaintive cry.

'Oh my Jesus! Oh, no... !' Grey with shock, Mrs Steiner stared at the chaos that had been wreaked in her home. 'No ... no ... ' She was shaking her head, her face dazed, as she walked slowly into the room. Then her gaze came to rest on the broken china.

'My Meissen! My precious Meissen! Oh, dear God, not... It's worth thousands of dollars! Thousands and thousands... It's irreplac—' With a soft whimper, she crumpled to the ground.

*

After that, reality seemed a blur to Tess. It seemed as if she had been sucked into the vortex of a tornado.

Paramedics, police, sirens, a prison cell . . .

It was three weeks before Nick found out where she was. Another week after that until he managed to see her. Tess had refused to name her accomplice; Nick had got away scot free.

But no one would have recognised him now. Not in the uniform and brutal military haircut.

He saw the green eyes widen as she took a seat on the other side of the security mesh.

He nodded. 'Yes, they've accepted me.'

'Congratulations . . . ' Tess still couldn't believe that he'd done it. Joined the establishment of his own free will.

He looked at her with compassion. She was also wearing a uniform. The blue prison shirt hung loosely on her slim shoulders.

'Tess . . . oh, Tess . . . ' He leaned closer to the screen that divided them. 'I've been desperate to find you. They're sending me down south at the end of the month. I had to find you before that.' The hubbub of the other remand prisoners and visitors in the long narrow reception area almost drowned out Nick's words.

'They won't keep you here, Tess. After all, the Steiner woman recovered. It was just a slight heart attack.'

Tess stared at him, her face set and hard. 'They're out to get me, Nick. That bitch is going to do everything in her power to see me permanently in this place.'

If only I could touch her, Nick thought. 'You've got to have faith, Tess,' he urged. 'After all, it's a first offence.'

Nick did his best to sound convincing but he was worried. How could they have known the Steiner woman was the mother-in-law of the mayor of New York? As a result, the case had received more than its fair share of publicity — and public sympathy lay strongly with the 'victim'.

All too soon the whistle blew, signalling the end of visiting hour.

Reluctantly Nick stood up. 'I've got to go now, Tess, but I'll see you next time.'

Another two weeks before he'd be allowed back again. How was he going to bear it?

All around them people were calling out their goodbyes. Nick leaned closer and whispered urgently through the mesh. 'I love you, Tess. I love you so much. The moment you get out of here we're going to get married. And then,' he vowed, looking deep into those beautiful eyes, 'I'm going to make all our dreams come true.'

It was twenty-one years before he saw her again.

CHAPTER

7

'Twenty-one years ...'
      Nick slowly repeated the words as he sat on the sofa in her living room. Empty coffee cups and half a bottle of white wine stood on the low, stone-topped table between them.

It was almost one in the morning. They had talked for hours. Mostly about the past. About how they had lost each other all those years ago.

'I tried to find you, Nick. I wrote. Three letters in a row. They all came back to me. No one enlisted in that name, they said. And after that I didn't know what to do.'

He shook his head in painful disbelief. 'God ... if only I'd known. As an enlisted man I was forced to use my father's name ... Teece. It was as simple and as complicated as that.'

The father he hated, Tess thought.

She told him how she'd never given up hope. How over the years she'd tried various avenues, even sought the help of a private investigator. But of course, she'd had no idea that he'd changed his name ...

'I just wanted to know that you were alive, Nick, that everything had worked out well for you.' Her voice was soft, yet intense. She felt a great relief, as if the last piece had been placed in the jigsaw of her past.

His jacket off, his silk tie loosened, Nick leaned back in his seat and stared at her. He drank in the sight of those amazing green eyes and thought to himself how little, yet how much, the years had changed her — inside and out.

The figure was still as ethereally slim, the skin as fresh and glowing, but the toughness of the child he had known had been overlaid with a different sort of toughness: the patina that comes from money and power and confidence.

He had seen the photograph by chance; he rarely had time to read anything but the business sections of newspapers these days. But he had been recently posted to LA, and was doing his best to familiarise himself with the local scene.

He had skimmed the article about the newly appointed female Executive President of WLS before glancing at the accompanying photograph. Something jolted inside him as he looked at the set of the jaw, the tilt of the head, and looked again at the name printed underneath.

'Tess . . . ' he murmured under his breath as he sat at the breakfast table opposite his wife. Surely it was Tess . . .

'It plagued me for days,' he explained when they were seated, drinks in hand. 'I had to make sure. I didn't think they'd let me through to you by phone, and I certainly didn't want to leave a message.' He looked at her over the top of his untasted wine. 'Your E-type was mentioned in the article so I made up my mind to . . . well, to do what I did.'

'Are you glad you did, Nick?' She asked the question with a simple directness, thinking how handsome he looked: his hair was still thick and blond, his eyes as clear and blue as when he'd been a boy. And neither age nor success, she was glad to see, had erased his gentleness . . .

'Yes.' He spoke the word softly. 'I loved you, Tess. Wanted to take care of you and give you everything you hadn't had in life. As it happened, it didn't work out that way. But,' his voice became gentler, 'there's something about first love. You never forget it. No matter what comes after, no matter how good. It's a love that's so unbearably innocent and pure. And no matter how hard you try you can never recapture it ... '

She looked away, blinking, murmuring a reply he barely heard. 'Yes ... ' she said.

A simple yes ...

He told her of his marriage to Helen. 'We're happy, — which is a great deal in this day and age — and she's a wonderful mother.' There were two children, a girl and a boy, and as he showed her the photo he carried in his wallet Tess wondered what they might have looked like had she been their mother ...

'And you were happy to relocate to LA, Nick?'

'It's a move in the right direction for me, Tess. Conroy Aircraft Corporation is one of the country's largest and most respected firms. I'm now vice-president of their entire West Coast operation.'

'So your dream of working with aircraft did come true?'

'I have the US government to thank for giving me my chance. As an enlisted man I received an education that really did change my life. When you come from the background I did, it's never an easy climb. It took guts and a lot of hard work, but I made it. I made the system work for me.'

'I'm glad it's all turned out so well for you, Nick.' *I'll even try to be glad about Helen too*, she told herself ...

'Hey, but listen,' he said, taking a swallow of wine and placing his glass down in front of him, 'enough about me. Tell me what happened after we lost touch. I tried so hard to find you but the last thing I could discover was that the charges had been dropped and you'd disappeared without a trace.' He laid an arm along the back of the sofa and looked at her expectantly. 'What happened,

Tess? How did you end up in the movie business, for heaven's sake?'

She looked at him for a long moment then shook her head. 'It's late, and it's a long story, Nick. Let's save it for the next time.'

She scared herself by wanting so much for there to be a next time.

It was late when she got to bed but Tess found it impossible to sleep. The reunion with Nick had brought so many memories rushing back; not only of the time they had spent on the streets, but of the years since.

She lay staring into the darkness, wondering whether she would ever be able to give a truthful answer to his question.

How she had ended up in the movie business . . .

At first light, exhausted by lack of sleep and her turbulent thoughts, she could resist the urge no longer.

Slipping out of bed, she dressed quickly in jeans and sweatshirt and let herself out of the house. The E-type roared into life at the first turn of the ignition, breaking the silence of the morning. Tess hoped she hadn't woken Lola.

The sun was coming up over the San Gabriels as she curved her way through the canyon towards her destination. There were few cars on the road and she would have enjoyed the drive had her mind not been on other things.

The tall ornate gates were already open and she drove through and stopped in the deserted car park. Then she made her way slowly along the well-tended paths, noticing two workmen in the distance. It was cooler at this time of day, she supposed. Especially for their sort of work . . .

She didn't come here often, and it took a couple of wrong turnings before she found the place she was looking for.

Suddenly, there it was in front of her. A carved

marble angel, its upright wings touched by the first pink of the morning sunlight.

As motionless as a statue herself, Tess stood and looked down at the names inscribed on the pale marble slab.

Ruth and Reed Hardy

Dead almost ten years. Killed in the twin-engined aircraft her stepfather had loved to fly.

But not before Tess had learned the truth.

As she stood by the graveside, her eyes darkened with emotion. *I'm almost there*, she whispered to the ghosts around her. *Nothing is going to stop me now.*

As she'd told Nick, it was a long story...

CHAPTER

8

Somehow they'd managed it.

But then, Tess thought scornfully, the rich could manipulate most things. Why should the law be any exception?

Just two days before the charges were to be heard in the juvenile court, she was surprised when an escort arrived to take her to the warden's office.

Waiting alone in the simply furnished room, Tess tried to figure out the reason for her summons. Was it because she'd sworn at that hard-faced bitch who'd tried to hurry her in the showers? Or perhaps because she'd demanded the right to remain in her cell during the mandatory recreation period? It wasn't that she didn't want to get out of her rathole, but it satisfied her in some small way to irritate the pea-brained jerks who gave the orders.

A moment later the warden of the youth remand centre strode into the room. Tess was surprised to see she was a woman. And black at that. She was even more surprised when Warden Hillard told her the reason for their meeting.

'You're a very fortunate young lady, Tess. Mrs Steiner has agreed to drop all charges. There'll be no record against your name.' She fixed the girl opposite with a stern look. 'You're getting a second chance. But let me assure you, if you continue with your antisocial behaviour you won't be so lucky next time.'

Tess wasn't interested in lectures. Relief flooded through her. 'I'm free then? I can get outta this dump?'

'There is one proviso, Tess.' Warden Hillard tapped the official-looking document that lay on the desk in front of her.

'Yeah? What?' Tess allowed her insolence to show. They couldn't touch her now. She was getting out of the place.

The warden ignored the provocation. 'You're to be released into the custody of your mother.'

It seemed to Tess that she'd merely exchanged one prison for another. The only difference was that the second one happened to be a glass and stone mansion in Bel Air, where the guards doubled as housekeepers, maids and chauffeurs . . .

She had protested loudly and forcefully at the terms of her release — to no avail. The court had made its decision, she was told, and that decision had to be upheld. Tess would have to remain under her mother's supervision until she was deemed 'socially conditioned', as the parole officer so quaintly put it.

Tess's anger and outrage were matched by her despair at losing Nick. Everything had taken place so quickly that she found herself on her way to California before she had a chance to see him again and tell him what had happened.

It made her hate them even more: the woman who wanted Tess to call her 'Mom', and the well-built, craggy-faced man who was her husband. It was Reed Hardy, her new stepfather, who had come to accompany her on the flight to California. It was the first time Tess had flown, but she took no pleasure in the journey.

'Your Mom's so looking forward to having you in her

life again, Tess.' Reed Hardy tried to make conversation as they sat beside each other. 'It was a terrible thing that happened. I know she wants to tell you all about it herself once you're settled in with us.'

Tess sat in stony silence. She didn't want to hear what Ruth Hardy had to say. No explanation in the world could account for what she had done. *First she ruined my childhood*, Tess thought bitterly. *Now she's ruined my future.*

Turning her head towards the window, she blinked furiously against her threatening tears. Nick, oh, Nick ... how am I ever going to find you again?

Ruth Hardy was trying her hardest.

'This is your bedroom, Tess. And here,' she opened a door and stood back, 'you have your very own bathroom.' She looked at the girl's impassive face and asked nervously, 'Aren't they pretty, honey? Don't you like them?'

Pain squeezed Ruth's heart when Tess turned coldly away.

The next day Ruth took the girl into her private sitting room and tried her best to explain.

'They say it can happen like that, Tess. One minute you're feeling absolutely fine, the next your life's hanging by a thin thread. The medical term is an aneurism, which means that pressure in the lining of my brain was causing a slow leaking of blood. I can remember tucking you up in bed that day of my birthday and then deciding to go to the corner store for a carton of milk. Apparently it happened right there on the sidewalk outside the store.'

Ruth Hardy nervously twisted the magnificent solitaire on her wedding finger. 'They told me later that the coma lasted eight months. When eventually I came out of it, my memory was gone. I didn't know who I was, where I'd lived ... couldn't remember anything that had gone before. It took another four years of intensive therapy and treatment before slowly — very slowly — I began to remember. It came in patches, in no specific order. I felt as if I were fitting together random parts of a huge jigsaw.'

There was a plea in her voice as she looked at the girl's cold face. 'Please try to understand, honey. When the authorities saw how bad I was, they thought there was very little chance I'd ever recover. That's why they took you away — without even trying to explain what had happened. Maybe they were justified, because it was years before I even remembered that I had a child. But then when I tried to find you, tried to follow the trail of orphanages and foster homes, I'd invariably finish up in a dead end. It wasn't until I saw that photograph in the newspaper . . . '

With a little sob, Ruth left her seat and threw her arms around the silent girl. 'Honey,' she was crying as she clung to that unyielding slimness. 'I'm so *very* sorry. You'll never know how sorry I am. I tried so hard to find you. I love you, Tess. I never stopped loving you.'

The icy green eyes stared back.

I hate you, they said.

'It'll take time, baby.' Reed Hardy did his best to comfort his unhappy wife. 'It's only been a month, after all; not long to adapt to such a radical change in her life.'

The knowledge that his wife had a child he knew nothing about had come as a surprise to Reed Hardy. Not once in the four years of their marriage had Ruth spoken of a daughter. Not, he told himself, that it made any difference to his love for the woman who had come so unexpectedly into his life.

Reed might never have noticed the newcomer to the secretarial pool in his busy law office if it hadn't been for the incident that occurred one evening when he was working late.

At fifty-four, Reed Hardy was one of Hollywood's leading show business lawyers; it was his job to sift through the fine print in studio contracts to ensure the healthy financial futures of his clients.

Divorced from his second wife, and working harder than ever to make up for the gap in his personal life, he ignored his doctor's orders to take things a little easier following a suspect cardiogram a few months earlier.

That night he had needed a secretary in attendance to deal with some urgent correspondence. Ruth had volunteered. Only recently arrived in LA, she had few friends and little reason to look forward to another evening alone in her uninviting apartment.

She was a little in awe of her boss, a tall, ruddy-faced man with a thick mane of white hair, who exuded energy and charisma. Reed Hardy, Ruth saw, was not the type to suffer fools gladly. She hoped she wouldn't make any errors in her note-taking.

It was after eight and Reed was just about to call it a night when suddenly his chest felt as if it were on fire. Christ Almighty . . . He could hardly breathe . . .

Ruth heard the grunt of pain, saw the beads of perspiration spring out on her employer's ashen face and knew at once what was happening. At thirteen, she'd seen the same symptoms in her own father. He had died in less than fifteen minutes.

'Mr Hardy . . . ' Instantly, she was by his side, loosening his tie, helping him to the chesterfield where he could stretch out. He was close to collapse.

The paramedics arrived within minutes of her call. Ruth found herself in the rear of the ambulance holding Reed Hardy's hand and listening anxiously to his laboured breathing through the oxygen mask.

He was in Cedars Sinai for almost ten days. His room overflowed with flowers from his rich and famous clients, but it was Ruth Jordan whom Reed Hardy wanted to see.

Two weeks later, back at work, he called her into his office. She was in her early thirties, he figured, and for the first time really noticed her slim prettiness and soft dark eyes.

'I have a lot to thank you for, Ruth. If you hadn't realised what was happening and acted so promptly I don't think I'd be talking to you now.'

'I'm just glad you're better, Mr Hardy.'

Locking his fingers together, he leaned back in his chair and studied her. 'Tell me a little about yourself, Ruth. Are you married?'

She shook her head. 'No. I'm a widow. My husband was killed in a motorcycle accident less than eighteen months after our wedding.'

Reed Hardy nodded as if digesting this information. 'That must have been very painful for you.' His tone was sympathetic. 'Have you been a widow long?'

'Over twelve years.' Ruth was a little surprised at the personal nature of the questions. Why should a man as important as Reed Hardy be interested in the details of her past?

The conversation seemed to be over and Ruth was on her way out of the office when Reed Hardy asked the question that stopped her in her tracks.

'Would you be free for dinner Saturday, Ruth?'

Ruth Jordan was the woman Reed had been waiting for all his life. She was ladylike and softly spoken, kind and even-tempered. But best of all, she loved him as much as he loved her. They were married within four months of that first date. And at last, with a loving wife waiting for him at home, Reed cut back on his work load. Other things seemed more important.

Before their marriage Ruth had told him about her illness; about those terrifying lost years. Reed had been generous in his sympathy.

But she hadn't told him about the child.

They were eating breakfast on the sun-drenched patio of their Palm Springs vacation home, when Ruth's sudden gasp brought Reed's head up from his newspaper.

'What is it, baby?' He frowned, noticing that the section of the paper she held was trembling in her hand.

'Nothing,' she'd replied.

But for the rest of the day Ruth had been very quiet.

That evening she'd mentioned that she might take a shopping trip to New York some time soon...

CHAPTER

9

It happened day after day for weeks.

Every morning as her eyes flickered open, Tess was assailed by the same sense of disorientation. It would take her a few seconds to remember. But then the comfort of the mattress beneath her, the smooth luxury of the fine cotton sheets, and the expensively decorated bedroom would remind her. The days when her bed had been a couple of garbage bags stuffed with newspapers, when the only way to keep warm was to wear all the clothes she had in the world and snuggle close to Nick — those days were over.

Her mind was a turmoil of emotions as she tried to adjust to her new life. The magnificent home, the servants, the racks of brand new clothes were beyond her wildest dreams. She wasn't even sure exactly how she felt about such wealth and privilege.

But it was the reunion with her mother that caused her greatest confusion. On one hand, the elegant, expensively-dressed woman was a total stranger, yet on the other, certain things about her — a particular way of tilting her head, the scent of her skin, the way she bit her lip when thinking — touched a chord in Tess's memory.

But the stirring of such memories frightened Tess. Over the years she had tried so hard to forget, to thrust away anything that would remind her of the mother who had abandoned her to such a harsh fate.

And even now, after an explanation which meant she could no longer blame her for what had happened, something still held Tess back from the closeness her mother so obviously sought.

The more her mother tried to draw her towards her, the more Tess felt herself incapable of responding.

It took a while before she realised that she was afraid to love. Afraid to become vulnerable, to lose once again what she had lost twice already. Somehow it might happen again — and Tess knew she could not bear that.

Ruth Hardy was close to despair. Months had passed and she'd tried everything. Nothing seemed able to break through the barrier the girl had built around herself.

She had talked about the past, the time before her illness, and tried to recapture with Tess the warm intimacy of those poor but happy days.

'Don't you remember, honey, how you used to put your arms around my neck and tell me not to miss your daddy because we had each other?' Ruth glanced in hopeful expectation at the teenage girl as they sat in the rear of the air-conditioned Rolls Royce. They were on their way downtown; Tess needed ski gear for a forthcoming vacation in Aspen.

'Tell me about my father.' Tess asked the question quietly without taking her eyes off the passing scene. It was another sunny day in LA.

Ruth Hardy bit her lip. 'He — he died before you were born. We were high school sweethearts and we married just two days after my seventeenth birthday. We — we loved each other very much. But even I couldn't get Jeff to give up his beloved motorbike. The accident happened one night on a wet road. They found the flowers he was bringing home for me in his saddlebags.

I'd rung him at work that very morning to tell him I was two months pregnant.'

Tess heard the tightness in her mother's voice. She turned and looked at her with angry eyes.

'Why do we always have to lose what we love?' she asked bitterly.

She had written three letters to Nick without reply. At night her dreams taunted her with the look, the feel, the taste of him, while her days were spent wondering why he didn't respond.

Surely the military would ensure her letters were passed on?

At last she wrote to the Pentagon itself. The reply was brief. 'We regret to inform you we have no one of that name within our ranks . . .'

She had lost him. Whatever had happened to Nick, Tess was now forced to accept that she was never likely to see him again.

As she came to terms with that painful realisation, she also spent a lot of time thinking about the days she and Nick and the others had lived together; about the daily battle for survival on the dangerous streets of New York City.

While sheer chance had turned her own life around, others, like Drummer, were trapped in their pitiful existence. Tess knew first-hand that there were so many who, through no fault of their own, had no reason to hope for a better future.

It was then she made her decision.

She would take advantage of the opportunities offered in her new life. In time she would be able to help those who couldn't help themselves.

School seemed easier after that. At first Tess had been withdrawn and angry, resentful of her fellow classmates, the privileged children of California's rich and powerful. To her, their interests seemed focused only on the pursuit of status and material gain.

Now Tess's reaction was to absorb herself in her studies. It was one way, she discovered, to help distract her thoughts from Nick — and she realised too that she had a lot of catching up to do.

Noting her efforts, the teaching staff were happy to offer extra help.

'You've got a quick brain, Tess.' Mrs Vallence her class teacher, was handing back assignments. She was delighted at the change in the girl's attitude. Tess was still a loner; she still refused to mix with the others, but that would take time, the teacher thought sympathetically. It was a sad story Ruth Hardy had confided while seeking enrolment for her daughter.

'I couldn't fault you on this,' Mrs Vallence smiled down at the slim, dark-haired girl. 'Any idea what you want to do when you graduate?'

'No, ma'am.' Tess kept her eyes lowered.

It was a lie. She knew exactly where she was aiming. She was going to be a lawyer fighting for justice for the homeless and dispossessed ...

'Just came to say good night, honey.' Ruth Hardy stood at the door of the study. It was after eleven and Tess was still bent over her books. At this rate, Ruth told herself proudly, Tess was sure to get into UCLA.

On an impulse she walked into the room and leaned over to kiss the girl on the cheek. 'Don't be too late, now. You're at an age where you need your sleep.'

There was no reply, and as Ruth closed the door behind her, tears misted her eyes. She had felt the girl freeze at her touch.

When's it going to end? she asked herself despairingly. *When am I ever going to get through to her?*

She tried to console herself as she walked down the

hall to her own bedroom. At least she's safe and well looked after; that's the important thing. Maybe, if she was patient, well ... one day things would change.

Tess hadn't wanted to attend her graduation ceremony, but in his easy-going way Reed Hardy had insisted. 'Hey, I want to see something for all the dollars I've spent on that fancy school.'

It was the right approach, and Tess relented.

Reed gets through to her better than I do, Ruth thought sadly as she dressed for the ceremony. *He treats her more casually. I try too hard and she reacts against it.* She sighed. It was one thing to understand the problem, quite another to solve it.

She took a final glance in the mirror, then crossed the room to the walk-in wardrobe. Shifting aside a false panel in the wall, she turned the dial on the small wall safe. When it clicked open, she drew out a soft velvet pouch.

Ruth hadn't had to think too hard about Tess's graduation present. The brooch was Victorian, ornate and pretty; just the sort of piece that had become fashionable again. It had been a gift to Ruth; a gift that could now, most appropriately, be handed on ...

As she was re-rolling the pouch to return to safekeeping, something fell out of it to the carpet at her feet.

Ruth saw what it was and her heart skipped a beat. Oh Jesus ... She picked it up. It was so long ago she had forgotten all about it. She stared at the object in her palm.

At that moment Tess tapped on the door. 'Are you ready?' She never addressed Ruth by name. 'Reed thinks we should go. The traffic — '

'Tess,' Ruth walked out of the 'robe, her palm held out. 'Tess, look at this.'

The girl caught the tone in her mother's voice. 'What is it?'

And then Tess saw it. The red plastic locket on its piece of green ribbon. And she remembered. Oh God ...

'It was in my pocket when they found me that day,' Ruth explained softly.

Both looked up. For a long moment neither said a word as they gazed into each other's eyes...

It was Tess's harsh sob that broke the silence. 'Mom, oh, Mom... Forgive me!' She flung her arms around Ruth's neck and clung to her as the tears ran down her cheeks. 'I do love you! I love you... I need you so much...'

As she held Tess close and listened to the words she had longed to hear for so long, two opposing emotions raged within Ruth.

One was joy, the other an irrational, nameless dread.

CHAPTER

10

The Christmas break did little to relax Mike Havelock. Made curious by Tess's challenging words, he'd started on the script she'd presented to him the same evening he'd brought it home.

Paula had tapped on his study door at about eleven. 'I'm going to bed, Mike — will you be long?'

Mike Havelock didn't raise his head. 'Give me half an hour, honey.'

Three hours later he was still reading. At two-thirty in the morning he finally put the folder aside.

'Jesus ... ' he breathed. The stuff was dynamite ...

Stiff from the hours of sitting, he got to his feet and stretched his lanky frame. His brain was reeling.

The next day as he sat at the head of the groaning festive table, his air of distraction was obvious.

'What's on your mind, Mike?' Paula gave him a curious look as the manservant topped up their wine glasses.

'Oh, just the usual ... business.'

'Well, if you let that turkey sit any longer, honey, it'll be stone-cold.'

With an effort, he brought himself back to the present, and joined in the banter with his two grown-up

WHISPER FROM THE GODS 83

daughters. But he knew that first thing Monday he had to talk with Tess. The script she had given him to read was a minefield of libellous action.

But, he was forced to admit to himself, if there was a way around that, then it sure made one helluva story. The sort of story that could shoot WLS straight back up to the head of the pack.

Tess nodded, her face serious as she answered her employer's question. 'Yes, Mike, every word of it's true.'

She had been expecting the summons; it had come just five minutes after she'd walked into her office.

Mike Havelock shook his head as he ran his thumb over the thick wad of pages. 'This is dangerous ground, Tess. There are names mentioned here that still carry a lot of weight in this town ... It's a fascinating story but I don't know — '

'Mike, you know my background. I began my career in the legal offices of these studios. My speciality was dealing with just this sort of material. Of course I'll double-check with Clay Davis,' she said, referring to WLS's presiding attorney, 'but I'm sure there'll be no problem we can't overcome.

'Look,' she continued earnestly, 'I don't think we can afford to delay on this, Mike. What we have here is box-office dynamite. This one project alone is capable of putting WLS right back in the big league.'

But Mike Havelock was still unsure. If they trod on all those important toes without having their facts right ... Jesus, the law suits ...

Caution conflicting with his business instincts, he asked, 'You still haven't said who your source is, Tess. Is it someone credible, someone we can trust? Who told you this amazing story?'

Her green eyes stared evenly into his. 'A woman who was Elizabeth Eden's childhood friend, who kept in touch with her throughout her career until the day she died.'

'So, who . . . ?' There was a hint of impatience in Mike Havelock's tone.

Tess spoke with quiet intensity. 'Elizabeth Eden's confidante was my mother.'

She told him everything then: about the diaries and letters that Elizabeth Eden had given her old friend for safekeeping. Names, dates, events could all be verified, especially where so many of those named were still alive.

His excitement growing, Mike Havelock listened as Tess explained. 'Elizabeth Eden was a very good and generous friend to my mother, Mike. Especially after my father died. My mother hated hearing the lies about Elizabeth over the years. The stories about her being a slut, a drug-taker and a drunk, a mentally-unbalanced trollop who cost the studios a fortune with her demands and tantrums. But the greatest lie of all, she insisted, was the one that Elizabeth had committed suicide.'

She saw her employer's startled response and nodded. 'My mother never believed that Elizabeth killed herself — and when the true story is told America will see that there were a lot of important people who, for very different reasons, would have liked to see Elizabeth Eden dead . . . '

After that things moved even more quickly than Tess had dared to hope.

Once assured of the validity of the story behind one of Hollywood's most controversial actresses, Mike Havelock wasted no time in going with the project. He was a risk taker, always had been, and now he determined that the story of Elizabeth Eden would be the launch pad for WLS's climb back to the top.

To Mike's relief, Clay Davis, the studio's chief attorney, agreed with Tess's assessment of the material.

'The one it's going to hit hardest, of course, is Ivor Golding's son,' the attorney pronounced. He was referring to Bernie Golding, the current owner of their major rival, Republic Studios. It was to Republic that Elizabeth Eden had been contracted almost all her working life.

'It's just a pity old man Golding himself isn't alive to take the shit he deserves,' Davis added. He shook his head and tapped the script in front of him. 'That poor gal . . . a very different story from the one Republic put around. Those bastards did their best to destroy her.'

And they did, Tess told herself silently.

Now they were going to pay for it.

'So our next problem is casting.' Mike Havelock faced the six executives seated around the boardroom table. Their enthusiasm for the project reflected his own. The fact that they'd also be kicking the ass of one of their major rivals did absolutely nothing to diminish their eagerness.

'I guess we'll be goin' for one of the big four.' It was Ralph Geraghty, head of creative affairs who spoke and for the next ten minutes the names of Hollywood's leading actresses were tossed around.

'Tess . . . ? What do you feel?' Mike Havelock turned to look at her. They had decided that, apart from Clay Davis, they would not reveal the source of their material. But it was obvious that Tess's input was important. So far she had volunteered nothing to the casting debate.

Aware that all eyes were upon her, Tess took her time in answering. 'I think,' she said quietly, 'we should talk to Jennifer Ross.'

For a moment there was total silence. Then Luke Tennant, one of the co-ordinating chairmen, exploded, 'Hey, come on Tess! You know where she's coming from. No one's touching Ross these days with a bargepole.'

Tess's eyes flashed as she heard Luke Tennant's sentiments echoed by the others. Jennifer Ross was an Academy Award-winning actress in her early thirties. But her vocal and ongoing campaign for female actors to receive financial rewards equal to their male counterparts had reduced her flow of work to a trickle. She was being told loud and clear that that wasn't how things worked in Hollywood.

'I know exactly where Jennifer Ross is coming from,' Tess interjected coolly, 'and that's precisely why I think we should use her — and pay her top money. Can you think of a better way to beat up publicity?'

Jennifer Ross, statuesque, tall, and blonde, was out by the pool being put through her paces by her personal fitness trainer when her agent, Maggie Blake, screeched to a stop in the driveway of the shingle-tiled, ranch-style house.

'Jen! Where the hell are you?' Pushing past the startled maid, Maggie hurried as fast as her 180 pounds would allow out onto the rear patio. 'Jen!'

Breathing heavily, sweat running down her strong-featured face, Jennifer Ross stopped at her thirty-fourth push-up. She collapsed and rolled over on her back. Squinting against the strong sunlight, she looked up into her agent's flushed excited face. 'What's wrong, Maggie? You look like you just found the way to heaven.'

'Maybe I have, babe, maybe I have.' Maggie Blake gave a sideways glance at the waiting male trainer. 'Come inside and I'll tell you how you might be able to join me there.'

Five minutes later, sipping on a fruit juice, Jennifer Ross listened in mounting excitement as her agent told her about the confidential fax she'd received first thing that morning. It was a rundown on a script from WLS.

'They didn't give much away, but enough to show me it's gonna be red-hot, Jen. Seems that the depraved public image of Elizabeth Eden was a creation of those who thought a studio contract bought you body and soul. Then, just as I'd had time to digest the fax, Tess Jordan herself came through on the line.'

Maggie Blake wiped the perspiration off her upper lip with a lace-edged handkerchief. She hated the heat.

'Jordan asks me if I had time to read the fax — did I have time to read it! — then asks if I'm interested. When I indicate this might be the case, she proceeds to tell me why they're particularly interested in having my client play the lead role.'

Face aglow, Maggie Blake counted off on her plump bejewelled fingers. 'Firstly, as Jordan put it, they want you because you're a "first-rate actress"; secondly, because you're the same physical type as Eden; and thirdly, to quote her again, because "Miss Ross and Elizabeth Eden share many of the same views about the treatment of women in this industry".'

That wasn't quite enough for Jennifer Ross. 'That's great, Maggie, great. And is Miss Jordan also clear on my views re the financial rewards to women in this industry? Does she — '

'If you'd just let me goddamn finish, Jen, I'll tell you exactly what she said on that subject. They're happy to talk "real money", was how she put it. Hoffman and Cruise type money, baby! You'd better believe it!'

Jennifer Ross jumped to her feet and threw her arms around her agent's plump shoulders. 'Oh, God, Maggie! It's the breakthrough I've been fighting for!'

Eyes shining, she began to pace around the cool, tiled floor. 'We've *got* to pull this off, Maggie,' she insisted, hitting a clenched fist into her open palm. 'Once the standard's set the others will be forced to follow suit.'

Jennifer Ross's battle with the studios had all but crippled her career, but she had been determined to fight on. Now, it seemed, she had won.

Only later did she find time to wonder how much it had to do with having a woman like Tess Jordan at the top of the shitheap . . .

Under strict security the script was couriered to Jennifer Ross the next day. By the time she finished reading it the adrenalin was pumping through her veins.

Every impression she'd ever had of Elizabeth Eden had been turned upside down. Those sonsofbitches had taken a normal, small-town American girl and done everything in their power to destroy her . . .

Jennifer Ross knew she was being offered the role of a lifetime.

CHAPTER

11

Adelle Madigan felt as if twenty-five years had suddenly disappeared.

The huge convention centre was filled to bursting with Madigan supporters — waving banners, cheering, chanting the Madigan name over and over again. Poised and smiling, easily spotted in her red Chanel suit, Adelle moved down the narrow protective corridor formed by police and secret service agents towards the central platform. For one fleeting moment as the television cameras whirred and the flashbulbs popped, she let her imagination run away with her.

Instead of Robbie and Sara, it was herself and Tom the crowd were calling for...

'*Madigan ... Madigan ... Madigan ...*'

Adelle's eyes glistened with memory as tens of thousands of voices took up the refrain, rivalling the thunderous waves of cheering and applause. Oh, the power, the sheer unutterable power of being the focus of such adulation!

With a wrench she brought herself back to reality. This time it was Robbie they were cheering for. Robbie and Sara were the focus of the deafening welcome and the feeling of worship.

But that was OK, she told herself. It was, after all,

how she had always planned it. All that mattered was that she was still a Madigan too. Still carried the name that made people lower their voices in awe, that brought instant recognition, respect, and homage across the length and breadth of America.

A few years after the assassination, there had been rumours in the tabloid press that the President's widow was set to re-marry. But nothing could have been further from the truth. There was not a man alive who could have made Adelle relinquish the Madigan name and heritage. The name that was once more about to take its place in the history books...

At last the Madigans, the Conroys and other senior Democrats were assembled on the elevated platform, all relishing the adulation of their supporters.

Sara, dressed on Adelle's recommendation in a Bill Blass aqua-coloured suit, stood smiling widely, hand in hand with her handsome husband.

It's greater than I ever dreamed, she thought dazedly, *the desire to see another Madigan as President of the United States*...

Then Robert Madigan was raising his arms high in acknowledgement of the tumultuous welcome. The air was electric. It seemed as if the ovation would never end.

But at last the uproar in the huge convention hall died away. The charismatic candidate for the Democratic Party moved closer to the microphone to begin a speech that would surely bring him another step closer to the White House.

Mike and Tess had agreed with the publicity department that at that stage a press conference would have the maximum effect.

'Let's arouse expectations,' suggested Jon King, the head of publicity. 'Start whetting the public appetite for what's to come — and if there're a few out there who decide to start squealing about lawyers and actions, all to the good. It'll raise the profile of the project from the word go.'

So it was Tess, flanked by Jon King, who faced a roomful of eager journalists, agog with curiosity about some of the movie highlights hinted at in the press release. There was nothing the media liked better, Tess thought drily as she faced the barrage of questions, than dirt and scandal.

'It seems to me, Ms Jordan, that there's a move to "rehabilitate" Elizabeth Eden.' The question was put with a hint of ironic emphasis by a stocky, bearded reporter in the middle of the room.

'If by rehabilitating you mean restoring a reputation that was falsely destroyed, then of course you're right,' Tess countered evenly.

'Has WLS given full weight to the possibility that some of those named in the storyline might seek legal redress?' The dark-haired man who asked the question seemed vaguely familiar to Tess.

'We are fully aware of the legal complications involved,' she replied. 'The facts presented will have complete verification.'

'Ms Jordan, you are meeting male salary levels for Jennifer Ross, who will portray Elizabeth Eden. Is that going to set new standards for female stars in the future?'

'I certainly hope so,' Tess answered crisply.

Forty minutes later when she stood up to leave, the press corps couldn't wait to file their stories.

Carl Harris was very happy. For two years he'd been very happy and in another four weeks he was about to become happier still.

Money was what put the famous smile on Carl Harris's face. He was smiling now as his agent told him what they were going for when they sat down in a month's time to renew his contract.

'You've toppled Cosby, buddy. Your ratings are outta sight. If they wanna make sure of getting you back next season, they're gonna have to stuff our asses with cash.' Len Viertel spoke in his usual flat monotone. No excitement. No pleasure. Just a statement of fact.

Thin to the point of emaciation, pasty-faced and undersized, he looked like an ancient dwarf sitting behind the huge modern desk that separated him from his client. Yet his frail, unhealthy appearance was deceptive. When it came to the art of the deal, Len Viertel had the strength and tenacity of ten tigers.

'How much, Len? What're we going for?'

Len Viertel saw the excitement in the face of the man opposite. Carl Harris was fifty-eight but at that moment he looked like a wide-eyed schoolboy.

The agent named a sum and the silver-haired actor thought he was going to faint with sheer joy. The money was phenomenal, a king's ransom, but with *Time Out* topping the ratings for the last four seasons, he knew the networks would be begging him to take their dough.

'Just leave it to me, Carl. All you'll have to do is sign on the dotted line.' Len Viertel made it clear the meeting was over.

Carl Harris unfolded his lanky frame from the chair. 'Sure, Len. Sure.'

The agent looked his client over as he walked to the door. Carl Harris was tall and trim, and while his hair was greying, there was still plenty of it. 'Make sure you keep lookin' good, Carl. You still takin' those shots?'

From the doorway, Carl Harris nodded and grinned. 'Sure thing. Every week. Makes me feel thirty-five again. Why don't you give the doc a go yourself, Len? You'd be able to put a smile on Lorna's face three times a night.'

'Leave the jokes to the writers, eh, Carl?' Len Viertel answered sourly as he picked up the telephone.

*

Carl Harris's good mood lasted almost all the way through his diet lunch at the Beverly Hills Hotel. He was waited on like royalty, given the respect and recognition rightfully due to someone whose prime time show was topping the ratings.

He ate alone, but not without interruption, as other famous faces stopped to say 'hi' and bask in some of his reflected glory. For the runaway success of *Time Out* had made Carl Harris a star all over again — this time at the age of fifty-eight, and after almost a dozen years in the wilderness.

The offer of a major part in a family sitcom had come just in the nick of time. Lousy investments and a dearth of any worthwhile roles had reduced Carl Harris's lifestyle to the point where it was almost impossible to keep up even a facade of appearances any longer. And even though the role of Danny Elwood, the rich but sour-faced daddy to a brood of assorted foster kids, hadn't seemed that promising at first glance, Carl Harris was hardly in a position to knock back something that promised regular work and income. To the surprise of nearly everyone, the show had been an instant hit. And how.

Overnight Carl Harris had resumed and then surpassed his former status. As a leading man playing opposite some of the screen's major female stars, he had certainly been a well-known actor in his day. But now television and *Time Out* had brought him a new and much wider audience.

Just when he'd thought he was all washed up, the quirky sitcom had brought him fame and, more importantly by far, money he'd never dared to dream of.

And now, he mused happily, sipping at his Perrier, Len Viertel was going to make him even richer. The thought filled him with an overwhelming sense of delight.

Five minutes later, just as he was about to leave, Carl learned the news from a passing publicist. The Executive President of WLS had just announced the studio was planning a no-holds-barred movie on the life of Elizabeth Eden.

Carl Harris felt himself go numb with shock.

Adelle rose early, her mind immediately focused on the triumph of the previous evening. She was dying to read the columns in the morning's newspapers.

Tossing on a fine Swiss cotton robe, she made her way out to the sun-drenched patio where breakfast and the papers were waiting.

While the maid poured the first of her three cups of strong black coffee, Adelle carefully spread a low-fat dairy substitute onto a slice of Melba toast. She didn't believe in exercise — only diet and massage.

She took her first sip of coffee and directed her attention to the newspaper.

Two minutes later, Adelle Madigan's future suddenly exploded in her face.

Dave Arnell and Larry Brandt arrived at the house at almost precisely the same moment. The former lifted a bushy eyebrow and shook his head as the maid showed them into the sunny sitting room. 'Goddamn stinking timing,' he muttered under his breath.

His colleague nodded. As the men responsible for Robert Madigan's election campaign, the last thing they needed at this crucial point was a no-holds-barred look at the short life of Elizabeth Eden . . .

Adelle didn't keep them waiting. She had dressed and made-up in double-quick time. Both men stood up as she swept into the room.

'Dave . . . Larry . . . ' She offered her cheek to each.

These were men who had stood beside her the day of Tom's Inauguration. They were the men she needed now.

Coffee was served, the door firmly closed, and no more time wasted on trivialities.

'You read it..?' Adelle opened a carved wooden box on the table in front of her and removed a king size filter tip.

Dave Arnell saw the slight tremble in her fingers and his heart went out to her. As the Chief of Staff in the White House during Tom Madigan's term, he had got to know the President and his wife well. He adored Adelle; had done so from their very first meeting. She was so... genteel, feminine, so utterly charming. It was in the breeding of course, he told himself. Her background was impeccable.

He studied her now, thought how little the years had changed her. She was the sort of woman, he mused, who would always remain ageless.

His wife had been desperately jealous of his devotion to Adelle Madigan. In the end it was what had caused their marriage to fall apart. When Betty had accused him of spending more time with the President's wife than with herself and their children, Dave Arnell couldn't deny it.

There was something so intriguing and vulnerable about Adelle. Something that made him want to do everything in his power to protect her...

Over the years since Tom Madigan's tragic death, they had gradually grown closer. So close that eventually, his almost unthinkable fantasy had come true: Dave had found himself invited into Adelle Madigan's bed. It was an experience he'd repeated joyfully on a number of occasions. Yet he knew better than to ever dare suggest marriage. He knew without being told that Adelle would never stop being a Madigan, and had resigned himself to a relationship that would remain their secret.

At least, he thought now, they were both free and there was nothing immoral about their liaison, no danger if their secret was suddenly revealed.

Not like there'd been with Tom...

All those years ago, only those very close to the President had been aware of what was going on.

When Adelle began to have her own suspicions, it was Dave Arnell she confronted for the truth. 'Tell me who it is, Dave. That's all I want to know.'

Her voice was steady, but he knew how much she must be hurting inside. It wasn't fair, he told himself angrily, it just wasn't fair for any man to play around on such a wonderful woman as Adelle. But he could see she wasn't going to rest until he told her the truth. If only she hadn't come to him.

Taking a deep breath, he told her the woman's name.

If he could have heard the words that reeled off in the mind of the cultured and genteel Adelle Madigan, Dave Arnell would have turned white with shock.

They discussed it at length: the ramifications, the dangers.

'Nothing must be allowed to get in Robbie's way. Nothing... ' Adelle was pacing the floor, her sixth cigarette held in her long tapering fingers.

In all the time he'd known her, Dave couldn't remember ever hearing her use that tone of voice before. He glanced at Larry, saw the same anxiety reflected in his colleague's face. It was important to them all that Robert Madigan win the forthcoming Presidential election. In Larry's case, Dave guessed, he probably had a point to prove on top of everything else: he would want to show he had the same magic touch that would get another Madigan into the White House.

Dave turned to Adelle, his voice firm with resolve. 'Believe me, Adelle, we're not going to let anything stop Robbie now. Are we Larry?'

'No way, Dave. No goddamn way.'

It was after eight before Christopher Stanley left the office. He'd finished his column for the next morning's edition almost an hour before, but as usual, had put off the moment of going home as long as possible.

He hated entering the empty apartment, hated the

silence and loneliness now that Carrie was gone. Even moving from the place they had shared at Manhattan Beach to the tiny nondescript condo at Santa Monica hadn't helped much. He still missed her dark eyes and smiling freckled face, still longed for her crazy sense of humour and penetrating wit. And at night, as he lay alone in the bed they had shared for almost two years, he ached with the memory of her long pale body and the love-making that had stirred his soul.

In the basement carpark he climbed into his third-hand Corvette and wound his way up the ramps to street level. Less than twenty minutes later he let himself into the no-frills bachelor apartment, carefully devoid of any sign of the woman he had loved.

Carrie was the past, he told himself repeatedly. He had to forget her, push out of his memory the horror of that night.

In the two years since it had happened he'd tortured himself with guilt. If only he'd been home when the phone call had come; if only he hadn't agreed when Bill Kelly had asked him to make a fourth for tennis that evening. Perhaps then Carrie might still be alive...

As it was, Carrie had taken the call and decided to stand-in for him. As a junior reporter struggling for recognition, it was the sort of assignment she'd jump at.

The LA Police Department figured they'd copped enough bad press; they were about to move in and arrest the leader of one of the gangs terrorising the city's streets, and sought a media presence to ensure a much needed shine to their public image.

So Carrie, always eager and determined to make her professional mark, had answered the call in his stead. When the arrest had erupted in violence, she'd been one of four victims cut down in the crossfire.

That had been over two years ago, but time had done little to heal Chris's sense of loss. There'd been a few women since, casual encounters, but the moment any of them had wanted more and pressed for a real commitment, he'd walked away. It was crazy, irrational, but somehow he'd felt as if he'd be betraying Carrie...

He ate his usual hastily prepared meal, tidied up, watched the ten o'clock news, then went to bed. If he was lucky he wouldn't dream.

The telephone memo was one of a dozen awaiting his attention when he got into the office the next morning. He read the name — Suzie Hawkins — and repeated it under his breath. Why did he think it was vaguely familiar?

It was almost ten before he found a moment to return the call. The number took a long while to answer and he was just about to hang up when a breathless voice sounded in his ear.

'Uh, yeah, hi. This is Christopher Stanley from the *LA Clarion*. Am I talking to Suzie Hawkins?'

'Oh, Mr Stanley, you got my message... I — I wondered if I could meet you sometime. Sometime soon. I have some... information that I'm sure will interest you.'

The woman's approach and nervousness made him wonder if he'd got another kook on the line. It happened all the time.

'What does this... information pertain to, Ms Hawkins?' It wasn't a young voice, but these days it didn't do to presume about a woman's marital status.

He heard her sharp intake of breath. 'I — I read your article last week. About... about Elizabeth Eden. You see, I was under contract to Republic at the same time as Elizabeth. We became friendly. She — ' The woman stopped abruptly.

'Yes... ' Chris encouraged, his curiosity aroused. After the press conference with Tess Jordan he'd done a two-page spread on the subject of WLS's forthcoming movie. It had appeared in the *Clarion* about five days ago.

He heard the woman breathing deeply on the other end of the line. Then the words came spilling out.

'There's something very important I have to tell you, Mr Stanley. Very important. But — but it'll cost you . . . '

Before the appointment he looked up the *Clarion*'s files and found about half a dozen short articles on Suzie Hawkins, 'one of Republic's up and coming starlets'. There were photographs too, revealing a standardly pretty brunette with a full bustline and a rather vacuous smile. After appearing in about a dozen or so forgettable movies, Suzie Hawkins, it seemed, had disappeared from the Hollywood scene.

She had insisted on seeing him as soon as possible, so the next afternoon Chris drove out to the address in the Valley.

Rainbow Glen was a complex of about three dozen apartments with a shabby neglected air. Dusty oleanders dotted the patchy lawn surrounding an old-fashioned swimming pool. As he walked past the murky water, Chris decided it looked capable of producing a whole new world of deadly diseases.

After a couple of wrong turns, he found apartment 22A.

She opened the door at once as if she'd been standing there waiting. 'Come in, Mr Stanley, come in . . . '

The first thing he noticed was the overwhelming stench — a mixture of cats and stale booze. The blinds were pulled down tightly over each window and it took his eyes a moment to adjust to the dimness.

'Please, take a seat . . . '

Three cats leapt aside as he lowered himself onto an ancient sofa.

He could see her better now and did his best to hide his shock. The pretty young woman had become a shapeless tub of flesh with thinning hair harshly dyed to the darkness of her youth. The face was a mass of wrinkles, the over-long false eyelashes a grotesque adornment.

'Now, Mr Stanley, what can I get you to drink?'

God ... at this time in the morning ... He caught the slight slur of her words and realised she must have been at the booze already. Chris settled for a beer which arrived in a tall chipped glass.

Clutching a vodka of similar size, Suzie Hawkins finally took a seat. She was silent for a long time, sizing her visitor up. Early thirties, she judged. Tall, dark, strong appealing features ... the sort of man she'd have been attracted to in her youth. Then, she recalled dolefully, she'd been able to have any man she wanted ...

She steadied herself with a long sip of alcohol. 'Mr Stanley, you see that photograph there? On the table behind you?'

He turned to look where she was pointing. A child, a girl aged about six, smiled out from a cheap plastic frame.

He nodded, turning back to the woman. 'She's very pretty. Is she — '

'My grandchild. My only grandchild,' she emphasised. 'I love her very much, Mr Stanley, and she's dangerously ill. Louisa is the only reason I'm going to talk about something I've never told another living soul ...'

CHAPTER

12

Carl Harris knew it was only a matter of time. The question had been inevitable.

The young female reporter from *LA Magazine*, was looking at him expectantly, waiting for his reply.

Harris felt his heart begin to pump harder, but his voice, thank Christ, was steady enough. 'Elizabeth Eden? Yeah, sure, I played opposite her in half a dozen films. A great looking da — , ah, lady.' The actor caught himself just in time. In these days of Affirmative Action, it wouldn't do his image any good to refer to a member of the opposite sex as a 'dame'.

But the reporter wanted more than that. 'The movie is meant to reveal a different view of Elizabeth Eden than the drug-taking, promiscuous screen goddess she has been portrayed as. Which image do you think is the right one, Carl?'

Christ, why couldn't the fucking broad drop it? Despite his superstrength antiperspirant, Carl Harris could feel the sweat begin to form in his armpits. 'Hey,' he kept his voice light, 'we just worked together. I never really knew the woman. She wasn't my type ... you know?'

His mouth went dry ... But Elizabeth Eden had certainly known what his type was ...

*

Chris Stanley could barely contain his excitement.

If what Suzie Hawkins had hinted at was true, then he knew it was the sort of opportunity that comes just once in a lifetime. In researching his article on Elizabeth Eden he had learned that an unknown woman had rung the police to report Elizabeth's death. If Suzie Hawkins could prove she was that woman . . .

For two days after his meeting with the aging actress, he deliberated how to make the most of what fortune seemed to be offering him. In the end it came down to Tess Jordan and WLS rather than the *Clarion*.

If WLS could be convinced that Suzie Hawkins really held valuable information about the night Elizabeth Eden died, he felt sure they would pay whatever it took to get it. That way, Chris figured, not only would Suzie Hawkins get the sum she had asked for, but there would also be something left over for himself. The art of the LA deal, he thought wryly. Not that it ended there. He had a further proposal he wanted to put to Tess Jordan.

Arranging a private meeting with Tess Jordan wasn't as difficult as he'd imagined. As he drove to their early morning appointment, he was curious about what the female president of WLS would be like face-to-face. He was interested to see what made her tick. In an industry as cutthroat as moviemaking, it took sheer guts and blind ambition to make it to the top.

As he drew up at the entrance to WLS and presented his ID to Security, Chris wondered what had motivated Tess Jordan.

A secretary showed him into a comfortable reception room where a wall of windows gave a riveting view over the City of Angels.

Chris settled down for the usual lengthy wait, but it seemed the president of WLS didn't play by at least one of the basic male executive rules: she didn't keep him waiting long.

Within five minutes Tess Jordan was shaking his hand, greeting him in a manner as professional as her blue linen suit.

As she offered Christopher Stanley a seat, Tess wondered why the tall dark-haired reporter seemed familiar. Then, as she pulled up a chair on the opposite side of the low coffee table, it suddenly came to her. She remembered the overlong hair and casual clothes from one of her press conferences. She noticed he was no more formally attired today, although a sports jacket had been added to the open-necked shirt and jeans.

'You're with the *LA Clarion*, I understand, Mr Stanley. What can I do for you?' Her manner was direct and indicated that her schedule didn't allow for wasted time.

'Actually I'm not here as a representative of the *Clarion*, Ms Jordan. Rather I'm acting as a middleman in the transfer of some information I hope will interest WLS.'

Tess raised an eyebrow at this unexpected approach. 'Information? To do with what, precisely, Mr Stanley?'

The formality of her manner in a city as laid-back as LA, made it easier for Chris to broach the subject.

'It's about the movie WLS is producing on Elizabeth Eden. I've had contact with a one-time friend of Ms Eden's — a friend who claims to have been with her on the night she died.'

He waited for the response, but saw only the slightly widening eyes. He had to admire her control.

'Who is this "friend"?'

'I'm not at liberty to tell you, Ms Jordan. She came to me as a result of an article I wrote on Elizabeth Eden. She claims not only to have been with Elizabeth on the night she died . . . but to have further information about the actress's death.'

Tess felt her heart beat faster. She said softly, 'I think you'd better tell me exactly what you want, Mr Stanley.'

*

It took just twenty-four hours to arrange.

For reasons of vanity — or perhaps confidentiality, Chris was not sure which — Suzie Hawkins refused to come to the studios. Instead she drove into Westwood, left her car at a parking station, and Chris took her from there to the downtown hotel where the meeting was to take place.

Tess was waiting, her eyes wary as Chris performed the introductions.

Suzie Hawkins sank her bulk gratefully into the modern sofa. She was dressed in a floating peach-coloured caftan, her thick neck entwined with a double row of cheap pearls. On the outer corner of her left eye, the end of a heavy false eyelash was beginning to lift off.

Tess came quickly to the point. 'Ms Hawkins, I've been told by Mr Stanley that you have some vital information about the night Elizabeth Eden died. I also understand that for the sum of $30,000, you're prepared to part with this information. Is that correct?'

Suzie Hawkins nodded, shooting a quick sideways glance at Christopher. They had agreed that he should have $5,000 of the money she was asking for. 'That's right,' she replied a trifle breathlessly. She needed a drink. Badly. But that morning had found a control she hadn't known herself still capable of.

Tess gave her a level look. 'What proof are you offering of your revelations, Ms Hawkins?'

Suzie Hawkins' ridiculous eyelashes fluttered nervously. 'I was the unidentified woman who reported Elizabeth's death to the police. There will be a record of my fingerprints on LAPD files.'

For a moment there was silence in the room.

Tess was the one to break it. 'But why speak out now, more than twenty years after the event?'

Suzie Hawkins ran her tongue over dry lips. 'I was frightened... My career was beginning to slide. I — I didn't want to be mixed up in anything that could bring me the wrong sort of publicity.' She gave a bitter laugh. 'Not that it mattered in the end. As it turned out I was just another naive hopeful whose dreams were never going to come true. But now,' the woman's tone grew firmer, 'I have a reason to tell what I know. My little grand-daughter's sick. Real sick. She needs the sort of treatment only big bucks can buy. If she doesn't get that we're going to lose her. I need that money real bad, Ms Jordan ... believe me.'

Bad enough to tell a lie? Tess wondered. But there was something in Suzie Hawkins's demeanour that made her trust the woman. And she had offered a very final sort of proof ...

Tess made up her mind. 'I'm going to put it this way, Ms Hawkins. You tell me here and now what it is you know, and I'll give you a cheque for half the sum involved. Once I can arrange for a check on the finger-prints, you'll be paid the rest of the money. Is that a proposal you feel you can accept?'

Suzie Hawkins's fat body seemed to slump with relief. She had bought back her precious Louisa's life.

'I'll tell you everything,' she promised solemnly.

Mike Havelock was listening in rapt attention. 'She was there when Elizabeth — ?'

Tess nodded. 'When Elizabeth was *killed*, Mike.' She gave emphasis to the word. 'This proves my mother's instinct was right. Elizabeth didn't suicide. In fact, according to Suzie Hawkins, she was in fine spirits that evening. Suzie had been at a party at the nearby home of a well-known director. As she tells it, the party was a disaster for her. She had a fight with her lover at the time — a big name actor, apparently, though she refused to elaborate. I get the impression the guy was married and refusing to leave his wife, despite Suzie's pleading. She began to drink heavily and when she left the party she was very depressed and reluctant to go home to her own empty apartment. That's when she decided to call on Elizabeth — even though it was then almost midnight. They had worked on a number of movies together and had become quite friendly and anyway, Suzie was too heartbroken to care too much if Elizabeth would mind such a late visit.

'According to Suzie, Elizabeth was surprised when she took the call over the security intercom, but she hadn't yet gone to bed. Suzie drove her car around the back of the house and Elizabeth let her in at the kitchen door. She hated live-in servants, only had a woman who came in a few hours during the day.

'So Elizabeth herself made coffee and the two women sat at the kitchen table where Suzie poured out the whole sorry tale into her friend's sympathetic ear.

'When Elizabeth invited her to stay the night, Suzie remembers she was only too pleased to accept. Not very long afterwards she went upstairs to the guest bedroom. She thinks she might only have been in bed about five minutes, she was just dozing off, when she heard raised voices: Elizabeth's and a man's. It was obvious they were arguing.

'It went on for a while and then suddenly there was silence. For a long moment, Suzie lay there listening. She thinks she might even have fallen back to sleep for a while. Then she heard the front door slam, so she struggled out of bed and looked out of the window. It was dark, but she could just make out the figure of a man. He got into a car parked in the driveway and started off down the drive. Disturbed, she felt the need to use the bathroom. When she walked out into the hall, she could see the house was still lit up.

'As Suzie tells it, she called out to Elizabeth but got no reply. Though still groggy from all the booze she'd put away that evening, she remembered the raised voices and decided to see if Elizabeth was all right.

'And that's when . . . ' Tess fought to keep her voice

steady. 'That's when she found her. In the upstairs bathroom, in a tub of cold water already turned bright red with blood from her slashed wrists . . . '

Chris didn't expect to have any problems. He had established a good working arrangement with the LA Police Department.

'Read they're makin' a movie about her now,' commented Constable Joe Cornello as he filled in all the correct procedural forms for the release of the fingerprint copy. He looked up at Chris and grinned. 'Think this is gonna help you find the mystery dame?'

'Gotta write something,' Chris replied easily.

Only later did he remember Suzie Hawkins's curious comment. 'I don't know why the cops never managed to trace me,' she'd said. 'I couldn't have been that hard to track down . . . '

'OK, Sandy,' Tess responded to her secretary's query, 'I'll take it.' She switched to her private line and answered the call. 'Yes, Mr Stanley . . . Can I help you?'

He had prepared his opening approach, but still Chris couldn't be certain how it would be received. He spoke quickly, succinctly, outlining his proposal to one of Hollywood's most powerful women.

At least she listened — didn't interrupt. At the end she said briefly, 'Perhaps we should meet and talk about this more fully, Mr Stanley.'

He was grinning with elation as he replaced the receiver.

This time they met in Tess's office. It was after six, the first moment she had had free all day, and she offered him a drink.

'Now,' she said when they were settled, 'tell me in detail what you have in mind.'

He did. He explained how Elizabeth Eden had always

fascinated him; how he'd been planning one day, when he had enough money saved, to take a year or so off work and write her story.

'She was a forerunner in the industry, Ms Jordan. She fought so hard to escape the dumb blonde, sex symbol image the studios insisted on tagging her with. She hated the movies they lined up for her, hated to think she was wasting her talent; but it seems to me that in her struggle to escape the system Elizabeth Eden stepped on some pretty important toes. It's my belief she was made to pay a price for that.'

He was leaning towards her, speaking earnestly. 'I haven't seen your script, Ms Jordan, I don't know exactly what areas of Elizabeth's life you're going to explore, but I'm sure there's still plenty more to find out. Men, sometimes very powerful men, were drawn to her like flies; and Suzie Hawkins's story indicates very strongly that Elizabeth didn't commit suicide.'

He saw those green eyes looking unwaveringly into his and he came to the point. 'What I'm saying, Ms Jordan, is that there are too many loose ends — loose ends I can follow up if I have the financial resources. With the backing of WLS, I'd be able to trace back over those last few months of Elizabeth Eden's life, see what I can find out. There'd be something in it for both of us: a book for me, and a chance for you to make a movie which, if it raises enough questions about Elizabeth's death, might see the case reopened and justice done.' Chris raised a questioning eyebrow. 'What do you say? Are you willing to take that gamble?'

Tess kept her expression neutral as she studied the lanky, dark-haired reporter, but her mind was swiftly weighing up his proposition. Chris Stanley was young, enthusiastic, keen to make his name. He seemed to understand the real Elizabeth Eden and seemed sincere in his desire to clear her name. But most importantly, Tess felt he might just be able to gain access to the sort of information the police would never pass on. Information pertaining to the evening Elizabeth had died ...

At last, she nodded. There was something about the man in front of her that inspired confidence. 'It's a deal, Mr Stanley.' She stood up and extended her hand.

He took it in his. 'Call me Chris,' he smiled. 'I'm easier with that.'

She returned his smile but not the favour, as she said goodnight.

CHAPTER

13

It was a decision Adelle Madigan had made alone. But she told Dave Arnell what she was going to do.

'I think Robbie has to know, Dave. If the media somehow get a whiff of it, they're bound to confront him. He has to be prepared.'

Dave Arnell knew how much Adelle would hate having to broach the subject with her son. Even just to hint at information which might damage Robert Madigan's image of the father he had worshipped would be anathema to her. But Dave was forced to agree; Robert had to be told.

Even if Adelle knew only half the truth...

It wasn't unusual for Robert Madigan to call on his mother a couple of times a week. It was on one such occasion two days later, that Adelle tried as delicately as possible to enlighten him.

'The campaign is going very well, Robbie. The Republicans must be running scared.' They were strolling arm in arm through the grounds of Adelle's Pacific Palisades estate.

'We haven't put a foot wrong, Mom. The polls are telling us that. I don't see how we can lose.'

She heard the note of confidence in his voice and

chose her words carefully. 'One can't ever get too compla-
cent in the business of politics, Robbie. Right up to the
last moment the opposition are always going to be looking
for dirt to throw.'

'Well, they're not going to find anything on me, are
they?'

'No, Robbie, not on you. But perhaps the past can
offer more ... lucrative possibilities.'

He stood still and frowned at her. There had been
something in her tone ... 'What do you mean?'

'I'm talking about your father, Rob. It — It's something I hoped you'd never have to hear about. But he was
the President, and a very handsome man to boot, and
women were inevitably drawn to him.' Adelle looked
away, her eyes hidden behind large framed sunglasses.
'He slipped only once. The woman chased him unrelent-
ingly; she was determined to get him, and she was smarter
than the rest. It meant nothing to him, of course, and
didn't last long. Only a few close aides knew of the affair
and luckily it ... ended before there was any damage.'

'But who ...?' Robert Madigan frowned in
confusion.

'An actress.' Adelle didn't bother to hide her contempt. 'Elizabeth Eden. A woman with a reputation all
over town. But the danger for you, my darling, lies in the
fact that at this very moment they're making the movie
that purports to tell the "true story" about Elizabeth
Eden's life ...'

Sara knew something was wrong. She and Robbie were
too close for him to have something on his mind without
her suspecting.

She waited a few days and then one evening after they
had made love, she asked what was bothering him.

Robert Madigan rolled away from his wife's embrace.
'Nothing, honey,' he murmured.

But Sara knew him better than that. 'You're worried

about something, Rob. That's obvious. Why won't you share it with me?'

And so, with a sigh of relief, he told her.

For a long time afterwards, Sara Madigan lay staring into the darkness. *Don't worry, Robbie*, she vowed silently, *nothing's going to take the Presidency away from you. Nothing.*

The next day she rang her father.

Walter Conroy missed his only daughter. As often as possible he would fly in his Conroy-built jet to California as much to catch up with Sara as to keep an eye on business.

Anne seldom accompanied him on these visits and for that Walter Conroy was grateful. As the years had gone by, he and his wife seemed to have less and less in common. It was his daughter who had become his closest friend and confidante.

Walter thought he detected a note of strain in Sara's voice when she rang him at home, asking if there was any chance he might be in LA in the next few days. 'Nothing wrong, is there, baby?'

'Just want to talk with you, Daddy,' was the noncommittal reply.

'Well, as a matter of fact I was planning on flying in some time soon. Got a new guy in charge of West Coast operations; wanted to see how everything was going.'

They made a date for lunch in two days' time.

Walter took his daughter to the Regency Club on Wilshire Boulevard. It had the ambience of an English club, and an incredible view of the city. Not on the usual celebrity list, the restaurant provided an ideal background for quiet conversation.

Sara waited until they were having coffee to confide her news. It had an even greater impact than she expected.

Walter Conroy's fleshy face went the colour of ash.

'Daddy,' she hastened to reassure him, 'we can't even be sure the relationship will ever come to light. It's just that even the possibility is too risky to contemplate. The opposition would do anything to cut Robbie out of this race. I — I just wondered if there was anything you could do to stop them making this film.'

Walter had recovered his composure. 'Leave it to me, baby.' He patted her hand. His fingers were as cold as ice.

The bombshell his daughter had dropped was making it difficult for Walter Conroy to concentrate on his meeting with his West Coast president.

'So those are the two points I intend to negotiate around, Walter. Do you agree?'

Nick was winding up his proposal for dealing with a major client of Conroy Aircraft Corporation. But he could tell that his employer's mind was on matters other than the business at hand. In all his five years of dealing with Walter Conroy, Nick couldn't remember another time when that had occurred.

The older man nodded distractedly. 'Sure, Nick. Uh — better give me the whole report to read over on the way back to Dallas.'

As Walter Conroy got up to leave, Nick wondered if he should mention the other problem that was worrying him. Better not, he decided. Walter looked as if he had enough on his plate at the moment. And anyway, Nick thought, he'd better be absolutely sure of his facts before presenting them to his boss.

Anne Conroy held the receiver to her ear and scribbled down the list of figures being relayed to her.

She was making her usual call to her stockbroker and her eyes were bright with pleasure as she saw how much movement there had been in the markets.

'Thanks, George. Talk to you soon,' she said crisply, and hung up.

For the next few minutes she studied the column of figures, tapping them into her cheap pocket calculator. Finally, she leaned back with a sigh of satisfaction. Over $170,000 profit on the bonds alone. Her timing had been perfect.

She stood up and walked over to the bureau in the small, sparsely furnished room. She thought of it as her office though there was no evidence to that effect. No fax machines, screens or teleprinters — and her files were kept locked in the bottom bureau drawer.

For a number of years now Anne Conroy had been building her portfolio. But it was her secret. A secret between herself and her broker.

Her capital had come from the 'housekeeping money' Walter allowed her. He had never showed any interest in how she spent the allowance and gradually, by thriftiness and cutting corners, Anne Conroy had acquired a substantial amount of working capital. Now she no longer needed to skim off her household allowance, but thrift was still a habit. It had been ingrained in her from birth.

The sixth of seven children, Anne had learned the lessons of poverty early. When she had met Walter Conroy in her late teens, she had seen the driving ambition and ruthless energy by which he intended to escape his own straitened circumstances — and as his wife she had worked energetically and willingly by his side to assure their common dream. It was a dream she'd never doubted would come true.

Anne Conroy smiled grimly as she locked away the list of figures in the bureau drawer. Walter had looked on her as a good workhorse, someone who'd be willing to carry the physical day-to-day burdens of achieving their goals. And that's what she'd been. But Walter had also made it patently clear that he considered her too stupid to understand anything beyond the domestic realm. Unlike his beloved Sara.

Well, Anne Conroy's lips tightened, they'd both learn differently when the time came.

Six years ago she had begun to study the finance pages of the major newspapers and leading investor magazines, making a careful scrutiny of a wide variety of stocks and shares. After a shaky start she had turned her starting capital into millions.

Her reason for doing so was simple.

Those half-dozen years ago she had found the first evidence that Walter was having an affair. Since then, her snooping had revealed there had been dozens of women. Anne had read the letters and notes, listened in on the telephone calls, and realised Walter was merely marking time with her until he saw his everloving daughter ensconced in the White House. After that, Anne felt sure, it would be only a matter of time before Walter left her.

And that was the day she was preparing for.

When it came time to settle on the alimony, she was going to be able to afford the best lawyers in town. She was going to take her betrayer to the cleaners and then, she thought viciously, let him see how many of the greedy bitches would hang around . . .

If she couldn't have him, she'd make damn sure no one else could either.

'You wouldn't believe what they wanted to charge for reframing those mirrors.'

Walter faced his wife across the dinner table. She was on her usual hobbyhorse: the same old litany of just which particular tradesman, attorney, or supermarket chain was ripping them off. Usually Walter let her speak, offering the occasional grunt of agreement. But tonight he couldn't bear the sound of his wife's voice. It grated on his nerves and was driving him to distraction in his present state.

He wiped his napkin over his lips and stood up, interrupting her in full flight. 'I won't worry about dessert tonight, honey. I've got a lot of work to get through.'

In the sanctuary of his study, he poured himself a stiff shot of Bourbon. He noticed his fingers were trembling. Christ, he was coming apart at the seams . . .

He threw back the drink in one swallow, poured another, and sat down in his favourite chair to ponder the nightmare that threatened to change his life.

Just one slip-up . . . That's all there'd been. And some sonofabitch smartass had started sniffing around.

Walter felt the sweat break out across his upper lip. He had been counting so much on Robbie winning the election. He'd looked upon that as his salvation. But now, even that might be put at risk . . . If he didn't do something about it.

Once again, they met in the reception room.

Chris had assured her he'd be able to turn up a copy of the fingerprints of the 'unidentified woman'. He had, and was there to prove to Tess Jordan that they matched exactly with those he had just taken from Suzie Hawkins.

'So, she was telling the truth . . . She really was there the night Elizabeth was murdered.' Tess never used 'suicide' to refer to the actress's death any more.

'It's going to make for one helluva movie,' Chris put in.

Tess nodded. Shooting was just about to start. Everything was running to schedule. There had been loud legal rumblings from Bernie Golding, the owner of Republic Studios, regarding the major role played by his late father in Elizabeth Eden's corruption. But so far nothing had happened to make WLS change their storyline. And now, they had proof of Suzie Hawkins's amazing revelation.

Chris Stanley was shaking his head in puzzlement. 'You really have to wonder why the cops didn't have their suspicions at the time. It seems to me in rereading the dozens of articles on Elizabeth Eden's death, that they never once considered it might have been anything other than suicide.'

Tess looked at him thoughtfully. 'There seem to be more questions than answers about a lot of things to do with Elizabeth Eden's death.' Then she stood up and put out her hand. 'Thanks for your assistance, Mr Stanley. If you see my office manager on the way out, she has a cheque ready for the rest of the money.'

Chris got to his feet and she accompanied him to the door. With one hand on the doorknob, he turned towards her. 'You know,' he mused, 'maybe there's still a chance of finding out the identity of the man who visited Elizabeth that evening. Because he almost certainly had something to do with her death.'

'I think we both agree on that, Mr Stanley,' Tess answered softly.

As she parked on the pebbled drive of Nick's rented Beverly Hills home, Tess suddenly wondered if she had done the right thing in accepting the invitation.

'I'd love to introduce you to Helen, Tess,' he'd said. 'I've told her about you and she's very keen to meet you. Would you be free for lunch Sunday afternoon? It'll just be us and the kids.'

And so here she was — complete with misgivings.

Nick welcomed her at the door with a warm smile and a kiss on the cheek. Tess wished he hadn't done that. It made something she'd long forgotten stir inside her . . .

Helen Teece was as warmly welcoming as her husband. 'So lovely to meet you at last, Tess. Nick has often spoken about you.'

When . . . What did he say . . ? Tess directed the questions silently at the attractive, dark-haired woman with the gentle eyes and perfect smile.

'It's a miracle that you both not only survived but

have become so successful,' said Helen as she led the way
to the back of the house where a table was set in the warm
enclosure of a glassed-in terrace.

'I guess the only way left to us was up,' said Tess
lightly, trying to make conversation with this pleasant
woman whom she should have hated on sight.

Lunch was a casual, relaxed affair. The two children
created plenty of noise and distraction, which made it
easier for Tess to camouflage her emotions.

How she envied Helen! She was the woman who had
borne Nick's children, who slept with him every night,
who would be there to share his old age. And the fact that
Helen was so obviously a lovely human being, somehow
made it even worse.

Will I ever find what Nick has? she wondered. *Or will
it evade me for the rest of my life . . ?*

By late afternoon the children were tired and beginning to squabble.

'I think I'll get these two into the bath.' Helen stood
up with a smile. 'Anyway, you two could probably do
with a little time on your own.'

She's so goddamn nice, thought Tess. How could she
dislike a woman who was so genuine?

'Let's go inside,' suggested Nick. 'It'll be more pleasant now that the sun's almost gone.'

Once Tess was comfortably seated in the den, Nick
poured them both a brandy and settled down opposite her.

'I'm so glad you made it today, Tess. I don't want us
to lose contact again. It was hell all those years ago when I
couldn't find out what happened to you.' He took a sip of
his drink and looked at her over the rim of his glass. 'Are
you ready to fill me in on the past, Tess? To tell me how it
all happened for you?'

Tess took a swallow of her drink. She would tell him
what she could. But it wouldn't be the whole story. Right
now not even Nick could know that.

Maybe he never could.

*

It was dark when she stood up to leave.

'Well, I'd better be going, Nick. It's getting late. Thanks for a lovely afternoon.'

Before she could move, he was beside her, his arms reaching out to enfold her. As he held her close, he spoke softly into her ear. 'What we had was special, Tess. Nothing can rob us of that. But I can see from your face you haven't found everything you're looking for. Don't let anything — career, power, money — stand in the way of the important things. Nothing's worth that.'

Something happened inside her then. Nick's words suddenly caused her passion and longing to be replaced by a sudden flooding of joy — a joy that had its roots in friendship, compassion, and concern.

They clung together for a long moment before walking silently to the door.

CHAPTER

14

She had meant to finish some work when she got home and then go straight to bed. But as she tried to concentrate on the documents in front of her, Tess found herself increasingly drawn to thoughts of her conversation with Nick.

In the end she couldn't ignore her compulsion any longer. It was after eleven, but she dragged the locked suitcase from its storage place. Kneeling on the carpet beside it, she snapped open the lid.

The photo album was buried beneath a pile of old newspapers and magazines. There was also a bundle of letters which Tess had read with awe-struck concentration years before.

Now she turned the pages of the album until she came to the place she was looking for. The half-dozen faded black and white photographs showed two laughing girls of about fourteen years old. One was taller than the other and already more voluptuous.

'Francie had the sort of figure other girls would die for,' she remembered her mother saying when she'd first showed her the photographs of her and her best friend.

Now, as she stared down at the pages of the well-worn album, Tess wished she could have told Nick the truth.

She had told him so much about the years in between. But not everything. Not the thing that mattered most . . .

'Got a date tonight, sweetheart?' Ruth smiled across the kitchen table at her tall, beautiful daughter.

'No, there's an assignment due Monday. I'm going to work on that.' Pushing aside her empty coffee cup, Tess got to her feet. 'May as well start on it now,' she announced as she left the room.

Ruth hid a sigh as she watched her go. Tess was in her sophomore year at UCLA, a brilliant student. But not once had she mentioned a boyfriend. When Ruth had tentatively brought up the subject, questioning her lack of social outlets, Tess had been disdainful in response. She had absolutely no interest in following college baseball or football teams, she declared, or in wasting her time at parties or proms.

'I'm too involved with my classes, Mom. After all that's what I'm there for, isn't it?'

Ruth couldn't disagree. But it still didn't stop her worrying that the girl was missing the sort of fun and good times only youth can offer. When she mentioned it to Reed he refused to take her worries seriously.

'Honey, I'm sure Tess is doing exactly what makes her happy, so why don't you just stop losing sleep about it?'

Deep down Ruth knew he was right, but still she wished her daughter would find a nice group of kids to go out with and enjoy herself.

Surely the boys must find Tess attractive, she worried. Despite her attire. It amazed Ruth to see that all the lovely clothes she bought for her daughter were ignored for her invariable choice of Levis and sweater.

At her age, Ruth recalled, I'd have given my eye teeth to have even one of the beautiful dresses Tess owns. But then she remembered that at eighteen she had already been married to Jeff, had turned her back on college and independence.

Tess knew her mother was concerned by what she perceived as a gap in her 'normal teenage development', but what Ruth had forgotten was that for Tess such a state had never existed. Life on the streets of New York City had accelerated the process of growing up and given her little in common with her soft, naive peers whose definition of hunger was giving up Hershey bars on their latest diet.

She didn't feel she was missing anything with the boys she met either. None of them came anywhere close to making her forget Nick. She kept them all at arm's length and it made no impact at all when she heard she was known as the Ice Queen.

Tess was fully committed to the path she had chosen. Her studies were what mattered most. As she slowly came to understand the labyrinthine workings of the law she felt a growing confidence in her abilities to make the system work for those who most needed its protection. Nothing was going to sway her from her path.

Certainly not Scott McNeill.

They met while researching an assignment on Class and the Law. Students had to work in pairs, and while their names were chosen at random, Tess and Scott discovered very quickly the similarity in their outlooks. Like Tess, Scott McNeill was also driven to change the system, to ensure that the protection of the law was offered to all who sought it.

In time the relationship grew beyond the common intellectual bond that had brought them together. While Scott's quick brain and bold confidence were certainly appealing, Tess was forced to admit that his thick glossy hair, trim body and mocking blue eyes were also part of the attraction.

They began to spend more and more time together and when eventually she brought Scott home, she could read the relief on her mother's face. Her daughter was 'normal' after all.

But Ruth's relief soon turned to concern as she came to understand how deeply Scott McNeill hated the rich and privileged. From a comfortable middle-class background himself, he was scathing in his rejection of its values.

'It's the reason for America's decay,' he would argue with Reed. 'The rich are bleeding the country dry with their greed for more and more.'

'The rich provide jobs and pay taxes, Scott,' Reed answered mildly. He knew the boy was contemptuous of his own particular area of the law, that he felt actors were grossly overpaid, and saw Reed's role as that of a parasite on a corrupt industry.

While Reed hadn't admitted it to Ruth, he too was beginning to dislike Scott McNeill and his increasing influence over Tess. But the only way to deal with it, he decided, was to keep an open door and an open mind.

Tess and Scott were still a couple two years later when Ruth insisted, over Tess's protests, in celebrating her twenty-first birthday with a lavish party.

Over a hundred guests were invited to the Country Club where a ten-piece orchestra would provide the background for a sit-down dinner followed by dancing.

Ruth was adamant too that Tess have something special to wear for the occasion. It took two days of scouring the boutiques of Beverly Hills, but at last they found the perfect gown.

On the evening of the party as she entered Tess's bedroom Ruth caught her breath at the girl's dark beauty.

'You look absolutely wonderful in that dress, honey. And your hair looks so pretty up like that.' Ruth tried her best not to gush; she knew how it irritated Tess.

But that night, as Tess looked at her reflection in the mirror, she recognised for perhaps the very first time that she was blessed with exceptional looks. The strapless hot pink gown set off her tanned shoulders and the dark hair curled with expert carelessness on top of her head.

I really do look lovely, she thought in happy surprise. *I never guessed I could put it all together like this.*

And for a fleeting moment she remembered the young girl who had slept in a ragged coat which she wore day after day . . .

'You're wearing your graduation gift, I see,' Ruth smiled fondly at the Victorian brooch pinned between her daughter's breasts.

'Yes,' Tess smiled and turned away from her reflection. 'It looks OK doesn't it?'

'Fine, sweetheart.'

'Where did you say you got it again, Mom?'

Ruth looked into her daughter's innocent eyes. 'It was given to me by your Aunt Francie . . . You remember her, don't you? She used to write to us now and then. She was always . . . always very generous.'

Tess hadn't heard the name for years. 'Whatever happened to her?' she asked.

Ruth looked away. 'I don't know. After my accident we — we lost contact.'

It was then, at that precise moment, that Ruth made her decision.

While it was against her natural inclination to seek the limelight, Tess had enjoyed her birthday celebration more than she'd expected. She knew her mother and Reed had certainly got a great deal of pleasure in marking the occasion. Their many friends had outnumbered the few Tess herself had invited to the party.

She was aware that her mother had never hidden the fact that she'd lost contact with her only child for so long. It was just on the details of how they had found each other again that Ruth had remained deliberately vague.

'Am I disturbing you, sweetheart?'

Tess looked up from her books to find her mother

standing in the doorway of her room. 'No, Mom. Nothing I can't do later. Come in.'

Ruth was carrying something in the crook of her arm. She entered the sunny study with its view of the garden and took a seat on the low-backed sofa.

'Come and join me, Tess,' she said, patting the cushion next to her, 'I've got something I want to show you.'

Tess rose from her desk, a little surprised at the interruption. Reed was away for a few days on business but even so, her mother rarely disturbed her when she was studying. As she sat down beside her on the sofa, Tess became aware of the tension in her mother's bearing.

'What is it, Mom? Are you upset about something?' She frowned, sensing some unspoken emotion barely held in check.

For one desperate moment Ruth stared in silence at the girl beside her, and almost changed her mind. It was so tempting to ignore the whisper from the gods that was driving her to this act of madness.

But then with trembling fingers, she opened the photo album she'd brought with her.

It was the girl's right to know the truth. She had decided that. *No matter the cost to herself...*

'*Aunt Francie... my mother...*'

Tess breathed out the words, her face pale with shock. Her eyes were riveted to the black and white snapshots of the two teenage girls. Her mind reeled.

She had only the vaguest recollections of the woman who had visited on those isolated occasions when she was a child. It was the gifts, the unexpected deliveries of toys, or party dresses, or flowers she remembered more clearly.

But her *mother*... It was almost too much to comprehend. Slowly she raised her head and stared disbelievingly at Ruth. 'But... how? Why...?'

Ruth swallowed, praying for courage. 'To — to tell you that, Tess, I have to go back to the beginning.'

CHAPTER

15

'I met Francie when I was just thirteen, and she was a couple of months older.'

Ruth Hardy spoke slowly, carefully choosing her words so Tess might understand how fate had played its hand.

'My father had just died suddenly of a heart attack and my Aunt Nell took me into her home. She was divorced with no children of her own and she did everything she could to help me adjust to losing Pa. In fact, Aunt Nell had tried to get Pa and me to come and live with her two years before, just after Ma died. We'd lost the new baby too and Pa was pretty shook up, but he refused Nell's offer then.'

Ruth gave Tess a sad smile. 'I was glad, you know. I wanted it just to be the two of us . . . But I guess even then I knew his refusal had a lot to do with his work. Pa had been a miner since he was sixteen; he didn't know anything else.

'At Aunt Nell's it was hard getting used to a new school. The semester was almost half over when I arrived and it seemed to me as if all the other girls already had their groups of friends; they certainly paid no attention to me. I was so blue and lonely . . . and then I met Francie.'

The memory brought a smile to Ruth's face. 'She

came up to me one lunchtime, to the spot where I always ate alone. Francie was tall for her age, and already her figure was bursting out of her faded cotton dress. I didn't know it at the time, but everything she wore was a hand-me-down — things her mother had culled from the charity donations to the local church. The other girls would snigger at Francie's terrible clothes but at the same time, they were openly jealous of her developing figure.

'But I didn't know any of that when Francie first spoke to me. What I remember most about that meeting was her wonderful smile and gentle manner. She sat down beside me, introduced herself as Francie Kovaks, and without any preamble said how much she liked my curls, and how she wished she had them too instead of her own dark straight hair.

'Everyone at school knew, of course, that my aunt owned one of the two beauty salons in town, but what Francie was keen to find out was if I'd ever had my hair done there. She told me then that her dream was to have her hair permed and styled in a real beauty parlour. She hated having her mother chop at it with a pair of dress-making scissors.

'So that was how our friendship began. Just two kids talking girl-talk. In just a short time we were close to inseparable. We did everything together. But only during school hours. The moment school was out, Francie had to rush home. Her mother, she explained, didn't want her roaming the streets, "getting into trouble".

'I discovered that Enid Kovaks worked as a house-keeper for Father Doyle, the local parish priest. When I complained to Aunt Nell about Francie never being allowed to visit with me after school, or even on week-ends, she filled me in a little more on Francie's mother. The rumour on the grapevine was that Francie's father had deserted Enid when she was six months pregnant. Aunt Nell thought that might have been what turned her so obsessively towards the Church — for solace. I already knew from Francie that her mother was quite fanatical about her faith.

'According to the way Aunt Nell read it, Enid Kovaks hated all men and was determined that no one was going to get his hands on her only daughter. When I thought about how strict Enid was with Francie, how she would barely let her out of her sight, I figured Aunt Nell had got it right.

'I knew Francie was very much under her mother's influence. She'd never have dared to cross her, at least as far as boys were concerned. According to Francie, her mother was always preaching that the only men a woman could trust were the "men of God". She meant, of course, the priests she worked for. Enid made it clear to Francie that all the others were creatures with disgusting appetites and obscene minds who were after only one thing. And for any woman foolish enough to give in to their demands, she warned, the Lord would ensure an "eternity in hell". By the time her mother was finished with her dire warnings, Francie was far too terrified to even look at a boy.

'And then on that one and only occasion, she plucked up the courage to defy her.'

Ruth sighed deeply and shook her head. 'I can still picture that awful night so vividly. It started out so happily, but ended in tears and humiliation for Francie.

'The school prom was coming up and we were all looking forward to it. I'd just started dating Jeff, and Aunt Nell had made me a really pretty dress to wear on the big night. But about two weeks before the prom I caught a cold and ended up missing three days of school. It was then Francie decided to take the chance and visit me instead of going straight home.

'I was delighted to see her, of course. Typical kids, being apart for just three days meant we had lots to talk about. But when Aunt Nell offered Francie a glass of milk and a sandwich she refused — she was too nervous about being late home. She stayed little more than ten minutes or so, and as she was leaving, Aunt Nell asked if she was going to the prom.

'I remember the look on Francie's face as she explained how her mother would never allow her to do that. And how, even if by some miracle she did, there'd be no money to buy her a dress.

'Well, something must have clicked with Aunt Nell then. She just couldn't see why Francie should miss out on her big night. And, of course, she knew how much I wanted to share the occasion with my very best girlfriend.

'So she began to plot for Francie to go to the dance with me and Jeff. "Every girl should have the chance to dress up and go to her high school prom," I remember her declaring. "We're going to see that Francie goes to that dance." '

A smile curved Ruth's lips. 'You wouldn't believe, Tess, how excited Francie was when I told her of Aunt Nell's plan. It was all her dreams come true, especially when she heard that not only was Aunt Nell going to make her a dress, but would also fix her hair in the salon.

'Of course, thrilled as she was, she was also petrified that her mother would find out what was going on. But Aunt Nell had thought of a way round that too. She rang Enid Kovaks herself and asked if Francie would like to earn a little extra pocket money by helping spring-clean the salon on that particular evening. One thing Aunt Nell knew for sure about Enid Kovaks was that she wouldn't turn her back on the offer of an extra dollar.

'And the ruse worked. Everything fell into place. I took Francie's measurements carefully at school and Aunt Nell worked on the dress so that by the day of the prom it was ready.

'Francie's fears of discovery were easily side-stepped in the excitement of seeing herself transformed under Aunt Nell's skilled hands. It was her dream of having her hair fixed in a real salon that seemed to please her the most. Aunt Nell set to, cutting and curling, and when she was finished, Francie was almost beside herself with delight. The new hairstyle, some lightly applied make-up, and a dress which was the first to ever fit her properly, and Francie's transformation was complete.

'When Aunt Nell finally allowed her to look in the mirror, Francie's expression said it all. You could see that she could hardly believe her own reflection. Her eyes shone as she stared at herself in the glass; she kept running her hands over the full taffeta skirts of the dress, repeating breathlessly: "I never dreamed I could ever look like this ... Never ... " '

Ruth paused, her eyes distant with memory, as she turned to the girl beside her. 'To tell you the truth, Tess,' she said softly, 'I think it was the happiest moment of Francie's life to date.'

She seemed lost in thought for a moment and then, with a heavy sigh, went on. 'But something terrible soon happened to spoil it all. And, oh God, it was awful ...

'We'd been at the prom for less than an hour. Francie was the centre of everyone's attention. The girls were openly incredulous and envious while the boys stood gaping in astonishment and admiration.

'She was so beautiful, Tess. All it had taken was for someone to care, to show her how to make the most of herself. That night, at the prom, Francie Kovaks stunned them all. No one was sniggering at her then, and the boys were knocking each other aside to ask her to dance. You could see how absolutely smitten they were.

'But then, it was all spoilt — made dirty and shameful. Enid Kovaks turned up.

'She burst into the hall and pushed her way across the dance floor to where Francie was standing surrounded by a group of admiring boys. Enid was a strong, well-built woman and she shoved them aside, her eyes burning with fury. Without a word, she drew back her arm and slapped Francie across the face with every ounce of her strength. By now people had seen what was happening, and even the band had stopped playing. It made it all the easier to hear the words Enid Kovaks began to scream at her daughter.'

Ruth shook her head. 'I couldn't repeat them, Tess. But they were the sort of words you'd never expect to hear from a woman as deeply religious as Enid Kovaks claimed to be. In front of all of her stunned classmates, Enid called her daughter the most foul and vile names, while she ripped at the dress with both hands.

'Francie seemed frozen to the spot, her face ashen except for the mark of her mother's hand. And then, some of the other girls who had been ignored while their boyfriends surrounded Francie, were ugly enough to laugh out loud, to enjoy her shame and humiliation.'

Ruth looked into Tess's stony green eyes. 'Jeff and I tried to calm Enid Kovaks down, to hush her from calling Francie any more of those filthy names. But nothing could stop the woman until finally she dragged poor Francie through the gaping onlookers and out into the night. It was all over in minutes.'

For a long moment Ruth was silent, reliving the scene that all these years later, was still so vivid in her mind.

At last she went on. 'You can imagine, Tess, how very hard it was for Francie to come back and face the others after that awful scene. But she had no choice. And the strange thing was, that despite her humiliation, despite the fact that she was back to her ill-fitting, second-hand clothes, the boys treated her differently. They couldn't forget what they had got a glimpse of that night at the prom. They surrounded Francie like eager suitors. And while she was too frightened to respond in any way, such male attention made her very unpopular with the other girls.

'Of course it didn't take Enid Kovaks long to discover Aunt Nell's role in the whole business. She was on the telephone at once, screaming abuse at Nell for "trying to corrupt her daughter" as she put it, and demanding that I go nowhere near Francie in future.

'Of course she couldn't really do anything to enforce that while we were both at school, but it made things difficult for a while. And then, one summer's afternoon, four months after Francie's seventeenth birthday, Enid Kovaks's hold over her daughter finally came to an end.'

Ruth bent her head and studied her hands. She could feel the girl's eyes burning into her as she gathered herself to go on with her story.

'Francie had started work behind the counter of the local bakery. The business belonged to Jack Byrne who was one of the stalwarts of the local Catholic Church. This particular afternoon he asked Francie to deliver a cake to Father Doyle at the presbytery; it was the priest's birthday and Jack Byrne wanted to surprise him.

'So Francie carefully carried the box the three blocks to the rambling wooden house built next door to St Augustine's. She knew her mother would still be at work there, so instead of knocking at the front door, she made her way round the side of the house to the rear.

'It was then, as she passed by Father Doyle's bedroom window that she heard what sounded like her mother's voice. But to Francie it sounded as if her mother was in pain; she was moaning, pleading with whoever was in the room with her . . .

'Afraid something might be wrong, Francie stood on tiptoe and peeped in through the window. She saw her mother lying spreadeagled on the bed. Father Doyle lay on top of her. They were both naked . . . '

Shock . . . Repulsion . . . And finally, outrage.

Tess knew the emotions she was experiencing at that moment must have been exactly what her mother had felt as she stared in at that bedroom window.

She became aware that Ruth was speaking again.

'I want you to understand, Tess, that Francie never told me what she'd seen that day till a long time afterwards. At the time, all I knew was that she was going to do something I'd never believed possible.

'She knew I'd be at Jeff's place later that afternoon and that's where she called me. I knew from her voice that something was wrong, but she wouldn't say what. Merely that she wanted me to meet her at the interstate bus depot at five-thirty sharp.

'Puzzled, I did as she asked and found Francie with two suitcases at her feet, the ticket for LA already in her hand.

' "I'm leaving, Ruth", she responded to my obvious bewilderment. "I'm getting out of here. Tonight."

'I couldn't take it in. I asked her what had happened, but she shook her head, refused to tell me. "Someday, Ruth," she said, "I'll let you know. But at the moment I've got to go while I've still got the courage; got to get right away from the filth and hypocrisy."

'I listened in astonishment, shocked by the bitterness in her voice. I asked about her mother; if she knew what was happening.

'It was then,' Ruth spoke softly, 'that something happened behind those lovely blue eyes. "My mother", Francie replied coldly, "is never going to get the chance to say anything to me ever again. She's imprisoned me for far too long with her monstrous threats and hellfire visions."

'And I knew then that whatever had happened had finally broken the hold Enid Kovaks had over Francie. Whatever she'd done, she'd lost her daughter forever.

'For many months I didn't hear a word, and it worried me sick. But then, at last, I received a letter and learned the truth about why Francie had run away.

'I understood then. All those years of her mother's preaching and self-righteous condemnation, the dire warnings and threats of eternal damnation — all aimed at stopping Francie from behaving like any other normal teenage girl . . .

'I wanted to go to her then, to comfort her, but Jeff

and I had just got engaged. We were planning our wedding and there was so much to see to. I hoped Francie would be able to come home to be my bridesmaid, but I could understand her reason for refusing. She didn't want to come anywhere near her mother. She had got a job, she wrote, as a sales assistant in a shoe store, and she was slowly finding her way around LA. "The most exciting place in the world", was the way she described it.'

For a moment Ruth was silent, once more lost in reverie.

Tess broke impatiently into her thoughts. 'So when did you see each other again?'

Ruth Hardy turned and looked steadily into the girl's green eyes.

'Eighteen months later. By then her name was Elizabeth Eden — and she came to beg me to bring up the child she had been carrying inside her for three months.'

CHAPTER

16

Elizabeth Eden...
Francis Kovaks had become Elizabeth Eden. The legendary actress. Her mother.

In the days following Ruth's revelations, Tess struggled to accept the reality of what she had been told. Ruth had talked long into the night; told her the whole story. And when they had finally kissed goodnight it was no longer as mother and daughter, but as friends bound by the secret of the past.

It was a secret even Reed Hardy had not been told.

'I saw no reason to reveal anything about it when we met,' Ruth had explained. 'I thought I'd lost you forever; there seemed no reason ever to mention that part of my past. Reed knew of my marriage to Jeff, of course, and about the accident that took his life a few short months later. And I told him what was almost the truth — that I'd been two months pregnant at the time. What I didn't mention was the fact that I had miscarried following the trauma of losing Jeff.

'Just a month before the accident we had moved to a small border town where Jeff had been lucky enough to find work. So no one back at home knew I had lost the child. At the time I couldn't bear the thought of more pitying looks, and Elizabeth was the only one I wrote to.

Then, just weeks later, she sent me money and asked if I could come to California. It was urgent, she explained.

'We met in a Long Beach motel room. When she walked through the door, she took my breath away. It was the first time I'd seen her since the evening she'd left. Francie Kovaks had disappeared forever, transformed into a glamorous, sophisticated woman. Her make-up was impeccable, her hair permed and bleached a stunning pale blonde, and she wore a dress that clung to every curve of her body. The way she walked, moved, spoke . . . the sexual aura was incredible.

'She saw my amazement, of course, and explained what had happened, how her life had taken an amazing new direction since she'd been signed on by one of Hollywood's leading studios.

'She called it luck, a matter of being spotted by the people who mattered, so that before she knew it she was under contract, being taught how to talk, to dress, to walk. At first, when they spoke to her about a big future she thought they were crazy. But by the time we met, Francie had come to fully believe in her own potential; she was determined to make her name as a serious actress.

'As she told me her ambitions, her eyes shone and her voice was full of resolve. It occurred to me then that Francie was determined to make up for the years of poverty and shame, for all the deprivation and suppression — she was going to grab the opportunity offered to her and climb as far as the ladder went. She was determined, she said, to be more than just another starlet. What Francie wanted was to be the best . . . to earn the respect, the admiration, the recognition of her peers. And it was for that reason she had sent for me.

'Tess, your — your mother loved the man who was your father. She would never reveal his identity, but when she spoke about him, it was obvious how deeply in love she was. Only the timing was wrong for both of them. Apparently his family were strongly opposed to a marriage, while Francie herself could see that a baby just then would have meant the end of her career before it had properly begun. At the same time, of course, an abortion for a girl of her upbringing could never be an option. Francie made it clear that I was her only chance.

'As I listened to what she was proposing, my mind raced ahead. I was lonely, missed Jeff dreadfully. My life seemed to stretch before me in a succession of dark joyless days. I saw that by helping Francie, I'd be helping myself as well . . .

'That's when I told her I'd do it. I'd do it for both our sakes . . . '

And so it had been arranged. Late in her sixth month Elizabeth escaped to a small town in New Mexico where she was joined by Ruth. Together they awaited the arrival of the baby. And when it was time, it was Ruth's name and details that Elizabeth gave to the hospital. A week later she was back in LA while Ruth, with the brand new baby, moved again.

This time to the anonymity of a small apartment an hour and a half's drive from Hollywood and Vine.

Now that Tess knew the truth, Elizabeth Eden became an overwhelming obsession.

Transfixed, she watched again and again the string of cloying exploitive movies, devoured the books, the newspaper articles and old fan magazines. The same picture emerged from all of them. Elizabeth Eden. Sex symbol. A woman who blatantly manipulated her sexuality to put her name on billboards across America, who indulged in promiscuous sex and illicit drugs, whose reputation by the time of her death had all but ruined her career.

The scandalous image might have been all Tess was left with, had it not been for the chance she was offered to know the real Elizabeth Eden . . .

The morning after her amazing revelations, Ruth had

handed Tess a large sealed envelope. 'I'm sure you'll want to read these, Tess,' she said gently. 'They'll help you understand what really happened to your mother in Hollywood.'

And so Tess had read the diaries and letters in horrified fascination — and with every word she came to understand how her mother's dreams had been turned to ashes. How a naive ambitious girl had been exploited by the studio system, a system which showed no mercy to those who dared to question its power and authority.

'Are you *serious*?' Scott McNeill couldn't keep the incredulity out of his voice. He had been dating this girl for over two years. How could he have misread her so badly?

'Are you really serious?' he repeated, and Tess could hear the beginning of anger in his tone.

She nodded, avoiding his gaze. 'Yes, Scott, I am.' She had been dreading the confrontation, but knew it was better dealt with sooner rather than later.

'I've — I've been thinking about it for a while now. Reed's made me see the potential involved. And it's a very interesting area.'

'*Interesting!*' Scorn and disbelief were written all over Scott McNeill's handsome features. He was no longer able to control his anger and contempt. 'Drawing up fat contracts for overpaid parasitic actors is *interesting*? Are you really telling me that's what you want to do with your life, Tess? Follow in the footsteps of your stepfather?' He looked as if he wanted to shake her. 'What the hell has gotten into you?'

Tess swallowed. She had known it wasn't going to be easy. She knew too if she made him hate her, he wouldn't ask any more questions.

'Reed knows everyone,' she replied, 'it'll be easy to get established.' The bile filled her mouth as she forced herself to say the words.

'Easy!' Scott McNeill spat out the word. 'Since when

did that become your motivation, Tess?' Eyes blazing, he looked at her as if he were seeing her for the first time. 'Jesus, Tess, I don't know how I could have got you so wrong! I thought we both knew where we were going; I thought we agreed that the law was shit; that the whole fucked-up system needed to be changed! Can't you — '

'Scott, please ... I've made up my mind.' She heard her voice, stifled, unnatural.

He looked at her in silence for a moment, searching her face for some clue to this sudden madness. All he saw was unshakeable resolve. When at last he spoke, he couldn't quite hide the tremor in his voice, the sudden flash of pain across his face. 'Then it's finished, Tess. You realise that, don't you? I don't have to spell it out.'

As she watched him turn and stride away, bright tears burned her eyes.

Forgive me, Scott, she cried in silent despair, *I haven't any choice. Not any longer ...*

'Are you quite sure, honey, that this is what you want to do?'

Reed Hardy was surprised. And delighted. He'd never dreamed Tess would want to involve herself in his particular branch of the law. Not for a moment would he have tried to influence her, but now, through her own free will, she seemed to want to follow his particular path. He wondered what had happened to turn her back towards the mainstream.

'Very sure, Reed,' answered Tess. 'It's something I've been thinking about for a while now. I want you to teach me everything you know about the studio system.'

And then, she made a silent vow, *when I understand it, I'm going to use it*.

To tell the true story about Elizabeth Eden ... To find out exactly why and how she died ...

CHAPTER

17

As she entered the sound stage where the stills were to be shot, an awed silence fell over the waiting crew.

In every last detail, from the pale blonde hair to the jutting bosom, from the full pouting lips to the sexy walk, Jennifer Ross was the reincarnation of the dead actress.

'Jesus . . . it's unbelievable.' Jerry Dario's voice faded to a hush. The sixty year old producer was overcome with wonder; he had known Elizabeth at the peak of her career. Now, with his eyes riveted on Jennifer Ross, he felt as if he were seeing a ghost.

Beside him, Tess gripped the arms of her chair, her throat suddenly dry.

It was Elizabeth.

Her mother.

This was the nearest she would ever come to seeing her in the flesh.

And then the moment of stunned wonder was broken by a round of spontaneous applause. Applause for the skills of the make-up and costume departments, for Jennifer Ross's uncanny ability to totally assume the persona of the dead woman.

The actress turned and faced her audience which included Tess, and Mike, and Jerry Dario.

'You like it?' The seductive open-mouthed smile was the ultimate effect.

'It's uncanny, isn't it, Tess?' Mike Havelock turned excitedly towards his executive president.

'Yes, Mike. Uncanny.'

There was only the merest tremble in her voice.

Jennifer Ross relaxed in her chair and let the make-up girl remove the platinum wig.

The role of Elizabeth Eden was everything Jennifer had dreamed it would be. She knew nothing else in her career was ever going to compare to this. The advance publicity was massive and tomorrow evening she would be flying to New York to appear on the Johnny Carson Show. Already she had made up her mind to use such widespread exposure to further advance the cause of her fellow actresses. Meryl Streep and the others had been calling for equal pay for years. Now it would be she, Jennifer Ross, who would lead the vanguard towards victory.

The photo shoot had taken hours but adrenalin had kept fatigue at bay. Only now, as her make-up was being removed, did Jennifer start feeling the effects of the last few hours. She had already discovered that there was nothing easy about emulating a woman whose looks and mannerisms were so universally recognised.

As she leaned her head back in relief she caught sight of someone entering the dressing room. It was Tess Jordan.

'Hi.' Tess pulled up a seat beside the actress as the make-up artist continued to clean off her handiwork. 'You all set for tomorrow evening?'

'Sure,' Jennifer smiled through the cold cream covering her face. 'The studio limo is picking me up at home, and when I arrive at the Waldorf I'll have a couple of hours to rest before going to the network.' Her smile grew wider. 'We're going to blow them away, Tess. This is the movie that's going to show how it really is for women in this goddamn industry — and that the time for change has now arrived. The days of the "boys' club" are finally numbered, and we've got you to thank for that.'

Tess accepted the compliment gracefully. Jennifer Ross's enthusiasm for the project had never been in any doubt. 'We've got a lot of things to prove with this one,' she agreed softly.

Busy as ever, Tess somehow found herself agreeing to squeeze in a meeting with Chris Stanley. He had called earlier in the week wanting to talk over some aspect of the script.

'What about we meet at a bar I know in Marina del Rey? It's discreet — we won't be disturbed.'

Tess hesitated. She never went to bars. She started to suggest that they meet again in her office, when he cut teasingly across her: 'Hey, come on, meet me on my own turf for a change.'

Used to calling the shots, Tess felt a moment's irritation. But then, she shrugged inwardly, why not humour the guy? He was just a kid, after all.

He was waiting for her at a corner table in the waterfront bar and restaurant.

'Hi.' He unfolded his lanky frame and got to his feet. He was dressed as informally as usual in jeans and a soft suede jacket. 'Best table in the house,' he grinned, pointing to the harbour view.

A waitress took their order and for the next half an hour they discussed the current script for the movie on Elizabeth Eden's life.

Chris Stanley couldn't hide his excitement. 'I didn't realise just how much background you'd got.' He had made a pact with himself to refuse to call her Ms Jordan any longer; he was determined that by the end of that afternoon it would be 'Tess' and 'Chris'. 'I mean, all that stuff about Golding trying to force her into having sex with his wife while he watched, and then when she refused, putting her on suspension for the next six months . . . And that time they had her committed — not because of her own "drug problems" as the public were told, but because she was about to reveal the rampant drug-taking and sexual harassment by Todd Raymor on her latest movie.' Chris was referring to one of the famous male stars of that time.

He shook his head. 'The revelations are amazing. I can't help wondering about your source.'

It was a leading question and Tess knew it. She looked at him over the top of her glass. Chris Stanley was on the payroll now, trying through his network of sources to come up with anything that might add to their knowledge about the night Elizabeth Eden died. It made no sense, she figured, not to put him completely in the picture.

And so she told him the same story she had told Mike; about how her mother and Elizabeth had grown up together and remained friends, about the diaries and letters . . .

'That's an incredible coincidence.' Chris Stanley gave her an appraising look from across the table. Tess Jordan intrigued him. He was trying to see past the formal professional air of the career woman to the real woman underneath. For a moment, as she had spoken about her mother's relationship with the dead actress, Tess Jordan's words carried an undercurrent of passion, hinting at something other than the cool, controlled persona she chose to project.

Tess looked at her watch. 'I've got to go. Don't forget Jennifer Ross is appearing on the Carson show tomorrow night.' She stood up. 'Thanks for the drink.'

'Sure.' He got to his feet. 'Let me walk you to your car.'

When she was behind the wheel, he leaned in the open window of the E-type. 'Call you as soon as I've got a handle on something, Tess. G'night.' He patted her arm and walked off.

As she turned the key in the ignition, Tess felt her irritation at the young reporter's familiarity at odds with another more puzzling emotion.

Under the hot studio lights Jennifer Ross was in full swing.

'This movie is a very important one for me and for every other actress who values her independence and self-respect, Johnny,' said Jennifer with total conviction. 'The real story of Elizabeth Eden is one of manipulation and coercion: one woman making a stand against the men and the system which tried to turn her into something they thought she should be, rather than what she herself aspired to. Too many times she was placed on suspension, or labelled box-office "poison" purely because she insisted on rejecting some of the mediocre and sexist roles she was being offered.'

Jennifer Ross fixed America's prime time TV host with a challenging eye. 'And even in these supposedly enlightened times, Johnny, the system still works against women. We're paid less than male actors, our working lives are shorter, and too often our role is merely that of sexual adjunct. It's those sorts of inequalities we're committed to change.'

Her voice resonant with emotion, Jennifer Ross was well aware of the irony inherent in sitting in front of cameras that took her into millions of American homes, dressed and made-up as a star the system had destroyed, while espousing the views of the modern actress. But it was the message that mattered after all, and whatever it took, she was determined to transmit that.

Johnny Carson was asking her views on working for a female boss.

Jennifer Ross left him in no doubt of her opinion. 'Having a woman like Tess Jordan in charge of a major studio means that the male dominance of the system is finally under threat,' she answered. 'Female actors will at last be given the chance to achieve success without allowing themselves to become the creations of Hollywood men.'

Jennifer Ross was about to elaborate further when her host smoothly changed the subject to the forthcoming movie. Enough was enough, after all.

Anne Conroy was making the most of her opportunity.

On the occasions when Walter actually made it home, she always looked for evidence. That usually meant a search of his suit pockets and, if he left it handy, a quick rifle through his briefcase.

Tonight Walter had gone to his den straight after a dinner during which he had exchanged barely half a dozen words with his wife.

Anne worked quickly. When the suit pockets revealed nothing of interest, she turned her attention to the burgundy leather briefcase that lay locked by her husband's bedside.

Her lips curved in a contemptuous smile. Walter thought she was so stupid, but months ago she had discovered the combination which gave access to his private papers. The security system in the Dallas house used the last few digits of their telephone number; the briefcase was unlocked by numbers corresponding to Walter's private line in LA. A simple process of deduction.

Anne flicked quickly through the pages of his appointments diary.

Eleanor Benson. Dinner two nights in a row on his last trip to LA.

Anne pushed the diary back into the case and reset the combination, her lips pursed in anger.

Slut.

Bitch.

Only the fact that that day's Dow Jones had closed thirty points higher helped her control her temper . . .

Closed up in his den, Walter Conroy took a long swallow of bourbon. His eyes were riveted to the television screen as he listened to Jennifer Ross. The movie, it seemed, was to begin shooting any day, and the actress was hinting at the revelations to come.

Walter felt his bowels turn to water. He was fully aware that there was a new puritanism in America these days. If the movie on Elizabeth Eden was set to reveal the details of the affair she'd had with President Tom Madigan while he was still incumbent in the White House, it must surely affect Robert's chances of gaining office.

Instead of the walkover Walter was counting on, there might exist the very real possibility that Robbie Madigan could lose.

Just the idea was enough to give Walter nightmares.

As the screen faded to a commercial break, he snapped off the set. He had heard enough.

He knew that the time for hoping was over. The time for action had arrived.

A tight-faced Adelle switched off the television and drew deeply on her cigarette. As she began to pace the room, she blew out an angry stream of smoke.

'We've got to stop this, Dave!' she hissed, the tendons standing out like strands of rope on her thin neck. 'I don't give a damn now what happened between Tom and her, but that slut's not going to be allowed to wreck things for me from her grave.'

Larry Brandt and Dave Arnell exchanged nervous looks. If Adelle only knew that it was so much more than that.

CHAPTER

18

Carl Harris inspected his face in the bathroom mirror. There were dark circles under the blue eyes that magazine articles called 'flinty, sexy and irresistible'. His skin looked sallow and slack.

Ever since the Carson interview with Jennifer Ross, he'd hardly had a wink of decent sleep. And the stress was beginning to leave its mark. His nerves were shot, and even the visits to the doc were doing nothing to help.

Harris turned away from the worrying sight in the mirror and made his way through the sprawling house to the plant-filled conservatory where his manservant was waiting to serve breakfast.

As he sat down in the upholstered rattan seat, he looked out at the pool, the heated spa, the landscaped grounds and tennis court and felt the now familiar spasm in his belly. This house, the condo in Palm Springs, the servants and cars, the respect and fame . . . he could lose everything if the movie on Elizabeth Eden went ahead.

The actor's hand shook as he poured low-fat milk on his cholesterol-reducing cereal. He had escaped once; he knew there was no way he could escape again. The past and Carlo Tollini had come back to haunt him.

For the first time in years Carl Harris allowed himself to remember the name he'd been born with . . .

'The boy's got the face of an angel, Moira.'

It was the chorus Carlo Tollini had grown up with. His mother's friends, the customers at his father's fruit barrow, the neighbours who shared the dingy, old-fashioned apartment block, all reinforced the message of his attractiveness.

His mother, Carlo knew, loved the compliments her son's good looks attracted. He heard the pride in her voice as she made her usual reply. 'It's in the blood. The boy couldn't help but be a handsome loon now could he?'

She was referring of course, to Carlo's Irish and Italian background. Moira Devlan had met Joe Tollini when she was only fifteen. It had been love at first sight and, despite the opposition of their families, they had married the moment Moira was legally of age.

Given their respective temperaments, the marriage was a volatile one, but even though their arguments were inevitably made up in bed, Moira proved unable to maintain her pregnancies and Carlo was their only offspring.

Carlo loved his mother with her flaming hair, big firm breasts, and loud lilting voice. As he grew older he found himself discomforted by the feelings in his body as he watched her move around the apartment in her unbuttoned robe, the heavy breasts swinging tantalisingly. He wondered if he would ever find a woman as wonderful as his mother.

By fifteen he was well aware of his own good looks and ready to use them to effect his first sexual encounter. He had seen the glint in the eyes of his friends' mothers and knew they found him appealing. The knowledge excited him. An older woman, someone as voluptuous and sensual as his mother, was what he was seeking to fulfil his unspeakable fantasies.

It was his history teacher, Lois Johnson, who provided

his first sexual experience. But the occasion was nothing like he had so breathlessly imagined.

Naked, Lois Johnson's appeal was suddenly and forcibly diminished. Where his mother was plump but firm, his teacher's soft flesh hung in ugly folds and her buttocks and thighs resembled lumpy sponges. Carlo could feel his erection falter as she drew him on top of her, gathered her loose breast and held it to his mouth.

'Suck me into life, sweetheart. That's my handsome boy ... ' Her voice was thick and raspy, her breath smelled sour in his face. But fighting back his repugnance, Carlo did as he was told.

But when the panting woman parted those flabby thighs to reveal the reddened ugly folds of the place he had dreamed of, Carlo thought he was going to be physically sick. His erection died at once.

With such beauty at her disposal, Lois Johnson did everything she could think of to arouse the boy again. But when, without warning, Carlo came suddenly in her hand, she covered her frustration with a disdainful laugh.

'That's not quite the way it works, honey. Come back and try again when you're more of a man.'

Burning with humiliation, Carlo Tollini never forgot the sound of her scorn. Or the sight of her ugliness.

Not given to introspection, he did on one or two later occasions, however, wonder if that had been the start of it all. Perhaps it was his overwhelming need to overcome the feelings both of inadequacy and sexual repulsion which had altered the focus of his desire. However that may have been, he was made aware of the changes within him just a few short weeks after the disaster with Lois Johnson.

It happened one hot summer's afternoon in a tiny dusty park not far from his home, whose faded baseball diamond and cluster of rusty climbing bars was a constant attraction for local children.

Carlo was standing under the meagre shade of the

park's few trees waiting for his turn to bat, when he became aware of a noise in the nearby bushes. Thinking it might be a fornicating couple, he moved stealthily closer. Through the tangle of leaves, he saw a blonde-haired child of about eight. He recognised her as Emily Kratz, the daughter of their local kosher butcher.

Carlo stood motionless, watching as the girl pulled down her panties and squatted amongst the bushes. His mouth went suddenly dry as he took in the perfect satiny flesh of her small firm buttocks and he felt the thick sword of excitement grow in his trousers.

He knew then he had to find some way of touching that wonderful creamy youthfulness.

Emily Kratz opened the door to a whole new world of sensation for Carlo Tollini. It was so easy to take what he wanted from vulnerable prepubescent girls — and through them he was able to restore the sense of authority, power, and manhood that had been stripped from him by his first humiliating sexual encounter.

Cured of his obsession with older women, Carlo had no interest either in girls his own age. On the evenings he left the apartment, his mother would occasionally enquire if he were meeting a date.

'Nah . . . ' Carlo made a joke of it. 'Who'd be interested in me?'

Moira Tollini joined in her son's laughter. Carlo was fussy, that was all; a good way to be. And anyway, she thought happily, until he found the right girl he would be hers for a little longer.

But then came the shocking allegations which lost her her son forever.

A thin, pale-faced girl of ten plucked up the courage to tell her parents what had occurred. And she could identify her assailant — she'd had the presence of mind to follow Carlo home after it was over.

Two police officers were at the Tollini apartment within the hour. Carlo denied the charges vehemently, while his mother swore in her thick brogue at her uniformed countrymen.

As part of their investigation, the officers talked to other young friends of the victim and the evidence mounted. But by the time they returned to the Tollini apartment with a warrant for Carlo's arrest, their prey was on a Greyhound bound for somewhere as far away from New York as it was possible to go.

LA. A city where youth and beauty could be all that was needed to open doors.

In the time it took to cross the continent, Carlo Tollini had become Carl Harris. He was three months short of his nineteenth birthday.

CHAPTER

19

In the privacy of the place he called the Shrine, the Idolator replayed the Carson interview again and again.

Throbbing with desire, he stared at the reincarnation of his dream.

She looked like Elizabeth.

She sounded like Elizabeth.

She was Elizabeth.

Chris hated himself for the way his heart began to race as he lifted the receiver. Jesus, how long had it been since he'd felt this way about ringing any woman? He couldn't remember.

He had waited till after nine. She was home and answered the phone herself.

'Hi, Tess, it's Chris Stanley.'

She greeted him without surprise. After all, she had provided him with her private home number. 'What can I do for you, Chris?'

He felt his breathing quicken. He'd planned a preamble — had decided to say something about Jennifer Ross's interview on the Carson program the previous week — but instead, he heard himself barging straight in.

'Actually, I'm ringing to see if you'd be free to go to a

Lakers game with me this Saturday night. I'm a dyed-in-the-wool fan and I've — I've got a couple of tickets.'

Dead silence from the other end of the line.

Tess was wondering if she'd heard right. The *Lakers* . . . ? This guy was asking *her* to a basketball game? She almost laughed out loud.

'The Lakers . . . ?' she repeated.

Chris could hear the incredulity in her tone. 'Yeah . . . Just thought you might like to see how the rest of America lives, you know.' He couldn't help his nervous sarcasm. 'We could even eat hot dogs and drink Coke if you really want to do the whole trip.'

It was his cheek, Tess thought. His barefaced cheek . . .

And then she surprised them both by saying yes.

'So . . . you survived.' He grinned at her across the table of the crowded bistro where they'd gone after the game.

'Sure. Even quite enjoyed myself, to tell you the truth. America in a microcosm. Families, patriotism, athletic rivalry, junk food . . . it had everything.'

'I couldn't believe you'd never seen a game before. What sort of deprived childhood did you *have*, for God's sake?'

He'd meant it as a throwaway comment, but something changed in her eyes and immediately he sensed his mistake. Swearing inwardly, he chastised himself for his big mouth. After all, what did he really know about the woman sitting across from him?

Helping himself to salad, he did his best to change the subject. 'So what do you do to relax, Tess?'

She raised an eyebrow and swirled what was left of her wine around the inside of her glass. 'I guess I don't have much time for anything but work these days. Sometimes, if I'm lucky, I might get home early enough to fit in a couple of laps of the pool.' She gave a rueful smile. 'As it is, my housekeeper manages to use it more than I do.'

Chris gave her an appraising look as he poured them each a little more wine. 'You must have been extraordinarily dedicated to climb the ladder as quickly as you have. And to do it at such a young age.'

Tess shrugged off the comment. 'Come on . . . I must be at least ten years older than you.'

He grinned at her. 'Well, I'm thirty-one . . . so how old does that make you?'

He really was quite incorrigible.

'Not quite as old as I thought, it seems,' Tess answered, green eyes flashing.

He couldn't stop thinking about her. It was the contradiction that intrigued him: the coolness and control on one hand, the glimpse of humour, compassion and fire on the other. Tess Jordan, he realised, was beginning to affect him in a way he had thought would never happen again.

Seven years younger.

Tess had never spent time with anyone like Chris Stanley before. She was used to men older, sophisticated, highly successful. Men of power and wealth who had aimed for and got exactly what they wanted out of life.

Men who inevitably felt threatened by her . . .

Carl Harris woke with a jerk, his body drenched in sweat. The dream had been so real.

He'd been back in the stinking rathole apartment he'd grown up in. The scandal had been revealed and he'd lost everything he'd worked his ass off to acquire.

It was just past two am but Carl Harris felt desperately in need of a drink. Down in the living room, he poured a stiff Scotch and waited for it to work on his shattered nerves.

But it was going to be all right, he did his best to reassure himself. He'd done something about it.

With one swallow he finished the rest of his drink and made his way back to bed.

But sleep eluded him and, against his will, he found his thoughts returning again and again to the day when Elizabeth Eden had discovered his forbidden desire.

He had always got on well with the make-up girls and Mary Kitter was no exception. If only, he shuddered in memory, she hadn't brought her eight year old daughter on location with her that time.

Mary Kitter had received special permission to have her child accompany her for the three-day location shoot in San Francisco. She hated to leave the girl overnight — because Holly Kitter was retarded. An accident of birth. And to all those who saw her, the most appalling aspect of the tragedy was that the child was blessed with a breath-taking beauty.

Carl could see that face now in his mind's eye. Huge liquid hazel eyes, delicate bones, and a mouth so sensual it was almost an obscenity on a child.

Carl's growing success in Hollywood had forced him to resist his dormant urges. As a well-known star, there was so much at stake. But faced with Holly Kitter, his resolve had shattered. He'd be safe, he told himself: the kid wasn't normal; there was no way he might be discovered.

But he hadn't counted on Elizabeth Eden entering his trailer at that precise moment. Ashen-faced, he had spun round to catch her look of appalled horror; the same expression was reflected on the face of the child's mother who stood close behind. They had come looking for Holly, had knocked on the trailer door; but in his excitement he hadn't heard.

Carl Harris had no defence. The child was sitting naked on the side of his sofa, while his penis was rearing out of the front of his pants.

He would never forget the look of hate and disgust on Elizabeth Eden's face as she snatched up the child and handed her to her sobbing mother.

'You'll pay for this, you bastard! You'll pay for this with everything you've got.'

But there was a way out. One chance of escape — if only Mary Kitter could be persuaded to agree. With Elizabeth Eden tied up on the set for the rest of that afternoon, Carl Harris made repeated and frantic attempts to convince the child's mother to listen to what he had to say.

At last he got her alone, and offered the shocked and angry woman his proposal. He promised Mary Kitter he would put up the money needed to educate and provide ongoing care for the rest of the child's life if only she would not go to the authorities. For if she did, Carl knew there was every chance the other charges would also come to light.

Mary Kitter loved her child. She knew she could never do for Holly what Carl Harris's money could. In the end she said yes. Not even her friendship with Elizabeth Eden could change her mind.

But that deal had ended years ago when Holly Kitter and her mother had died in an automobile accident on the San Bernadino Freeway on Christmas Eve. Carl had greeted the news with joy and delight. With Elizabeth Eden dead as well, he was free at last.

Until now.

What worried him was that among the new material around which the movie on Elizabeth Eden was to be based, the story of Mary Kitter might come to light.

But, he reminded himself again as the dawn light crept through the blinds, he had taken steps to see that would never happen . . .

Jennifer Ross could feel the eyes drilling into her as she followed the maitre d' past the other well-known diners to where her agent sat waiting at the very best table in the house. There was now probably no one in the industry, the actress realised, who wasn't aware of her role in the forthcoming film being made on Elizabeth Eden's life.

Jennifer Ross felt a sense of real responsibility. It was up to her to show how Elizabeth had been slandered and betrayed, to reveal how the industry treated those who refused to obey its rules. For she knew that while things might be better now for those who had actually made it, for others, those still fighting to realise their dreams, too many of the same traps and dangers still existed.

But Jennifer was clever enough to know that it was her career as well as her ideals that were at stake. If the movie was a flop, then her outspokenness, her identification with the problems highlighted in the Elizabeth Eden story, would surely mean no major studio would touch her again.

That's why the movie just *had* to succeed. And not only for the sake of her own future but for Tess Jordan's as well: the woman who had been brave enough to take on the Boys Club that still maintained so tight a grip on the movie-making industry; the woman who had caused the first real cracks to appear in that edifice of male power.

As Jennifer arrived at the table, her agent, Maggie Blake, rose ponderously to her feet. Her small dark eyes gleamed out from folds of flesh as she grinned her welcome.

'Hi, babe. Glad you got here.' She kissed Jennifer effusively on both cheeks. 'Sit down quick before those eyes bore a hole right through you. Now, what'll it be? Dom? Krug? There ain't nothing too good for my favourite client.'

Jennifer hummed softly to herself as she steered the open-roofed Mercedes around the curves of the Malibu coastline. She had enjoyed her lunch with Maggie. The bottle of Krug they'd shared had been just enough to relax her yet hadn't left her feeling too sluggish to browse through her favourite Beverly Hills boutiques for an hour or so afterwards.

Blonde hair streaming over her shoulders, Jennifer smiled to herself at the thought of the shocking pink Claude Montana she had found in Lina Lee's. The moment she slipped it on, she knew she had to have it.

It was one of those rare overcast days in LA. Although it was only late afternoon, Jennifer turned on the parking lights of the Mercedes. She didn't expect to pass much traffic on this section of the road at this time of day, but better safe than sorry, she thought to herself.

The other car appeared out of nowhere.

One minute Jennifer had the road to herself, the next the battered sedan was virtually riding on her tail. Annoyed, she stepped on her brakes, tried to warn the dangerous driver off. To no avail.

As the next steep incline approached, Jennifer's irritation grew. This time, she blared her horn, glaring into her rear-vision mirror.

What happened next made her blanch. Instead of backing off, the driver of the decrepit Ford rammed hard against the Mercedes' tail bar.

Jesus . . . ! Jennifer Ross swore loudly as the action was repeated. Some nutcase was trying to ram her off the goddamn road!

She gripped the wheel tightly, stepped on the gas as much as she dared on the treacherous curve and tried to pull away.

But the other vehicle was moving faster too, and to her horror, she suddenly felt a bone-jarring thump on her side of the car. The bastard was right alongside her! Forcing her closer and closer to the edge of the road!

There was a sickening crunch as once again metal scraped against metal. The next moment the Mercedes crashed through the guard rail and plunged over the cliff face . . .

The call reached Tess just as she was about to leave the office. Stopping only to phone the news through to Mike, she drove grim-faced and as fast as the traffic allowed to where they had taken Jennifer Ross.

The news services picked up the incident in their late evening bulletins. It was reported that the actress Jennifer Ross had been injured in a car accident on the Malibu coast road. First reports suggested her late model Mercedes sportscar had been deliberately run off the road. Only a miracle had thrown the actress clear as her vehicle had crashed through the guard rail. She was being treated for shock and minor abrasions in Cedars Sinai hospital where she had been transferred.

'Some hood desperate for a few dollars, according to the cops.'

Mike Havelock handed Tess a drink from his well-stocked bar. It was two days after Jennifer Ross's accident and they were discussing the worrying incident in the privacy of Mike's office.

The lanky businessman took a sip of his drink and continued. 'Yeah, seems he was probably trying to scare her into pulling over so he could get his hands on her purse, when things went too far.'

Tess was aware of the police report. While she realised such random attempts at robbery happened all the time in LA, she still somehow felt uneasy.

Perhaps, she consoled herself, she would feel better after visiting Jennifer this evening and getting her own version of the accident which had almost cost her her life.

The actress smiled up from her hospital bed. 'It was good of you to come, Tess.'

'They tell me you're going home tomorrow.'

'Yes. Thank God the shooting schedule won't have to be delayed.' She rang a finger over the wads of gauze that were taped over her cheek and neck. 'Just superficial scratches, they tell me. I'll be as good as new in a couple of days.'

'You were very lucky, Jennifer.'

The other woman shrugged. 'Guess you could say I was both lucky and unlucky. Unlucky enough to be on the road at the moment that sonofabitch was looking for his next victim, lucky that I survived with so little damage.'

'You didn't get a close look at him then, or make a note of the licence plate?'

Jennifer Ross shook her head. 'No. As I told the cops, the whole thing happened so damn quickly . . . '

'Well,' Tess patted her hand, 'the main thing is you're fine. Now just you take it real easy over the weekend and we'll see you when shooting starts Monday.'

'Sure, Tess and thanks again for — '

She was interrupted by a hospital worker who entered the room carrying an enormous bouquet of flowers. 'You got more people love you than you thought, Miss Ross.' The woman smiled as she looked around the room that was already overflowing with floral arrangements. 'Heavens to Betsy knows where I'm gonna find room for these.' She detached the small greeting envelope and handed it to the patient in the bed. 'You wanna read who these're from, while I go find another vase?'

Tess got to her feet as Jennifer removed the plain white card from its envelope. 'Well, I guess I'd better — ' Her words were cut off by the other woman's sudden intake of breath.

'Oh, Jesus . . . Oh God, no . . . '

Tess knew she had to speak to Mike at once. She called him from the hospital and was relieved to find him home.

'Sure, Tess, come on over.' But the unexpected call and the overtone of tension in her voice made him ask, 'What's up? Anything wrong?'

'I'll be there as soon as possible, Mike. I'll tell you then.'

As she drove towards the Havelock mansion, Tess replayed in her mind the words of the note sent to Jennifer Ross.

The threat had been explicit.

'This time you were lucky. If the movie on Elizabeth Eden goes ahead, don't count on luck saving you a second time.'

As she'd read those words, all Tess's earlier suspicions had been confirmed. Jennifer hadn't been run off the road by some chance crook. It had been a deliberate attempt on her life ...

And she realised that the same thought had occurred almost simultaneously to the ashen-faced woman on the bed.

She had done her best to comfort the frightened actress. 'Jennifer, let me handle this. I'm going straight to Mike Havelock with this note. It seems obvious someone wants to scare us out of making the movie on Elizabeth Eden. But we'll get to the bottom of it, I promise you. Mike will know exactly what to do. It's difficult, I'm sure, but just try to stay calm.'

The colour was coming back into the actress's face. 'I — I'll be okay, Tess. It was just such a shock ... ' Her voice grew stronger. 'Don't worry, I'm not going to let this frighten me. Nothing's going to stop me making that movie.'

'We've got to find out who's behind this, Mike. Jennifer's being brave, but it's obvious whoever it is meant to kill her, not merely scare her.'

Tess was seated in Mike Havelock's comfortable living room, a stiff drink in her hand.

Her employer tapped the note that lay on the coffee table between them. 'Leave this to me, Tess. I've got connections in the LAPD. This can be handled quietly, I'm sure. That way, Jennifer will be safe and there'll be no adverse publicity connected to the movie.' He gave a derisive snort. 'Of course, if it did leak out, we're just as likely to be accused of engineering the whole thing as a deliberate publicity stunt.'

Tess finished her drink and stood up to leave. She felt

better now that Mike had all the facts and had agreed that the situation was serious and warranted immediate action.

'Give me twenty-four hours to organise something, Tess. In the meantime, I'll make sure Jennifer Ross's security has top priority.' He patted her arm as he walked her to her car. 'Don't worry too much. I'm sure it won't take too long for the cops to find out who's behind all this.'

But as she drove away, Tess wondered if the task of discovering the culprit would be quite so simple. The range of suspects, she was slowly realising, was wide open. It could be any one of the directors, producers, fellow stars who had played a part in the ruin of Elizabeth Eden's reputation and career.

Then another idea came to her with icy force: what if it was more than that?

What if the pressure to stop the movie was somehow linked to Elizabeth's death . . . ?

CHAPTER

20

'Oh, God, Larry. I feel like those twenty-five years in between never existed. The same sense of excitement . . . so many of the same faces . . . the utter certainty that we're going to win.'

Adelle Madigan's thin, bejewelled fingers clutched at the dinner jacket sleeve of her son's campaign manager. 'Doesn't it feel like that to you too?'

Larry Brandt nodded in agreement. 'We're gonna make it, Adelle. No one can stop Rob now.' His voice was calm, but he shared Adelle's excitement. So far the campaign had gone like a dream. Not a single hitch. Like Adelle, he couldn't help but recall that night over twenty-five years before — that other campaign which had attracted as enormous a crowd of California's famous and powerful as this evening's, and to this same grand ballroom in the Beverly Hills Hotel.

History really was repeating itself, he mused. As Adelle had said, many of those present then were also present today, their hopes now focused on the son of the father. The heady scent of victory was in the air and, as campaign manager, Larry Brandt was only too happy to have his own role acknowledged in pointing another Madigan towards the White House.

He watched as Adelle moved away to join her son at

the centre of a group of powerful admirers. The kid had everything it took, Larry reckoned. He was young, only thirty-seven, but he'd been a Senator for almost ten years. And while the name, looks and charisma weren't exactly drawbacks, Robert Madigan's credentials went much deeper than that. In the legislature he had established an impressive record for liberal reform while his knowledge of domestic and international affairs revealed he was every bit as intelligent as his late father. He would more than hold his own against older and more campaign-hardened opponents.

Larry Brandt grinned to himself. Rob Madigan was the easiest product to sell since the motor vehicle.

As regal as any queen, Adelle moved around the grand ballroom of the Beverly Hills Hotel dispensing charm and good humour to all those who had forked out the five hundred dollars a head admission to pay homage to her son. Elegant in a plum-coloured Givenchy gown, she could sense the excitement of the assembled guests; could feel the outpouring of their love for the handsome young man who was so certain to restore the Democrats to power.

Adelle had just stopped to chat with one of Holly-wood's leading money men when suddenly the smile froze on her face.

Lips tightening, the beginnings of panic fluttering in her belly, she swivelled her head, searching for the one man she could trust to solve the problem.

With his usual instincts for Adelle's wellbeing, Dave Arnell was already by her side.

Adelle hissed out of the side of her mouth, her face a mask of controlled anger, 'What the hell is that bitch doing here, Dave? If I'd known she meant to come . . . '

'Take it easy, honey,' Dave Arnell kept his voice low. 'Let's not overreact. Let's not assume she's here to make trouble . . . You just keep doin' the rounds, I'll keep an eye on her.'

Adelle forced herself to relax. She would trust Dave. Dave always took care of everything.

As she entered the grand ballroom of the Beverly Hills Hotel, Tess vowed that for this evening at least, she was going to push her worries to the back of her mind.

It was almost a week since Jennifer Ross had received the threatening note and, so far, despite all the discreet investigations initiated by Mike, the police had come up with no leads.

'They're not giving up, Tess.' Mike had done his best to reassure her. 'Something'll come to light sooner or later. In the meantime, having Jennifer Ross driven back and forth from the studio by our own security staff means she's not likely to be faced with any further unpleasant incidents.'

In the crowded function room, pre-dinner cocktails were still being served and, as Tess moved through the milling, elegant crowd, smiling a greeting to those she recognised among California's rich and powerful, she found it difficult to suppress her cynicism. How many of those present, she wondered, firmly believed in the Democratic Party platform, and how many were there merely to be seen in the presence of the man who was almost certain to be the next President of the United States?

Tess's own firm commitment to Democratic ideals had been forged by personal experience. Her time on the streets had given her a sympathy and understanding for all those who so desperately needed the help of a compassionate and caring government. She felt sure that Robert Madigan was going to spearhead such an administration.

'Tess! Hi! Come join us.' Rory MacTiernan, managing director of a major broking house, smiled a welcome as he beckoned her over. He had been one of those responsible for negotiating the sale of WLS to Mike Havelock. As she moved to join the group of high-powered businessmen it occurred to Tess to ponder how out of place someone like Chris Stanley would be at a function like this. In the world of politics, Hollywood glamour, and sophisticated high finance, Chris Stanley — young, naive, guileless — would stand out like a sore thumb.

Just moments before the guests were invited to take their places for dinner, Tess found herself face to face with the powerful charismatic candidate who was so certain to return the Democrats to the White House.

Robert Madigan smiled and shook hands with his supporters as each was introduced by his aides.

'And this is Tess Jordan, Senator. Ms Jordan has recently been appointed President of WLS. Seems that things are really starting to move there now.'

'So, I've heard ... So I've heard ... '

With her hand held in Robert Madigan's firm grasp, Tess felt the directness of his intense blue eyes. He was staring at her as if ... as if ...

As if he hates me, was her stunned conclusion.

'Walter? What's the matter?' Anne Conroy frowned at the expression on her husband's face. She followed the direction of his gaze and saw it was fixed on a tall, dark-haired woman in a black lace dress who was one of a group being introduced to Robert Madigan.

'What is it, Walter? Who is that woman?'

Walter Conroy barely heard his wife's questions. His heart had begun to beat harder in his chest. Just when he had at last taken the necessary steps, Tess Jordan's unexpected appearance made him wonder if he had left it too late. Did the woman have some ulterior motive in coming here tonight? Was she here to taunt them with her presence, remind them of the devastating exposure she was planning on movie screens across America? An exposure that could cost Walter everything he had slaved and worked his guts out for ...

WHISPER FROM THE GODS 167

He got a grip on himself. Surely nothing would happen here tonight. Not now when he had at last put his plan into action . . .

'Walter, they're serving dinner. Let's go sit down.' Annoyed at her husband's distraction, Anne Conroy scowled as she linked her arm through his. She wished the evening were over; she was having a lousy time. She hated leaving Texas. For one thing, how could she be sure what wasteful extravagance the help were indulging in when she wasn't around to keep them in line?

Tess found herself seated between one of the country's richest oil magnates and a leading newspaper owner. Both were men in their fifties; both bored her rigid. She could tell that neither was comfortable in her presence either. Accustomed only to dealing with other powerful males, they were unsure of how to treat her. It was a scenario Tess had had to confront time and time again. Men of their generation were simply at a loss when it came to dealing with women of equal status and power. It unnerved them, broke all the rules they had learned so well.

'So, tell me, what's it like working for the mysterious Mike Havelock?' It was, not surprisingly, the newspaper proprietor who put the question.

Tess understood at once. Focus the conversation on the absent male and, apart from what you might just be lucky enough to dig up, you also avoid the problem of relating to the threatening female.

Tess smiled sweetly as she dipped her spoon into her vichyssoise. 'Mr Verner, do you media people always work overtime?'

The main course had just been served when Tess felt a tap on her shoulder.

It was one of the hotel managers. Bending over, he spoke softly into Tess's ear. 'Ms Jordan . . . forgive me for interrupting your meal but I have Mrs Paula Havelock on the line. She wishes to speak with you urgently. Perhaps you'd like to take the call in my office?'

With a frown, Tess stood up and excused herself from the table. She could feel the curious eyes on her as she hurriedly followed the manager out of the grand ballroom. What could be so urgent to cause Paula Havelock to phone her here?

The manager closed the door discreetly behind him as Tess picked up the receiver. 'Paula? What's up? Is something wrong?'

A sudden chill gripped her belly as she listened to the other woman's rapid explanation.

CHAPTER

21

By the time Tess arrived at the main entry gates to WLS, a horde of reporters, television crews, and curious onlookers were already blocking the roadway.

But the studio's own security staff were out in force and the easily recognisable E-type was waved speedily through the checkpoint.

'Over on Lot 14, Ms Jordan!' A burly uniformed guard stuck his head in the car window. 'Mr Havelock's there with the fire crews. They're — '

But Tess had hit the accelerator.

Lot 14. The sets for the Elizabeth Eden movie.

She could see the red glow of the flames while she was still blocks away. Jesus...

Her progress was finally impeded by a row of fire trucks. Tess jumped out of her car and ran towards the frantic fire crews, trying not to trip over the thick hoses that crisscrossed the ground.

'Hey, lady! You can't go in there!' Tess heard the words being shouted over the roar of the flames. Next moment a uniformed fire officer had her by the arm.

Yanking herself free, Tess pulled out her ID and shouted back, 'I'm Tess Jordan! I'm President here! What's going on? How bad is it?'

'We're trying to keep it isolated to the back stages,

ma'am.' The man was deferential now, but spoke quickly, obviously unwilling to waste precious time on explanations. 'If we can contain it there, we've got a chance of keeping the whole place from goin' sky high.'

The whole place . . .

Tess swallowed. 'How did it start?' She had to ask the question.

The man's mouth set in a tight line. 'Deliberate . . . no doubt about it. Some crazy sonofabitch . . . Who the bejesus knows why?' He turned and was gone.

Tess stood rooted to the spot. The man's answer came as no surprise but still she was stunned. Who? Who was behind —

'Tess!'

Spinning round, she found Mike at her side, his face streaked with dirt, his features strained.

'Oh, Mike . . . ' She grabbed his arms, looked despairingly into his eyes. 'Are they going to be able to save it? Is there a chance?'

'They're doing their best, Tess.' His voice was flat. 'Let's get the hell outta their way and leave them to it.'

It was a sombre gathering at the Havelock mansion: Mike, Tess, about a dozen other executives and key personnel.

While Paula Havelock organised drinks and a cold supper few could look at, Mike kept in constant touch with the LA fire chief at the scene. His face was grey with fatigue and worry as he turned back to those in the room with still nothing positive to report.

At last, after another inconclusive phone call, he addressed the room at large. 'Look, there's no need for all of you to hang around. Why not go home and get some sleep? It's up to our own crew and the LA fire department now. Staying up all night isn't gonna make one scrap of difference.'

Tess, reluctantly, was the last to leave. It was almost

four and the streets of the city were, for once, relatively clear of traffic. As she made her way home, she listened to the car radio. All stations were reporting the fire raging at WLS studios.

She had just put her key in the front door when she heard the phone ringing. She snatched up the receiver.

It was Mike, his voice a mixture of fatigue and relief. 'They did it, Tess. Lot 14 is a total write-off, but they managed, thank God, to keep it from spreading.'

Tess was too much the professional to do anything but echo his relief. It was not the time to start asking all the questions that needed to be asked.

'I'm gonna grab a couple of hours' sleep now, Tess. I suggest you do the same. We've still got a lot to sort out about what happened tonight.'

But Tess couldn't sleep. Neither she nor Mike had exchanged a word in front of the others, but she felt sure he must be as certain as she that this was another attempt to stop them making the Elizabeth Eden story.

Adelle Madigan was enjoying her breakfast more than usual. Wrapped in an ivory silk pegnoir, she sat on her sunny patio sipping at her third cup of black coffee.

A selection of the morning's newspapers lay on the marble-topped table in front of her, and as she bit into her thinly-spread Melba toast, Adelle's knife-tightened eyes were bright with delight behind her sunglasses.

The fire at World Link Studios had made the front page of all editions. Estimates of the damage varied; arson, while strongly suspected, had yet to be officially confirmed; yet one thing was absolutely certain: the damage to Lot 14 had been extensive.

When asked what effect the fire might have on the progress of the Elizabeth Eden movie, the owner of WLS, Mike Havelock, had been noncommittal. 'We'll have to see what can be salvaged,' he had been quoted as replying.

A smile of satisfaction played around Adelle Madigan's lips as she read the columns of print. Let them try. She'd take a bet they'd never get the troubled project off the ground now. Mike Havelock was a businessman; and he wasn't in the business of throwing his money away.

Lighting her second cigarette of the day, Adelle stood up and walked back into the house. She felt suddenly suffused with a warm glow of gratitude towards the man who had never failed her. For she didn't doubt that what had happened overnight at WLS had been organised by Dave Arnell. Not that they would ever discuss it; Dave was too protective of her for that. The problem was solved; that was all that mattered. She had trusted Dave. And as always, he hadn't let her down.

Her mouth suddenly tightened. It was more than she could say for the man she had married...

Carl Harris read the newspaper headlines with equal delight. The problem had been solved.

It had cost him, but he was in the clear. He felt sure the financial position of WLS would mean the Elizabeth Eden project was a dead duck.

A smile played around his lips. Crazy boy Gino had fixed it good.

Gino Cozzi was Carl Harris's cousin. They had grown up together and Gino was the only family member with whom Carl had kept in touch. Whenever his cousin was in LA they hit the town and had a ball.

Gino had always had 'interesting' connections. And on a couple of previous occasions he'd come in handy when Carl had been faced with some irritating shit in his life. Like the broad who'd fallen pregnant and threatened to squawk to the tabloids if he didn't come up with the dough. She'd left town twenty-four hours after Gino had paid her a midnight visit.

And this time, Gino had pulled it off again.

When Carl had explained the problem he'd made it

clear Gino had free rein. 'Handle it any way you like, as long as that fuckin' movie is killed stone dead.'

Carl Harris smiled to himself as he tossed the newspaper aside. Gino hadn't wasted any time. A fire on the set, and the whole goddamn back lot up in flames.

It has cost him thirty thousand bucks but it was worth every cent.

Chris Stanley's call at seven the next morning woke Tess from a brittle sleep.

'Tess! Forgive me for ringing so early. I tried to get you a dozen times last night then realised you must have already been at the studios. It goes without saying they wouldn't let me into the place.'

Still half asleep, Tess started to reply but Chris cut across her. 'Look, first reports suggest the fire was started deliberately... on the lot where the Eden movie was being made. Is that true, Tess? Do you think it was an attempt to stop the movie?'

Fighting off fatigue, Tess pushed herself up in the bed. 'The evidence found at the scene was pretty conclusive, Chris: empty containers of flammables. And yes, Lot 14 was certainly the target.' Then, for a split second, her voice cracked with emotion. 'Jesus, it was so close! For a while there it looked as if the whole goddamn place was going to go up.'

At the other end of the line, Chris realised it was the first time he had been allowed a glimpse behind the cool facade. 'Tess, that strange accident with Jennifer Ross... and now this... The press are beginning to say there's a link between the two. Do you think..?'

She knew then that she was going to have to tell him everything.

'Chris,' she glanced at the bedside alarm, 'I can't talk now. I have to get to the studios and see Mike as soon as possible. Are you free this evening? Can you come and see me here? Around eight?'

As he copied down the address, Chris suddenly realised he'd been offered the invitation he'd been hoping for.

Only not in these circumstances.

Mike Havelock looked as if he'd had as little sleep as Tess, but his energy didn't flag as he held the impromptu executive meeting in the boardroom off his office. In front of him he had the hastily assembled reports from the City's fire chief, the investigating police, and the studio's own security personnel.

'There's no question it was arson, as you'll clearly see when you read these reports.' Mike addressed those seated around the gleaming oregon boardroom table. 'What *is* still a question is how security was breached and access gained to the compound. But at the moment that's a problem I'm leaving to others.'

He faced his silent, watching staff. 'What we've got to decide here is how we're going to handle the sort of publicity the media have already begun to serve up. There were a number of articles in the morning press linking Jennifer Ross's accident and this fire on the lot of the Elizabeth Eden movie. Our decision must be how to use that publicity to work in our favour. Don't you agree, Jon?' Mike turned to look at his head of publicity and promotions.

Jon King looked ill at ease. 'I don't like it, Mike. We're all set to invest big dollars in the story of Elizabeth Eden — not forgetting that already there's the taint of what it's going to do to lots of reputations in this town. Maybe the incident with Jennifer Ross, and now last night, means the whole project is gonna be too messy, gonna attract all the wrong sort of publicity to WLS just as we're trying to get back on our feet. Maybe,' he sighed and tapped the point of his pencil on the pad in front of him, 'we should just scrap the project altogether.'

'*No!*'

WHISPER FROM THE GODS 175

The unexpected force of Tess's reaction made her the focus of attention. She composed herself in an instant. 'I mean — I don't think what's happened will have any lasting detrimental effect on the finished product.' Her heart seemed to be beating at twice its normal rate. 'Look, no one can prove that what happened to Jennifer Ross was more than an accident. And as for the fire, well, by the time the movie hits the screens, all that'll have been forgotten.' She turned pleading eyes to her employer. 'You agree with me, don't you, Mike? There's been so much groundwork done on the Elizabeth Eden story, and we've aroused so much public interest, we'd be crazy to toss it away at this stage.'

Tess felt the intense gaze of her employer. Suddenly she worried that she had revealed too much. Was she making too obvious her unusual emotional commitment to the project? Yet surely, she told herself, Mike wouldn't give credence to Jon King's fears? Fears, she remembered with a sudden coldness in the pit of her belly, that were certain to be compounded if he and the others were to learn about the threatening note to Jennifer Ross. Yet Tess knew that so far Mike had said nothing about that to the rest of the executive staff.

Then she remembered. Tonight she was going to put Chris Stanley in the picture as well. Was going to tell him everything that had happened. Because, she told herself, he was helping her search for the truth.

Because, the unexpectedness of the realisation caught her by surprise, *she wanted to see him again . . .*

Mike Havelock made his position clear. 'I don't think there's any reason to go overboard about this. The project will go ahead. I want a twenty-four hour reconstruction schedule operating immediately on those damaged sets. In the meantime, let's get our asses into gear and concentrate on getting the handful of location shoots in the can.' He gathered up his reports. 'Jon, I'll expect a watertight PR angle for release to this afternoon's press.'

Tess gave no outward sign of her relief as the meeting came to an end.

It was the sort of house which made you feel immediately at home, Chris thought, as he settled himself on the comfortable sofa and looked out through tall glass doors to the pool and garden beyond. The room was softly lit, something classical was playing in the background, and as he accepted his drink, he found himself wishing that this could have been a social rather than a business call.

Hey, he chided himself inwardly as he took the first sip of ice-cold Corona, come down to earth, Chris, baby: she barely knows you exist except as an employee ...

Sitting across from him in a high-backed wicker chair, Tess was trying to remember how long it had been since she'd sat in her own living room with a male companion.

These days when she did finally make it home, it was usually to spend a few more hours at work in her den before falling into bed. But, she told herself, that was the way she wanted it; that way she had no time to miss — She pushed such dangerous thoughts out of her head.

'Chris, I'm sorry. I should have told you all this earlier. But there's been just so much happening, I've been flat out ... ' She gave an apologetic shrug and put down her wine glass. 'Let me bring you up to date ... '

'And the cops are working on it? You're sure about that?' Chris had listened in frowning silence until Tess was finished.

She nodded. 'Mike's organised it so that the investigation is being carried out with due discretion. Obviously the last thing we need out of all this is adverse publicity. He's hoping the statement he made this afternoon — that the fire started with an electrical fault on the sound stage — will help kill off the rumours.'

Chris's expression was serious. 'Someone's very

frightened, Tess. That's more than obvious. The problem is finding out who might have the strongest reason for wanting to stop the movie on Elizabeth Eden. Before,' he added quietly, 'something really tragic happens.'

Tess frowned. 'But it could be anyone... Those letters and diaries blow the whistle on any number of big names: producers, directors, fellow stars — all those who played a part in Elizabeth's betrayal and corruption.'

'Sure,' Chris said slowly, 'and here's a movie that's going to reveal all that... but even more importantly, it's going to reopen the question of her death... I think that's what all this is about, Tess. Elizabeth's death.'

She stared back at him. 'So do I, Chris.'

Tess assured herself it was only good manners that prompted her invitation.

Their glasses were empty in front of them, as she glanced at her watch. 'No wonder I'm starving. It's almost nine-thirty. Look, uh, if you don't have to rush off somewhere, I can throw us together a steak and salad.' She gave him an apologetic smile, aware at the same time that his response was more important than it should have been. 'Cooking isn't quite my forte, but it'll save having to disturb Lola.'

Chris shrugged with an easy smile. 'Only thing I have to rush off to is a messy condo without even a goldfish for company.' He spoke the words as casually as possible but his eyes never left her face.

He wondered later if it had been merely wishful thinking or had he really seen that brief glow of pleasure cross her features?

The weather was typically balmy and they ate on the terrace overlooking the pool with its underwater lighting.

'How's your steak?'

'Terrific. I must admit, I'm super fussy as far as steaks are concerned. Hard to convince anyone I like it this rare. Carrie used to — ' He stopped abruptly.

'Carrie . . . ?' She was watching him from across the table, those wonderful green eyes holding his own.

'I . . . She was a girl I — ' Chris looked away. The pain was still there. It would never leave him.

'I'll get coffee,' she said softly, pushing back her chair.

Another one with a problem . . . In the kitchen Tess flicked on the faucet with a little too much force. Another typical wounded and bitter LA male. Well, she gave an inward shrug, why should she have thought Chris Stanley would be any different?

CHAPTER

22

The night of the fire at WLS, Nick was on a business trip east. As soon as he read the headlines and saw the television news, he resolved to call Tess the moment he returned to California.

He could imagine how she must be feeling. The afternoon she had come to the house to lunch she had mentioned only briefly the movie about Elizabeth Eden. Yet even so Nick had sensed her dedication to the project. The movie, Tess had announced, was going to blow apart the Hollywood dream, was going to propel WLS straight back to the top.

Now, three days later, as the company jet took him back to the west coast, Nick made up his mind to catch up with Tess as soon as possible. His schedule was every bit as hectic as her own, but surely it would be possible to fit in a lunch one day soon. Fate had brought them together again after so many years, and nothing, not even the demands of their high-powered careers must be allowed to interfere with their bond.

But as he emerged from the terminal into LA's relentless sunshine, Nick was met by his worried-looking assistant, Reuben Nelson. On the drive to the company headquarters on Wilshire, Nick listened to his assistant's disturbing news, and realised that a meeting with Tess would have to be put on hold.

'It's about that chopper crash last week near Big Bear, Nick. Pilot and both passengers killed. As you know, the preliminary investigations seemed to suggest it was the motor at fault; nothin' to do with any specific Conroy parts. But then, first thing this mornin' I get a call from the FAA investigation arm.' Reuben Nelson's jaw was set in a tight line. 'They want to talk with us. Urgent. Couldn't get anythin' more out of them except that it's got somethin' to do with the rotor blades.' He shot his boss a hard look. 'It doesn't sound good, Nick.'

'Let's not panic till we see what they're getting at, Reuben.' Nick's voice was calm, but he was thinking of the alarm bell that had rung in his mind a few months previously when, newly arrived in California, he had begun to go through his predecessor's files.

He remembered the two-paragraph letter that had first aroused his suspicions. It would only have meant something to someone with his detailed knowledge of the industry. At a consequent meeting with Walter Conroy he had decided the time was not right to raise the matter. Firstly, because his employer had seemed so obviously distracted on that occasion, but mostly because Nick had wanted time to pursue his investigations more thoroughly. Then the pressures of everyday business had taken precedence and he'd been forced to leave the problem till later.

And now, thought Nick, feeling the first stirrings of anxiety, perhaps the Federal Aviation Authority was going to pre-empt him.

The FAA didn't waste any time.

The two senior investigators were in Nick's office first thing the next morning.

The elder of the two, a ruddy-faced man with a crew cut, came straight to the point. 'At first we felt pretty sure it was the starter motor at fault. But then, when we couldn't pinpoint anything in that direction, we naturally started looking elsewhere. That's when one of our team found something strange about the rotor arms.'

'What do you mean, "strange"?' Nick surveyed his visitors coolly from behind his expansive modern desk.

The two hard-eyed professionals told him exactly what they meant.

And now Nick knew he had no choice but to bring the matter to the attention of Walter Conroy as soon as possible. The FAA wanted answers and they weren't going to go away without them.

In all the eight years Nick had worked for Walter Conroy, he had never seen his employer so angry. His face was purple, his dark eyes bulged, the spittle flew from his lips as he gave vent to his rage.

'What the shit are those motherfuckers trying to pin on us! I'll sue the fuckers for every goddamn red cent! The Conroy reputation's the best in the business!'

Nick watched as his employer slammed a huge fist down on an antique occasional table. They were in Conroy's lavishly appointed penthouse in the Century Plaza Hotel.

Tall and powerfully built, Walter Conroy looked as strong as an ox, but for a moment Nick wondered if the sheer force of the man's temper was going to cause him to have a heart attack.

Conroy's mood made it all the more difficult for Nick to ask his question. But he knew it was one that couldn't be sidestepped.

'Walter ... You don't think there might have been something going on with the previous management, do you? Something that could have some bearing on the FAA suspicions?'

Walter Conroy immediately spun round to face him. 'What the fuck are you driving at?'

Nick knew then that what he was about to say might cost him his job, yet he had no option but to reveal what he'd discovered.

'I was going through my predecessor's files not long after I moved to LA. Most of it was the usual, straightforward stuff, but then I came across a letter ... It — it seemed innocuous enough on the surface but on a closer reading, I picked up on some of the codes and serial numbers being referred to. What it seemed to suggest was that certain rejected stock might still be offered as new if it could be got away with. I haven't had the time to follow through as thoroughly as I'd like, which is why I didn't mention it to you before, but on first examination it doesn't look as if the suggestion was in fact adopted as policy.'

'What are you trying to say to me, Nick?' Walter Conroy's voice was soft now. Soft and dangerous.

'I guess what I'm saying is that it's bad enough the FAA are suspicious about the standard of rotor blades on that chopper, but with further investigation a real possibility unless we can prove those blades were the genuine article, that's a dangerous letter to have on file. Even if it could be proved that nothing ever came of it.'

To Nick's surprise, his employer's response was immediate. Walter Conroy didn't seem to need to absorb what he had just been told. He gave his instructions curtly and precisely. Almost, thought Nick, as if he'd already been prepared to face just such a problem ...

'I want that letter in my hands first thing tomorrow morning — you got that? Then, in exactly a week from today, you're going to set up a meeting for me with each of those FAA bastards separately. I don't care what you tell them, just make sure that's how it happens.'

He turned and left the room.

Nick knew when he was being dismissed.

Usually Eleanor Benson's full, voluptuous figure was the perfect antidote to Walter's stressful routine.

But this evening even his beautiful young mistress failed to bring the relief he sought. As he'd undressed, he'd tried, but hadn't succeeded, to shut out the conversation with Nick Teece. The last thing he needed just now was those sonsofbitches from the FAA poking their fucking noses into things. It was absolutely vital that he shut them up until the Pentagon was —

'Honey ... you OK?' Eleanor Benson stopped her pelvic grinding to frown up into her lover's face.

Walter swore under his breath and rolled his bulk off her pale body. 'Sorry, babe. Business. Somethin' on my mind. Next time I'll be fine.'

Eleanor Benson made the appropriate soothing noises. As she snuggled close and stroked the grizzled grey hair on her lover's chest, she hid her relief. For one terrifying moment she'd been worried that Walter Conroy might be losing interest in her. But thank Christ it wasn't that.

Her ingenuous blue eyes took in the luxuriously appointed bedroom. The apartment and all utilities were provided by the heavy, ugly man beside her. The man she was determined to make her own.

It wasn't easy, but Nick managed to arrange a quick drink after work with Tess about two weeks after Walter Conroy held his meeting with the respective FAA officers.

Provided with no information as to the outcome of these meetings, Nick could only assume — when no further investigations were ordered into the Conroy Corporation's role in the Big Bear crash — that Walter had satisfactorily answered all the investigator's questions.

But still Nick felt uneasy about the whole episode. Walter Conroy was a powerful and wealthy man. If those rotors *had* been faulty, could he have done some separate deal with each of those guys? Offered them money to —

'Nick ... You're miles away. You've hardly said a word in five minutes.'

'Oh, God, Tess, I'm sorry.' He was instantly contrite. 'You're right, I've got things on my mind at the moment.'

She gave him a sympathetic look. 'Business?'

He nodded. 'Yeah. Settling into this new position isn't without its problems.' With an effort Nick shook himself out of his reverie. He could think about his problems in his own time. Leaning across the table, he placed a hand over hers. 'Hey, things have been tough for you too. How's it going now? Is everything still full steam ahead on the movie?'

Tess sighed. 'It's slowly coming together. Rebuilding the sets is what's taking time. But we're getting there.' Her voice grew more positive. 'Believe me, Nick, nothing's going to stop me getting that story on the screen.'

He studied her in the soft lamp light. They were sitting in the Art-Deco splendour of the Rex, a bar on the ground floor of the historic Oviatt Building. Essentially a fine restaurant with the ambience of a 1930's cruise liner, it was also an elegant escape from the noisier, more trendy downtown drinking spots.

'This project's really got under your skin, hasn't it, Tess? Is it because you can relate to the crap Hollywood dishes out? Is that why you want to show how it was for Elizabeth Eden?'

It was then, for just a split second, that Tess wanted nothing more in the world than to tell Nick the truth. Wanted to tell him the real reason behind her drive and commitment to the Elizabeth Eden project.

But at once she fought back the impulse. This was her secret, a secret she had carried in her heart for almost seventeen years. It was almost as if she couldn't bear to let anyone, not even Nick, come between her and the mother she had never known . . .

'It's a story that has to be told, Nick. Elizabeth Eden was destroyed by a system that was evil and corrupt. Degraded by rumour and innuendo, made to work in roles she despised, she was robbed of her innocence and potential. And as well as that,' she added softly, 'there are still too many unanswered questions about her death.'

Nick saw the intensity in those green eyes he had never been able to forget. 'Taking on the establishment is never an easy task, Tess. Don't knock your head too hard against the wall.'

Gently he smoothed a strand of dark hair behind her ear as he tried as tactfully as possible to say what was on his mind. 'Honey, I admire your persistence and courage, but it seems to me that you're just living for your work these days. Isn't there... ?' He hesitated, reluctant to pry.

Tess finished the question for him. 'A man?' She looked away, shaking her head. 'No. Nothing's worked out like that for me. In my position, men either resent me or find me intimidating.' She forced a little laugh. 'But listen! There's no need to worry about me. Life's good, believe me. Great job, great money, terrific home. I'm happy. Really I am.' As she uttered the words, she almost came close to convincing herself.

Twenty minutes later they kissed a warm goodbye in the lobby before getting into their cars. Neither of them noticed the well-dressed man who had followed them out of the Rex. With his bland, regular features he was rarely noticed.

That was why he was so good at his job.

As she made her way home, Tess pondered Nick's words and her own response to them. There was no denying she lived for her work. That much was obvious. And as she had said, it had brought her an enviable life style... power... money. But — had it made her happy?

Much as she had stressed her contentment to Nick, Tess faced the fact that her personal life left a lot to be desired. Whereas Nick was now driving home to a loving wife and children, to people who shared his life and goals, who supported and cared for him, she would enter a lonely home with only her housekeeper for intermittent company. And even Lola, Tess thought with rare self-pity, had children at home in Mexico, and had parents, brothers and sisters who cared what happened to her.

It was that unaccustomed mood which made Tess react to an equally unusual impulse. Picking up her car phone, she found herself dialling Chris Stanley's number. He was probably out, she told herself. Why would an attractive single guy be sitting alone at home?

He answered the phone on the third ring and she was almost caught by surprise.

'Oh — hi, Chris . . . Tess Jordan. Look, I know it's short notice but I was wondering if you're free to come over this evening? The LAPD haven't come up with anything yet on the fire, or the incident with Jennifer Ross. I think we've got to have a talk about the whole business, don't you?' The excuse sounded horribly weak, even to her own ears.

There was dead silence at the other end of the line and immediately Tess felt like kicking herself. Goddamn it, why had she let the conversation with Nick get to her? She enjoyed her own company. She didn't need to beg this guy or anyone else to —

But Chris Stanley was speaking. 'A good idea, Tess. I've put out a few feelers myself. No pay dirt yet, but I guess I should fill you in on them.'

His voice was warm and friendly and, almost hating herself, she gave in to another impulse. 'If you haven't eaten, I'm sure I can rustle something up.'

'Sounds good to me. But it'll be tough walking away from the three-day old can of tuna I was looking forward to.'

Tess was smiling as she hung up. Whatever Chris Stanley's hang-ups, at least he had a sense of humour.

This time Lola cooked one of her impressive chicken dishes and again they ate on the terrace. The conversation was light — books, films, music — until the meal was over and they had retreated to the living room where the coffee pot on the warmer meant they wouldn't be disturbed.

'Great meal.' Chris watched as Tess poured their two coffees.

'Lola's a terrific cook. I'm sure she's delighted when she has more than just me to cater for.'

Does that happen often? Chris wondered to himself. Or is it just someone like me you ask home, someone who wouldn't do much good to your image to be seen with in public?

He swore under his breath at his own crazy musings. He was here to talk business again. That was all. No need to allow his paranoia to get in the way . . .

Tess handed him a cup and settled herself next to him on the sofa. 'So Chris, tell me about these feelers you've been putting out.'

He added two spoons of sugar and stirred slowly. 'I'm concentrating on the night Elizabeth Eden died, Tess. Details of the police reports aren't easy to come by, but I've managed to get the names of the two officers who were first on the scene that night.'

Tess gave him an enquiring look.

'One was Rick Feldstein,' he continued. 'He retired from the force a very short time afterwards. Moved to Palm Beach where he seemed to make his living from the track. The horses must have been good to him too. He was living pretty well by the time he died.'

He saw her sharp look. 'Yeah. Died of a heart attack about ten years ago.'

'So,' Tess looked disappointed. 'No lead there. But there were two cops, you said. What about the other one?'

'From what I can gather, the other guy, Les Donovan, is still alive. Unlike Feldstein, though, he was dishonourably discharged from the force. Did time in jail for accepting bribes in a couple of drug cases. By the time he was released his marriage had broken up, and so far I haven't been able to track him down.'

'What do you think he could tell us even if you could find him, Chris?'

'Who knows? But he was *there*. He might know something that to him at least doesn't seem remotely pertinent. But perhaps in hindsight, pieced together with what Suzie Hawkins saw and heard that night, things might add up. It's a chance anyway, and I'm doing my darndest to find that guy.'

Tess heard the determination in his voice. 'You're spending a lot of time on all this, Chris. Are you sure it's going to be worth it for you? What about your work with the *Clarion*?'

'I've got time to kill, Tess. Nothing in my life these days but work.'

Just like her . . .

She kept her question casual. 'Don't your girlfriends object to that?'

His eyes met hers. 'It's been over two years since there was anyone special in my life, Tess. After Carrie was killed, work was all that kept me sane.'

She said nothing, continued to hold his gaze. And before he knew it, he was telling her about Carrie.

'I'm sorry.' Chris glanced at his watch and gave her an apologetic look. 'I — I didn't realise how time was getting on. I've been talking too much.'

'I think it was something you needed to talk about,' Tess answered gently.

Chris nodded. 'You're right. That's really the first time in two years I've talked to anyone about Carrie or that night. I — I guess I was never ready to before.'

'It's never easy when you lose someone close to you, Chris. Especially in — in tragic circumstances.'

He looked at her more closely. Some undertone in her softly spoken words made him wonder if perhaps she, too, had experienced some similar loss. It brought home to him once again how little he knew about her.

He reached for his jacket and rose to his feet. 'Well, I've kept you long enough. Guess I'd better be going.'

She walked him to the door, where he turned and smiled down at her. 'Thanks again for saving me from the tuna. Lola's got a great way with chicken. It was a very pleasant evening. I — I enjoy your company, Tess.'

She was looking up at him, aware of the sadness still lingering in those direct dark eyes. Perhaps it was compassion, a spontaneous gesture of sympathy, that made her suddenly lean forward and kiss him on the cheek. But as she tasted his skin, caught a whiff of some lemon-scented after-shave, Tess felt her senses assaulted by a more powerful, violent emotion.

She drew back, not daring to look at him, jolted by the current of pure physical response.

'Tess . . . ' Chris breathed her name, stunned by the unexpectedness of her action, by the undeniable electricity between them. Gently he turned her face up to his, looked deep into those startled eyes. Whispering her name again, he lowered his lips to hers. The kiss was tentative at first, then lingering, caressing, until finally they broke apart.

Breathless and shaken, they stared at each other in silence. Seconds later, arms entwined in a tight embrace, they were kissing again, this time with open-mouthed intensity.

It was Chris who broke away first. 'I've — I've got to go, Tess. It's been a lovely evening. Thanks. Thanks a lot.'

And with a quick squeeze of her hand, he was out of the door and starting the engine of the Corvette.

For the next half-hour as she prepared for bed, Tess was confronted by a whole range of confusing emotions.

Chris Stanley. Her junior . . . A colleague . . . She had kissed him like . . . like that . . . And he'd responded. She, with her unbreachable rule of *never* getting involved with a co-worker.

Well, she told herself, firmly, she wasn't involved. Chris Stanley was carrying too much baggage from his past. He'd made that clear. Nothing would go any further than this evening.

So why did she feel so disappointed?

Confused and angry, she pushed that thought away.

She had just slipped between the sheets when the telephone rang beside her.

'Tess ... It's Chris. I'm sorry to disturb you.'

Disturb her? Her insides hadn't stopped churning since he'd left.

'Tess, I can't stop thinking about what happened tonight. I — it caught me unawares, and I wasn't sure if — ' He stopped, took a deep breath. 'What I'm trying to say is I feel something special could be happening between us — and if I fight it I might be crazier than I think.' She heard the intensity in his voice. 'Tess, I guess I'm asking if you'll see me again. Soon. Real soon.'

Her fingers were clutched tightly around the receiver. A million reasons for saying no were running through her head.

'I'd like that, Chris,' she heard herself reply. 'Very soon.'

As she hung up, Tess felt as if something inside her had just been unfrozen. Released.

Carl Harris's legion of admiring fans would have been shocked to hear the language pouring from their idol's lips.

It had taken time to track Gino down but finally Carl had reached him.

'Don't you read the fuckin' newspapers?' the actor bellowed down the line. 'Those motherfuckers are still movin' on the project! I paid you thirty thousand big ones, pal. Do something! And this time make it stick!'

Slamming down the receiver, he reached for his drink with trembling fingers.

CHAPTER

23

Jennifer Ross yawned as she released the button on the intercom and punched in the code which activated the security gate. It was quarter to six, the sky was just beginning to lighten, and the studio limo was right on time as always.

She gulped down the rest of her coffee. It was far too early to eat anything.

Dressed in her usual working uniform of blue jeans and casually expensive sweater, her face devoid of the make-up she'd be forced to wear for the next ten to twelve hours, Jennifer grabbed her leather hold-all and let herself out of the house.

The uniformed driver stepped out of the sleek white Cadillac.

As she turned to pull the front door closed behind her, Jennifer called a greeting over her shoulder. 'Hi, Danny!'

A split second later, she spun round in surprise. Instead of waiting by the open car door, the driver was bounding up onto the porch.

Jennifer Ross's eyes widened. 'Hey! You're not Da—'

Then she saw the long-bladed knife in his gloved hand.

'Open the door!' The man in the sunglasses and chauffeur's uniform caught her in an iron grip and held the knife to her throat.

Rita Colby left her battered station wagon out of sight at the rear of the house and let herself in at the back door.

In the kitchen the first thing the black housekeeper did was open the refrigerator. For the next ten minutes she concentrated on making one of the super sandwiches with which she always started her day now that her employer was out of the house so early. Fancy cheeses, succulent ham, tiny ripe tomatoes, crisp cos lettuce ... Rita stuffed them all between two thick slices of sourdough.

At the kitchen table, she munched slowly, in no hurry to begin her day. Hardly a thing to do anyways, she thought, washing down her snack with a glass of freshly squeezed orange juice. Woman lived alone, never messed the place up. Most days all Rita had to do was tidy the main bedroom and bathroom, and keep everything else looking spick and span.

When she'd finished eating, the housekeeper carefully cleaned away all evidence of her meal. Not that she figured her employer was likely to mind, but why the heck go lookin' for trouble?

Tying on her apron, she adjusted her Walkman and made her way to the main bedroom.

She stopped at the open door, surprised for a moment at the unaccustomed messiness. Bedclothes strewn across the floor, one of the antique bedside lamps knocked askew, a pair of jeans and a sweater flung carelessly in a corner.

Rita frowned. Musta been one helluva night.

Then, as she bent to retrieve the discarded bedclothes, she saw something out of the corner of her eye. Something lying on the tiled bathroom floor.

Straightening up, Rita moved closer. And suddenly what she had been staring at took shape.

A scream of terror ripped from her throat, just moments before the undigested sandwich followed suit.

'There's no way you could have kept *this* from the press, Mike.'

Lieutenant Ric Buchanan stared at the set, strained face of the owner of WLS. 'I did my best for ya with the other business, but JC himself couldn't have kept this a secret.'

'I know, Ric. I know.' Mike Havelock couldn't sit still. He moved restlessly round his office, shaking his head in disbelief. 'I thought we'd taken care of that angle. I thought we'd done all we could to take the threats seriously.'

'You can't blame yourself, Mike. It was so simply done.'

'Has the call to the limo hire firm been traced?'

Both men looked over at Tess as if they had forgotten her presence. Numb with shock, she had sat without speaking for so long that they probably had.

The lieutenant shook his head. 'Nope. And it probably won't be. Not from a payphone.'

'But why didn't they *check*!' Tess's voice rose with unaccustomed shrillness. Her fingers were trembling — as they had been ever since the news of Jennifer Ross's murder had reached her an hour and a half ago.

'Hey, take it easy, ma'am. They're no more to blame than Mike here.' The officer shrugged. 'They get a call saying a car won't be needed that day, why should they bother to check?'

With a stiff nod, Tess stood up. 'You're right, of course, Lieutenant.' She turned to her employer. 'Mike, I'm sorry. If you don't need me any longer ...'

He saw the tight lines around her mouth, the chalkiness of her complexion. 'Sure, Tess. It's up to the lieutenant now, anyway — to handle this ... this tragedy.' He put a hand on her elbow and walked her to the door, speaking softly, comfortingly. 'Don't torture yourself about this, Tess. No one can expect to foresee what a madman's going to do.'

She shrugged free of his hold. 'I'll be in my office if you need me again.' Quickly she walked away.

A madman...

Face buried in her hands, Tess sat motionless at her desk, tortured by images of what had happened during Jennifer Ross's last hours.

She had forced herself to listen as the lieutenant described the scene which had met them as a result of the housekeeper's hysterical call.

A nutcase. A loony with a capital L. Ric Buchanan was certain of that. For not only had Jennifer Ross been raped and savagely stabbed to death, but her sexual organs had been mutilated with a terrible ferocity.

For Tess however, the horror of the crime went beyond even those monstrous bounds.

According to the police report, the acts of violence and perversion had been carried out while Jennifer Ross was dressed and made-up to resemble Elizabeth Eden: the platinum wig, the slim-fitting gown that was almost a replica of that worn by Elizabeth in her debut movie... A gown that in the frenzied attack had been shredded almost to ribbons.

'I'm so sorry to disturb you, Ms Jordan,' her secretary's voice came over the intercom, 'but there's a gentleman at the main gate who insists on seeing you. He refuses to move his vehicle until you've been told he's there.'

'Who is it?' Tess was sifting through the pile of telephone messages awaiting her attention. The phones had been running hot since the news of the murder had broken.

'Mr Nick Teece. We've got him on monitor.'

Tess flicked a switch by her desk and checked the

security monitor for the main studio gates. It *was* Nick. Caring, wonderful Nick.

'He's a personal friend. Let him in at once.'

'As soon as I heard the news, I had to come.'

'I'm glad you did, Nick. I'm OK, but it's still hard to believe what's happened.'

They were in the plush private reception room off her office. Nick took her hand in his, his face creased with concern. 'Tess, what's going on? What is there about the Elizabeth Eden movie that's made someone desperate enough to kill?'

She shifted her gaze from his. 'It's — we're stepping on some big toes, Nick. We knew that at the start. Only we never dreamed it would come to ... this.'

She could feel his blue eyes fixed intently on her face.

'Somehow I feel there's more to it than that. I'm not sure why. But maybe one day you'll tell me what's behind this obsession with Elizabeth Eden.'

Her face still turned away, she answered softly, 'The truth, Nick. That's all I want. To find out the truth.'

The strength of Nick's concern and the depth of their friendship sustained Tess as she did her best to get through the rest of the day.

Further comfort came in one of the dozens of phone calls she took in the following half-hour.

'Tess!' It was Chris. 'Thank God I've got through to you at last. Are you OK?' His concern was obvious.

'I'm coping. The phones haven't stopped. Where are you?'

'At the precinct. I'm going to hang around with the cops for a while and see if there's anything more I can piece together here.' He lowered his voice. 'Tess, the way she was found ... the dress, the blonde wig ... This has to have some link with that other death.'

'I think you're right.' The calmness of her tone

amazed her. 'Look, it's not easy for either of us to talk now. Are you free to come round this evening? About nine?'

'I was about to suggest the same thing. I'll keep trying every angle I can here, and catch up with you then.'

It was around seven, just when she was about to make her escape, that she received the summons from Mike.

'Won't keep you too long,' he promised on his private line. 'But I think it's pretty important you know about this before tomorrow.'

Later, Tess realised she should have been prepared.

But she wasn't. Not even when she walked into her employer's office and found three other executive personnel there, including Jon King, head of publicity and promotions.

Responding to subdued greetings, Tess took a seat. As she gratefully accepted a drink, she could see from the faces around her what a toll the day had taken. On this occasion, at least, the violence endemic to LA had touched each of them.

She had just taken her first sip of vodka when Mike's opening words almost made her drop her glass.

'Tess, I don't think we've got any choice but to drop the project on Elizabeth Eden.'

'I should have seen it coming. But when he said it, it was like a bolt from the blue!'

They were in Tess's living room. As she related what had occurred with Mike Havelock, Chris realised this was the first time he'd ever seen her lose her cool.

'And he refused point blank to reconsider,' she continued. 'No name actress, he said, would go anywhere near the role now.' Tess shook her head in exasperation. 'Well, I don't believe that, Chris. This role doesn't even need a big name. It'll *make* an unknown. I'm certain of that.' She gave an angry shrug. 'But nothing could shift

Mike. The project's off. Finished. He's frightened that any more bad publicity will mean the death of WLS before we're even up and running.'

Chris did his best to soothe her agitation. 'I can understand you're upset about the movie, Tess. But that doesn't mean to say we have to give up.' He frowned as he nursed his beer. 'The message I'm getting is that the story behind all this is even bigger than we thought. Someone is desperate. We've got tragic evidence of the lengths that person's prepared to go to stop this movie.'

He put down his glass, got to his feet and paced restlessly round the room. 'I'm not going to sit back and wait for the cops to act on this. There's *got* to be that one undiscovered or unrecognised factor that's going to help crack this story.'

Tess rose to face him, her eyes dark with emotion. 'Then find it quickly, Chris. Otherwise the whole truth about Elizabeth Eden will never come to light.'

Chris put his hands on her shoulders, his expression as intense as her own. 'I know how much this project means to you, Tess. It's important to me too. Believe me, I'm not going to let it go until I find out the truth.'

He drew her towards him and she drank in the comfort of his embrace.

As his arms tightened around her, their lips met. This time no barriers existed between them. Tess felt her pulses begin to race as his tongue and lips explored her own, his hand on the small of her back holding her close against him.

They kissed again and again, time and place receding, as each surrendered to their hunger and need. Then she felt his breath warm against her hair, as he whispered, 'I want you so much, Tess. You can see that. But we're going to wait, aren't we? Until there's a better time than this?'

She nodded against his chest.

*

Suzie Hawkins was panting with fear. First the 'accident' and now this. The gruesome murder of Jennifer Ross.

Her thick fingers were unsteady as she dialled the number. He was home.

'Mr Stanley ... it's Suzie Hawkins.'

Chris heard the tremor in the woman's voice. He could guess why she had called. 'Yes ... what can I do for you?'

'Mr Stanley, I don't like what's going on. I don't know how you're reading what happened to that actress, but something tells me plain as day she was murdered so that that movie doesn't get made.'

Suzie Hawkins' breath rasped noisily in her throat. 'Whatever role you're playing in all this, I'm just begging that my name be kept right out of it. You hear what I say? I'm frightened, Mr Stanley!'

CHAPTER

24

'Think the cops're gonna nab the psycho who made mincemeat of that actress?'

As he polished glasses behind the counter, the barman nodded at the television screen fixed in one corner of the dimly lit bar.

His solitary customer, on his third bourbon, was looking contemptuously at the screen as LA's chief of police did his best to answer the media's questions.

'Listen pal,' he gestured dismissively, 'too many times the cops are made to work with both hands tied behind their backs.'

'You reckon?' Todd Larson was making easy conversation. It was mid-afternoon, the slowest time of the day. Still a couple of hours to kill until happy hour when things would start to get busy again in the tiny Santa Monica saloon.

'Yeah, I reckon.' There was something belligerent in the man's tone. 'You can work your butt off on a case, but if someone at the top don't like what y're findin' out, you don't go no further.'

Todd gave his customer an appraising look. Late fifties, overweight, balding — a loser, he guessed.

'Sound like you know somethin' about it. You been in the force?'

'Yeah.' The man's lips curled back in a sneer, revealing bad teeth. 'Long time ago. But I don't forget. They mighta shut me up, but I don't forget.' He shoved some change across the counter. 'Gimme another.'

Todd Larson cleared away the man's empty glass and made him a fresh drink. The customer took a deep swallow then seemed keen to resume his conversation. 'I knew sure as Moses there was no way that movie was gonna be allowed to go ahead.'

'Yeah?' Todd was only half listening, his eyes on the television screen where some fat woman was sounding off about welfare fraud. Whole goddamn country'd be on welfare soon, he figured, they kept on the way they were goin'.

'An' I know why.' The drinker wasn't going to be ignored. 'I was there that night. I know what I saw.' The words were slightly slurred now as the liquor began to take effect.

'What night?'

'The night Elizabeth Eden was murdered.'

The man saw he had at last caught the barman's attention and for a second a triumphant expression flashed over his soft, pudgy features.

He nodded emphatically. 'Yep, Lieutenant Les Donovan I was then. Me and my partner were the first at the house that night. Rick's gone now, so there's only me left who knows the truth.' He lowered his voice conspiratorially. 'Knew at once it weren't no suicide. I seen lotsa bodies before and believe me, that baby didn't kill herself.'

Todd Larson was listening carefully. Very carefully. The guy could be another crazy, but you never knew . . . 'Why'd ya think they said it was suicide then?' His voice was soft and encouraging.

'Ha!' Les Donovan snorted angrily. 'They were coverin' up, weren't they? Coverin' up for — ' He stopped abruptly. A muscle twitched in his right cheek.

'Coverin' up . . . ? Who the hell they'd be doin' that for, Les?' Todd Larson was doing his best.

The man stared at him, and now there was the beginning of fear in his bloodshot eyes. He swallowed the last of his drink in one gulp. 'You wouldn't believe me if I told you.' Les Donovan slid off his stool and walked quickly to the exit.

By the time he rounded the bar, all Todd Larson had time to note were the numberplates on the departing old model Dodge.

Hurrying back inside, he scribbled the figures on a beer coaster. Two minutes later he was using the pay-phone by the men's room to place his call.

She knew by his tone it was urgent.

'I can't discuss this on the telephone, Tess. You able to get away? Can you meet me somewhere?' Chris thought quickly. 'What about outside the Griffith Park Observatory? That OK?'

Tess glanced at her watch. Almost quarter to four. She had no more meetings scheduled for that afternoon. 'Sure. Give me half an hour.'

Located high above the Hollywood Hills, the Observatory looked over the sprawl that was the City of Angels. But as she listened to what Chris had to tell her, Tess was barely aware of the view.

'Todd's someone who keeps his ear to the ground for me. People talk when they've had a few drinks, and he's helped me on stories before. But if what he's telling me this time is on the level . . . ' Chris was keeping his voice low, but his excitement was obvious. 'This could be it, Tess, the break we've been waiting for.'

Tess felt her heart begin to race. The officer who had been first on the scene the night Elizabeth died. A man who was certain there'd been a cover up . . .

She looked at Chris, her eyes bright with anticipation.

'We've got to find him. You've got his name and licence number. Surely . . . '

Chris grinned. 'Easy when you know how, Tess. Started the wheels turning the moment I got off the phone from Todd. Donovan lives in Orange County, at El Venjo. It's an industrial town outside of Laguna.' He gripped her hand in excitement. 'I think we're gonna have to take a trip south this weekend, don't you?'

He saw her to her car and leaned in the window as she turned the key in the ignition. 'I'm absolutely certain this is it, Tess. Donovan's the lead we've been looking for.'

'I hope you're right, Chris. Oh, God, I hope so.'

They kissed a quick goodbye, neither aware that behind a group of chattering tourists, a man was watching them intently.

The two men were seated together in the back seat of the limousine. A glass panel divided them from the driver but still they kept their voices low.

'You saw the network news before you left? Havelock's made it official — he's called off the project.' It was Larry Brandt who spoke.

'Yeah, I heard.' Dave Arnell ran a finger round the stiffly starched collar of his dinner shirt. 'Who's crying?'

Larry Brandt grinned. 'Great timing, I'd say.'

The campaign manager was looking forward to the evening ahead. A dinner for thirty hand-picked guests at the home of oil man, philanthropist, and staunch Democrat supporter, Seymour Van Weiss. It'd still be 'work' but Larry could stand the pace. He might be over fifty, but he prided himself on his energy. His usual routine of a fifteen-kilometre early morning run, plus a hard game of racquetball at his club whenever he could find the extra time, had kept him in shape. Tonight he felt in top form.

Dave Arnell was speaking softly again. 'But there might still be a problem, Larry. You know what I mean?'

Larry Brandt gave his colleague a sharp look. 'You're working on that though, aren't you?'

Dave Arnell nodded. Yes . . . he was working on that.

Seymour Van Weiss was not only a very rich man but a generous one as well. And as a major contributor to the Democratic Party's campaign, he fully expected to have the ear of the next President of the United States. This evening, as on other occasions, he made no attempt to hide his self-interest. As the first course was cleared away, he was seeking Robert Madigan's views on a new oil price-fixing authority.

Seated at the right hand of her host, Adelle beamed her public consumption smile but felt her concentration wandering. The dinner was wonderful, and Seymour Van Weiss's antique-filled mansion, built to resemble a seventeenth century French chateau, was a sensational setting. But Adelle didn't really feel at ease.

Her gaze kept drifting to Dave who was seated further down the long candlelit table, and now and then her smile would slip, replaced for a fleeting moment by a worried frown. Adelle was perfectly aware of the strength of Dave's feelings for her. He loved her completely, as her husband never had, yet for all these years he'd accepted that she would never give up the honour and prestige afforded her by the Madigan name.

Dave understood what it meant to be a Madigan and he was totally committed to seeing Tom Madigan's son make it into the White House.

But, had he really . . . ? Could he have actually . . . ?

Adelle did her best to push the unthinkable out of her mind.

Carl Harris felt as sick as he looked.

He closed the door against any intrusion by the servants and took a seat opposite the big-shouldered man with the short dark hair and broken nose.

'Why'd you do it, Gino? Why'd you do it like that? I told you to handle it, but I never — ' He stopped, did his best to swallow past the lump in his throat. 'Christ, Gino, the fuckin' cops are gonna be swarmin' all over the fuckin' place. Couldn't you have — '

'Hey . . . hey . . . ' Gino Cozzi held up a thick-fingered hand. 'You got it all wrong, Carlo. I had nothin' to do with knockin' off that broad. You're safe, believe me. Seems like there might be a few others don't wanna see that movie made.' A grin split his heavy face. 'You just got lucky, that's all. No star, no more movie. Relax.'

Gino saw the relief begin to dawn on his cousin's grey face and he rose to his feet. 'Gotta be goin'. You take it easy — there ain't no more problem, right?'

He patted the other man's shoulder and made a speedy escape. No point in sticking round to answer any more fuckin' questions.

'I can't believe you're really trusting me to drive this brilliant piece of machinery.'

Chris flashed Tess a sideways grin as they headed south on the San Diego Freeway. They'd left early, deciding that they would see Les Donovan first, then stop for lunch on their way home.

Relaxed in the low leather seat beside him, Tess answered teasingly. 'I could tell at once you had a way with cars — and women.'

Without taking his eyes off the road, Chris reached over to pat her hand. 'Only clever ones with wonderful green eyes.'

It was that sort of day. Nothing was going to go wrong.

Or so they thought.

The registration address for the Dodge turned out to be hopelessly out of date. The manageress of the shabby two-storey boarding house informed them that Les Donovan hadn't lived there for almost eighteen months.

Chris swore inwardly. 'Any idea where he might have gone?'

'Nope.' The woman with the faded ginger hair was singularly disinterested.

'Well, did he have a job? Would you remember where he worked?' As he asked the question, Chris slipped a twenty dollar bill out of his wallet.

The woman licked her lips, her eyes on the money. 'Can't rightly say. Not real sure that he had a proper job.' Her tone was a little more helpful.

Chris added another ten to the twenty.

The woman frowned in concentration. 'Now that I come to think of it ... I remember Les sayin' somethin' about some part-time janitor's position.'

'He was a janitor? Where? Can you recall?'

The woman's face screwed up into a map of wrinkles as her frown deepened. 'Now where the goddamn *was* that? I just can't — Hey, yeah!' her face cleared. 'I remember. A school! It was one of them high schools on the south side. Redburn ... Rayburn ... somethin' like that.'

Her fingers closed greedily around the notes as Chris thanked her for her help.

'This has got to be it — Redland High.' Chris pointed to the name. They'd pulled in at a gas station to consult the area telephone directory.

'But it's Saturday, Chris. How are we going to —'

'Kids play sport Saturdays. Let's find the place and take it from there.'

No wonder he was good at his job, thought Tess, as she sat in the car watching Chris approach the group of teenagers arranged around the baseball diamond next to Redland High School. She began to believe they'd find this Les Donovan after all.

A moment later she changed her mind.

'Kids say he *used* to work at the school,' said Chris as he opened the car door. 'Had to toss it in about four months ago when he put his back out.'

As he slipped into the driver's seat, Chris saw Tess's disappointment. 'Hey, no problem... they know where he lives. Five minutes away.'

The apartment was the smallest in the run-down block.

A thickset, balding man opened the door to their knock. He was wearing an overtight T-shirt, the armpits stained with sweat.

'Yeah? Whadda ya want?' He eyed them suspiciously, obviously unused to visitors.

'Mr Donovan, my name is Christopher Stanley, and this is Tess Jordan. May we speak with you for a moment?'

'What about? Who are you?' The man's manner was no less surly for the introduction.

'May we come in?' asked Tess.

'You sellin' religion?' Les Donovan scowled and made to shut the door. 'If so, I'm not buyin'.'

'No, Mr Donovan, we're not selling anything. In fact we might be able to — to buy something from you.'

'What're you talkin' about?' But Tess could see she had aroused a wary curiosity and a moment later they were being ushered into the tiny living room littered with old newspapers and the residue of fast food containers.

'Mr Donovan, I believe you were once an officer with the LAPD.' Chris found a seat amongst the clutter and came straight to the point.

The man stiffened. 'So what if I was?'

'I'm a reporter from the *LA Clarion*, Mr Donovan. We're here because we have reason to believe you were one of the two police officers who were first on the scene the night Elizabeth Eden died.'

The man's head jerked up, and the colour drained from his face. 'Is that why you're here! Well, you get the hell outta the place this instant!' He lunged across the room and fastened his thick fingers around Chris's upper arm, dragging him to his feet.

'Mr Donovan, please. We just want to ask you a few questions.' Chris was stronger, fitter, he could have resisted — but if the guy didn't want to talk, what could they do?

'Please, Mr Donovan . . . We need your help.' Tess was on her feet also, her plea falling on deaf ears as Les Donovan pulled open the door.

'Get outta here! And don't come back! I don't know nothin', do you hear? I've forgotten everything about that night!'

And with a resounding crash the door was slammed behind them.

He could see how upset she was, how bitterly disappointed.

Donovan had been their only starting point, and while they hadn't thought it would be easy, they'd counted on being able to prompt him to part with his information — with a cash inducement if necessary. But they'd never even had a chance to make the offer.

Chris did his best to cheer her up. 'Look, we know where he lives now, Tess. We can try again. Let's not get too down about it all.'

She was sitting stiffly, staring straight ahead as they headed back to the freeway.

'I'm trying not to, Chris. But to be so close to perhaps finding out something . . . ' She bit her lip, shook her head in frustration.

'Listen, Tess, I'm absolutely certain of one thing. Donovan knows something. Something that he's too frightened to tell — at the moment. Well, I'm not giving up until I find out exactly what that is. You've got to trust me on that.'

*

Because of the delay in locating ex-officer Donovan they ate a late lunch, opting to divert to the stylish Laguna Beach area. 'I know a great place to eat,' Chris told her. 'You'll love it.'

She did. The restaurant was spectacularly sited on the cliffs overlooking the ocean, the beach, and much of the town. Because of the hour, they managed to get a table on the outside patio.

'How did you know about this, Chris? It's wonderful.'

He shrugged. 'Man of the world.'

No need to mention that he'd brought Carrie here the last Christmas they'd spent together.

The prices, he saw as he was handed the menu, hadn't got any better.

Tess was noting them too. At Las Brisas the view didn't come cheap. How, she wondered, was she going to handle the delicate problem of the check. Eat first, she decided, think about that later.

The restaurant specialised in Mexican-style seafood and they both ate with gusto. The bottle of robust white wine was the perfect accompaniment.

Later, over coffee, Tess stared out over the breathtaking panorama and murmured, 'Makes you hate the idea of going back downtown, doesn't it?'

Ignoring the scenery, Chris was staring at her. 'Well, why go back, then?' he asked quietly. 'Why don't we spend the night here? You got anything special to do tomorrow?'

She turned, and her green gaze held his. 'What a wonderful idea . . . '

At that moment the waiter brought the check, placing it diplomatically centre table. With a teasing light in her eyes, Tess pushed it across to Chris. 'You handle the lunch, I'll find us a great hotel.'

'Goddamn independent women . . . ' he murmured, stroking her hand.

*

Taking the advice of the restaurant manager, they settled on the Hotel Laguna. 'It's a landmark,' he explained. 'The oldest hotel in town, but the rooms have just been totally refurbished. It's close to the beach and the gardens are charming.'

'Sounds perfect,' Tess replied.

'If you like, I'd be happy to ring and reserve you a room,' the manager offered cheerfully.

Their reservation confirmed, they drove into the town.

'We'd better buy a hold-all of some sort or they'll think we've just picked each other up in the street,' Tess joked.

At a local supermarket they purchased a few toiletries, dropping them into the soft canvas bag in which they'd left the packing paper for bulk.

Tess raised an amused eyebrow. 'Think that'll fool them?'

'Our passport to respectability, for sure,' Chris grinned.

The sun was just beginning to set and they took a stroll along the beach before checking in to the hotel. By unspoken agreement both realised this was a moment to savour.

With the wind in their hair, the taste of the salty air on their lips, they tried to forget, for the present, the aborted visit to Donovan. By the time they returned to the car and eventually headed for the hotel, they shared a mood of excited anticipation.

Tess took a shower first and was lying naked between the fine cotton sheets by the time Chris joined her.

There was no awkwardness, no hesitation in their embrace. They caressed each other's bodies with passion and delight, fighting to control their eagerness, breathlessly prolonging that longed-for moment of union.

As she felt the cool touch of Chris's hands against her skin, sliding over her hips, brushing her taut nipples, Tess moaned in pleasure at the exquisite torment.

Neither of them could bear to wait too long. Chris's hard body covered hers and Tess arched to meet him so they were flesh against flesh, beating heart against beating heart.

She heard his groan as he moved deeper into her warm ripeness, and she shuddered with pleasure. Then together they began that slow steady rhythm, that primal dance which edged them closer and closer to the edge of consciousness.

Finally, inevitably, their tempo became more urgent until they were losing themselves in that dark world of the senses, that spinning vortex of passion and burning blood, of joy and fiery possession.

For a long time afterwards they lay in each other's arms, neither needing to speak. The complete abandonment of their lovemaking was message enough of the depth of their feelings.

As she lay with her head against Chris's chest, Tess realised this was the first time since Nick that she had felt so close to a man. She had never lost herself so completely with any of the lovers in between.

He was younger. He was so different. But, she thought in silent wonder, *I love him. And I trust him* ...

The night seemed to go on for ever.

They ordered a room service meal and ate it wrapped in the terry-towelling robes provided by the hotel. They could barely keep their hands off each other, and as soon as the meal was cleared away returned to bed.

'I could stay like this forever,' Chris whispered into her hair. 'I'd never need anyone else.'

Tess didn't trust herself to reply.

And then he was ready for her again, his hardness electrifying her, awakening a depth of sexual response that was almost frightening in its intensity ...

CHAPTER

25

It was after eleven when Les Donovan left his familiar neighbourhood bar. That night, as on most Tuesdays, the place was pretty quiet, but as far as Les Donovan was concerned, it beat going home to the stifling loneliness of his apartment.

Since the problem with his back had forced him to give up his janitor's job, his only real source of company was his local bar.

A shit of a life, he was muttering to himself as he made his way across the darkened car park. Sometimes he —

The first blow struck him across the back of the head. He staggered, then fell, hands tearing on the rough bitumen as half a dozen sledgehammers seemed to be hitting him at once. Instinctively, he curled up, trying desperately to shield himself from the rain of blows. But next moment there was a sharp crack, agonising pain, and he knew they had got his ribs.

'My wallet . . . ' he gasped. 'You can have — '

But it wasn't Les Donovan's few dollars his attackers were after.

'See what happens when you talk to the wrong company, pal?'

The words reached Les Donovan through a thick curtain of pain.

212 WHISPER FROM THE GODS

'Now we're gonna shut your fuckin' mouth for good!'

Les Donovan knew then what it was all about. Knew it was all over. The past and its dangerous ghosts had finally caught up with him.

'HEY! What're you motherfuckers up to!'

As abruptly as it had begun, the avalanche of blows ended. From the epicentre of his pain, the injured man was vaguely aware of the sound of pounding footsteps, of scuffles and wild yelling. Seconds later he lost consciousness.

Les Donovan knew what he had to do.

As soon as it was light, he'd staggered out of the local emergency centre where some trainee medic had done a painfully awkward job of strapping up his two cracked ribs.

Les knew they'd be watching his apartment, determined to finish the job properly this time. Only sheer good luck in the form of the local cleaning crew had saved his life, and Les Donovan wasn't betting on being lucky twice in a row.

He made his way to the Greyhound terminal, every step agony. Open twenty-four hours a day, he knew it would be the perfect place to wait. He'd be safe there. With a grunt of pain, he pushed open the grimy glass doors and saw the change of expression on the tired faces of the three waiting passengers. No wonder, he thought, if his own mug looked anything like it felt.

It had just gone six. As he made for the payphone in the corner, Les Donovan hoped there'd be someone at the *LA Clarion* to take his call, someone willing to give him Chris Stanley's home number.

Chris had just stepped out of the shower when he heard the telephone ring. Grabbing a towel, he picked up the receiver. Next minute his heart began to race as his caller identified himself and began to speak.

'Stay there,' he ordered. 'I'm coming to get you.'

As soon as he hung up, Chris put a call through to Tess. He explained the situation as succinctly as possible. 'I've just had a call from Donovan. He wants to talk. I'm going to pick him up straight away and take him to my apartment. Will you be able to meet us there?'

He gave her the address.

Tess handed the ex-cop his second stiff bourbon, suppressing a shudder at the man's swollen, bloodied face. It was obvious that whoever was responsible for the attack had certainly meant business.

'So what's this all about, Les?' Sitting on a straight-backed dining chair, Chris gave the man on the sofa a questioning look. There had been little conversation between them on the drive back downtown. Donovan, it appeared to Chris, had been gathering his thoughts.

Now the ex-cop said, 'That thing on?' He pointed at the taperecorder on the low table between them.

'It is now.' Chris pushed the button.

'But... that's incredible!' Tess's face was a mask of disbelief. 'Are you trying to suggest that Elizabeth Eden might have been... murdered by *Tom Madigan*? By the *President of the United States*?'

'That's exactly what I'm saying, lady. And that's why an attempt was made to kill me last night. Because they know I know. And because someone had started asking me questions.'

Chris was as shaken as Tess. 'Let me get this straight... You and Feldstein answered that emergency call and were first on the scene that night. You found Elizabeth Eden's body in the bath with both wrists slashed. And what you're saying is, while it *looked* as if it could have been suicide, you were suspicious of the extensive bruising on the body?'

'Yeah.' Les Donovan nodded. 'And then, among the bedclothes, I found the unmistakable evidence . . . '

Tess, her voice still breathless with shock, finished for him. 'The cufflink with the President's own seal . . . '

'But Chris, it just doesn't make sense . . . '

It was late evening on the same day. With Les Donovan ensconced in a cheap, out-of-town motel until they could decide what step to take next, Tess had arranged for Chris to meet her at home as soon as they both finished work. There was so much they had to discuss.

They had eaten a simple meal and were now sitting on the terrace still trying to make sense of what Donovan had told them.

Tess was openly incredulous. 'I really can't . . . Chris, Donovan's trying to tell us the President of the United States could have been capable of *murder*!'

Chris frowned, shook his head. 'I know it sounds crazy, Tess, but we can't completely disregard the guy's story. As he tells it, there *was* an attempt on his life. And there's all that other stuff . . . what happened to him following that night.'

Tess knew what he was referring to. According to Donovan, he had paid a high price for attempting to find out the truth.

'Just minutes after we arrived on the scene that night,' he had told them, 'a whole swarm of plain-clothes tough guys turned up. At the time I thought they were the Feds — because of who Elizabeth Eden was an' all. It was obvious they wanted us two dumb cops outta there real quick. But before we were bundled out, I handed over the cufflink I had found to the guy in charge. I explained what it was, said I'd seen pictures in magazines, read about the special cufflinks that were made for each President with the Presidential seal and his own initials. Well, the guy just took the thing from me without a word, and stuck it in his pocket.

'Only later, maybe five or six weeks afterwards, when I never heard nothin' more about it, did I start to wonder what had happened to that amazing piece of evidence. By that time the Coroner was about to bring down his verdict and no one was suggestin' anything other than Elizabeth Eden committed suicide.

'When I asked my boss what had happened to the cufflink, he looked at me like I was nuts. Told me there'd never been no cufflink. But I wasn't gonna let it drop; I made that plain and clear. I *knew* what I'd seen, and Rick Feldstein had seen it too. So I tried to contact Rick — we hadn't been rostered together since that night — and you coulda knocked me over with a feather when I discovered he'd resigned from the force and moved with his wife and kids to Palm Beach...

'Well, I had my vacation comin' up and I decided to go visit him there, ask if he'd back me in tryin' to get at the truth.

'When I eventually tracked him down, I found him livin' in a real fancy house in one of the classiest areas, and I couldn't help wonderin' how he managed a lifestyle like that on just his pension from the force.

'I couldn't say he was real happy to see me, and after I told him why I was there, his mood turned even dirtier. He told me point-blank that he hadn't seen anythin' that night, and that I must have been imaginin' things.

'At first I didn't believe what I was hearin' but then, suddenly, everythin' fell into place... The fancy house, the sudden move from LA... It was obvious Feldstein had been paid off.

'That's when I lost my cool. I told him I was goin' to see justice done even without his goddamn help; told him I'd wasted enough time and now I was goin' right to the top.

'But as it turned out, I never got the chance to take it further. Less than twenty-four hours after my return to LA I was suspended from duty — charged with acceptin' bribes from a couple of big-time coke dealers. It was a set-up. I'd never seen the guys before in my life. But my protests were ignored, and when it finally came to a trial, I got eighteen months and lost my pension entitlement.

'I had plenty of time to stew things over in the can. It seemed obvious to me there'd been a cover-up — and on reconsiderin', I figured it wasn't the FBI there that night, but the Secret Service. Destroying whatever other evidence they might find that proved President Madigan was with Elizabeth Eden the night she died.

'But by openin' my big mouth, I'd ended up losin' my freedom, my job, my pension, and even my marriage. By the time I was released, I'd made up my mind never to talk about what had happened.'

Tess remembered the intensity in Les Donovan's voice as he'd spoken his next words. 'But now I've *gotta* talk about it. The only way I've got a chance of stayin' alive is if they know I've talked; if they know it's all on tape.'

And it was, thought Tess. Locked in a safety deposit box downtown was the tape containing allegations that were political dynamite...

Her mind was still reeling at what they'd been told. She turned to Chris. 'Do you think we can believe him? Is he really telling the truth?'

'The guy's frightened, Tess, I know that much for certain. We've got to give some credence to his story.'

'But you and I both know from what we've read of Elizabeth's letters and diaries that there are at least a half a dozen names — many of them still important in this town — who would give anything to stop that movie getting to the screen. How can we be sure Donovan's putting us on the right track?'

'We can't, Tess. Not yet. But let's not forget one thing. Tom Madigan's son is running for the Presidency. And by all indications, he's going to be a clear winner. Unless... unless attention was about to be refocused on Elizabeth Eden and the night she died...'

'But . . . ' Tess bit her lip. 'The shocking way Jennifer Ross was killed . . . surely they wouldn't . . . ? How does that make sense in all this?'

'I don't know yet, Tess. But I sure as hell am going to do my best to find out.'

They lay wrapped together in the darkness. Caressing, teasing, consumed with desire.

Tess felt the electricity of her lover's touch; shuddered as his hands and lips hungrily explored her body. Yet this was so much more than sexual desire. In Chris's arms she felt flooded with uncontrollable joy; felt the sense of belonging she'd been searching for for so long. And best of all, she knew he felt it too.

Their lovemaking transported them. At once gentle and passionate; wild, yet overflowing with sweet emotion. When both were satisfied, Chris held her in his arms, listening as her breathing evened and she fell asleep.

But his dark eyes were troubled as he stared into the darkness. Suddenly there seemed so much at stake. So much more to lose. He loved Tess to the core of his being. And that's why he was afraid. To continue with the investigation meant putting them both at grave risk. If they really were facing such powerful foes, he couldn't afford to underestimate the danger.

As he held the woman who had awoken his heart, he remembered what had happened to Carrie. Through her involvement in his work, Carrie had lost her life.

He couldn't let the same thing happen to Tess.

The security checks seemed endless and merely served to heighten Walter Conroy's tension.

He had had no choice but to respond to the summons from the Pentagon but was determined to keep his nerve. Attack and stall would be his defence.

All he needed was time, he assured himself as he followed the uniformed aide down the labyrinth of passages that formed the heart of US defence head-quarters.

It wasn't Walter's first visit to the legendary five-sided building in Arlington, Virginia. But his previous visits had been under more auspicious circumstances: to sign lucrative contracts for the supply of military hardware by Conroy Aircraft Corporation.

Now, at today's meeting, if he didn't handle things properly, Walter knew CAC and everything he had ever worked for would be destroyed.

The thought made the sweat prickle in his armpits.

With an effort he got a grip on himself, reminded himself that after the federal poll no one would be able to touch him. In just a few short months, Robert Madigan was certain to be the next President of the United States. There was now no longer even the remotest danger he would lose.

The Elizabeth Eden problem had been taken care of.

Walter swallowed. Oh God, yes . . .

Three hours later, the President of Conroy Aircraft Corporation was jetting out of Washington. He had bought the time he wanted. For a moment, though, it had been touch and go.

Seated in the dark-panelled office, addressing top ranking brass and various stony-faced aides, Walter had been fearful of really pulling it off.

But he had. Using all the cunning and skills honed by a lifetime of wheeling and dealing, he had managed to stave off the moment of disaster.

Of course, he had promised, manufacturing schedules and distribution details would be forthcoming. Like all of them, he wanted nothing more than to 'get to the bottom of this dreadful business' . . . It was 'absolutely vital' that he clear CAC's good name . . . And he had not the slightest doubt that he would.

It was just that it was taking a little more time than

he'd counted on to trace back, he explained smoothly, to follow through on everything involved ...

In the end, Walter had got the Pentagon's grudging agreement to another precious couple of months' grace.

Sara Madigan was surprised by the phone call. Her father usually let her know when he was due in town.

'Couple of unexpected things cropped up I had to take care of, honey.' The lie rolled smoothly off Walter Conroy's tongue. 'And I know it's late notice, but are you guys free to grab a bite to eat with me this evening by any chance?'

Sara checked her schedule. Rob had a dinner meeting with his media people, but they wouldn't need her. She'd ask her father to the house for a home-cooked meal. He always liked that.

'So ... how's it all goin'?'

Walter faced his daughter across the dining table. He'd enjoyed the simple but tasty pot roast she'd cooked for him.

'You mean with Rob?'

Walter nodded. What else was he interested in these days? That was why he had flown to LA instead of returning to Dallas. He needed the comfort of sharing in the final approaches to victory.

'Fine. Everyone's working harder than ever, but there're no complaints now we're so close to home.'

The words were spoken easily, but Walter detected something in his daughter's tone.

'Somethin' wrong, honey?'

'No ... ' Sara was on her feet, gathering up their plates. She stopped when Walter put a hand on her arm.

'Tell me ... what's the matter?'

Sara Madigan held her father's gaze. Then with a heavy sigh, she resumed her seat. 'I could never fool you, could I, Dad?'

'My business to know when somethin's troublin' my little cutie-pie.'

She gave a half-smile at his use of the childhood endearment.

'It's —' She bit her lip, took a deep breath. 'I'd never tell this to another living soul but you, Dad, but . . . Rob isn't happy. Just recently he's been saying that he's not sure whether he's running for the Presidency because *he* wants to, or because so many other people want him to. On a couple of occasions he's even wondered if perhaps he should pull out.'

She heard her father's sharp intake of breath and added hurriedly. 'Oh, I'm sure he doesn't mean it! It's just the stress and strain of these last few weeks.' Sara Madigan gave a heavy sigh. 'I only wish I could help him snap out of it.'

Walter Conroy didn't answer. His face had gone deathly white.

CHAPTER

26

Adelle had never liked Walter Conroy.

First and foremost, he was a Texan. To Adelle, that meant boorish, loud-mouthed, vulgar and un-cultured.

While she had to concede that Walter mightn't be the worst of his breed, that still didn't make her interested in encouraging a relationship that was any closer than strictly necessary.

The campaign, of course, had drawn them more often into each other's orbit. So when Walter rang and asked to meet with her sometime soon — 'Just the two of us' — Adelle had no reason to be surprised.

'Of course, Walter. Why not come here for lunch? Then we can be sure no one will disturb us.' She wasn't dragging herself downtown for anyone.

They checked their respective schedules and settled on a day the following week.

Luckily Walter's appetite had all but disappeared these days or he'd have been ravenous after sharing what Adelle termed 'lunch'. How, he wondered, did anyone exist on that sort of vegetarian shit?

They were taking their coffee in Adelle's study, sitting beside each other on the pair of tapestry covered wingbacks.

Walter knew that the large antique desk by the window had once graced the Oval Office, while the dozens of photographs displayed on the half-panelled walls were further evidence of Adelle's reign as First Lady.

Adelle, he felt certain, would do everything in her power to ensure her son fulfilled his destiny. But was she aware of Robert Madigan's present state of mind?

'So,' he said, putting down his empty coffee cup, 'what's Rob's personal feeling about the campaign? Now that we're on the home stretch, I mean.'

Adelle knew instinctively that Walter wasn't making idle conversation. All through lunch she'd waited for him to get to the point of his visit. She clicked open a gold cigarette case and took out a filter tip. 'He's worked very hard, Walter. I don't think there's any doubt that he's going to win.'

Walter nodded and reached for the heavy onyx lighter to light her cigarette. 'These next few weeks are going to be even tougher, of course.'

Leaning back in her chair, Adelle blew out an impatient stream of smoke. 'Walter, why don't you just come straight out with it? What's on your mind?'

He told her.

Adelle didn't believe it, of course. She was certain nothing would make Rob throw away this opportunity. This was the goal they had set their sights on from the start. And now the dream was so close to fulfilment — the dream held by so many for so long.

Sara was overreacting, Adelle told herself. She was on edge and reading things into what Rob was saying. Nothing, Adelle was certain, would sway her son from the path to victory.

Chris watched closely as Gordon McLean, the *Clarion's* editor-in-chief read through the article.

At last McLean lifted a wry eyebrow. 'This is gonna stir the shit,' he announced laconically.

Chris nodded.

The editor rolled the ball of gum around his mouth and skimmed the article again. It dealt with the New Puritanism in America, the growing expectation among Americans that the personal lives of their leaders in government and business had to be blameless and squeaky clean.

Chris had listed recent careers that had been cut short by revelations of adulterous behaviour — and then offered the provocative suggestion that perhaps some of the big names of the past would have had trouble meeting the high expectations of a modern public, not to mention passing the scrutiny of a more aggressive media.

Among the names he referred to was that of the late President Tom Madigan...

Madigan, he wrote, with his dashing good looks, his charisma and aggressive self-confidence, had been a magnet for women. Certainly he was known to have sown his oats before marriage, but, the article pointed out, the women hadn't gone away just because Tom Madigan had a wedding ring on his finger. And as President he would certainly have been even more irresistible a challenge.

Did Madigan, or any of the other former Presidents, Chris hypothesized, ever take advantage of their positions? Did they lead secret lives? Lives that the press either didn't know about or were reluctant to reveal?

Gordon McLean chuckled as he straightened the copy. 'A few feathers are sure gonna fly. But it seems to me you've kept just on the right side of the wind, Chris. Don't think there's anything concrete enough for anyone to start screamin' for their lawyers. Just to be sure, though, I'll check it out with our boys, OK?'

'Sure, Mac.' Chris did his best to hide his excitement and relief.

*

The clearance from McLean came through less than twelve hours later. Chris had phoned Tess at once with the news.

'Is it too late to come over?' It was almost nine-thirty.

'Of course not.' As she replaced the receiver Tess had suddenly felt happier than she'd been all day.

Now they were propped up in bed, sipping champagne.

'So it's going in this coming Saturday?'

Chris nodded. 'Yeah. Without a word cut either.'

She heard the pride in his voice. He had never made any secret of his ambition. She knew Chris was determined to join that elite group of journalists who had established themselves as national names.

But while sharing his excitement, Tess also felt a stab of apprehension. The article would be like waving a red flag. And Chris's name would be on the by-line.

'It's a starting point in flushing out who're behind all this,' Chris had stated when he'd showed her what he'd written. 'It'll help us see if there's any truth in Donovan's story.'

Tess put down her empty glass. She curled up beside Chris, and laid an arm across his chest. 'What do you think will happen?'

'We have no way of knowing, Tess. But if the Madigan camp *is* involved they'll do something, you can bet on that. If they fixed the movie, they'll want to put a lid on this as soon as possible too.'

Later, as they began to make love, his own words preyed on his mind, adding to the intensity of his feelings. The publication of the article was bound to make him a target. For himself, he was prepared to take the risk. But as always he couldn't help remembering what had happened to Carrie because of her involvement in his work.

If Tess were to be in any danger . . .

He buried his face in her hair, breathed in its sweet scent. *Oh God, he couldn't bear to lose her. He loved her so much. So very, very much.*

*

Larry Brandt read it first.

Back at his apartment after his usual early morning run, he sipped at a glass of fresh carrot juice and began to sift through the major morning newspapers. As always, he was alert for any reference to the campaign.

The article was in a prominent position on the feature pages of the *Clarion*. He read it quickly, his heart pounding. Next moment he was dialling Dave Arnell.

Adelle felt as if she were choking. Fury bubbled in her throat, shortened her breath as she read and reread the half-page feature.

Beside her on the patio, Dave Arnell watched in silence. He had come at once; he hadn't wanted her to face this alone. He knew how it would affect her.

Finally, with one furious movement, Adelle swept the newspaper off the table. Dave winced at the words that spat from her lips.

Rob Madigan kicked off the side of the pool as he somersaulted into his thirtieth lap.

Even exercise couldn't calm him today, couldn't do anything to ease the way he felt inside.

He had read the article in that morning's edition of the *Clarion*, and an anger like nothing he'd ever felt before had raged inside him.

As he ploughed through the water, he asked himself what it had all been for. Hadn't his father done his best for his country? Even died for his country? And now, over twenty years later, they could do nothing better than to try to muddy his name.

The *Clarion* article was the first to ever suggest that Tom Madigan might not have been faithful to his wife. That there had been 'other women' during his term of office. Not that any names had been mentioned, of course; they wouldn't dare go that far. But the slur on Tom Madigan's reputation and morality had been established.

Robert Madigan hadn't forgotten what his mother had told him about the one time his father had slipped. But that, she'd made clear, was because the woman had 'chased' his father 'relentlessly'; Elizabeth Eden's reputation had been 'notorious'...

Robert Madigan churned angrily through the water. Why did they always expect you to be a saint...?

Stopping short of his usual hundred laps, he heaved himself out of the pool. His mother had phoned earlier. Expect her by ten, she'd said.

Adelle was pacing furiously, the usual cigarette held between her perfectly manicured fingers.

'They're not going to get away with this, Rob! I can promise you that. Everyone knows Paul Berger is a Republican supporter.' She was referring to the owner of the *Clarion*. 'That goddamn article will be treated with the contempt it deserves.'

Her son swung round to face her, his hair still damp from his swim. They were alone in the room. 'Don't bet on it, Mom! That article is the main topic of conversation on this morning's talk-back radio. Seems like once a man's dead they'll say any goddamn thing about him.'

Adelle couldn't bear to hear the bitterness in her son's voice. 'Rob, I won't let this harm you. I promise you that, darling. I promise you.' She left her cigarette smouldering in the nearest ashtray, and stood before him, gripping both his hands in her own, her face a mask of determination.

He shrugged off her hold and turned away. 'Do you really think it's worth it, Mom? Is it worth all the sacrifices? The hurt? The neverending scrutiny?'

'Rob!' Adelle was aghast. Sara had been right. He really was having doubts... She rounded on him again, trying to make him look her in the face. 'Rob, what are you saying? Are you trying to tell me you'd let some scurrilous two-bit article sidetrack you? Darling, you're the Democratic candidate for the *Presidency* . . . Isn't that what you've always wanted? What you've worked all your life for? The chance to follow in your father's footsteps . . . To continue his work . . . '

Robert Madigan's eyes went dark and his tone was harsh with recrimination. 'Maybe I never had a chance to know what *I* wanted, Mom! All my life I've felt the weight of this burden: of living up to a dead man, of doing what was expected of me. Well, I'm damned sick of it. They're not *my* dreams I'm fulfilling, they're *yours*! All that matters to you is getting back into the White House. Recapturing your days of glory! That's what it's all about, Mom, isn't it? *Isn't it?*'

He came to an abrupt stop, stunned by his own outburst. He realised he had just given vent to feelings he'd never dared admit even to himself before.

Shocked into silence, mother and son stared aghast into each other's eyes.

CHAPTER

27

Les Donovan refolded the piece of newsprint and stuck it back into his well-worn wallet. He almost knew the words from memory by now, but they still gave him the same warm glow of vindication. It might be years after the event, but at last, he thought, there seemed a chance of justice being done.

The article by Chris Stanley hadn't mentioned Elizabeth Eden by name, but Les Donovan guessed they had to be careful. He knew to his cost that the enemy was both dangerous and powerful.

He could tell Chris Stanley was beginning to be convinced of that. The young reporter called the motel a couple of times a week just to check Les was okay. The last time they'd spoken, Stanley had warned him of the article which was about to appear in the *Clarion*.

'So how much longer you want me to stay out here?' Les was beginning to get bored with sitting around the motel all day.

'Until it's safe. Until we find out who's responsible for everything that's happened. Up till then, keep your head low and don't take any chances. Your testimony is going to be vital when we finally get to the bottom of all this.'

'Yeah. Sure.'

But Les Donovan was sick of being cooped up. Each day he swam a dozen breathless laps of the motel pool, watched endless TV, ordered room service when he wanted food or more beer... But what he was really missing was a game of pool and some male company.

Damn it all, he thought, he couldn't sit around like a rat in a cage for God knew how long. A man needed a break. And some company.

He walked the six blocks to the nearest suburban mall where he found what he was looking for.

The pool room was attached to the rear of a small smoky bar and a group of noisy locals were taking odds on the players. Les's eyes lit up as he ordered a beer and strolled over to join in the fun.

It was almost midnight when he left. He'd stayed later, and drunk more than he'd planned, but what the hell, it beat sitting watching the box in his stifling motel room.

He could see the motel's neon sign in the distance when it happened.

He had just stepped off the curb to cross the dark, quiet street when suddenly, out of nowhere, the car came screeching round the corner.

Les Donovan moved as quickly as his alcohol-affected body allowed, but he didn't have a chance. The speeding vehicle mounted the curb and before ex-officer Donovan could even open his mouth to scream, he took the full force of the impact and was flung high over the windscreen.

It was all over in seconds.

'You're looking great, Tess. Things going better for you now?'

Nick smiled at her across the table. They had met for a quick lunch at the long established Scandia restaurant on Sunset Boulevard. She really was looking so much happier, he thought. Maybe now that the Elizabeth Eden project had been scrapped, the strain had been eased. She was no longer obsessed.

Tess took a sip of ice water. 'I'm feeling great, Nick. A lot's happened since I saw you last. I guess I should bring you up to date.'

Her tone, and the shine in her eyes put him on the right track. 'It's a guy, right?'

'Hey, come on,' she teased, 'does it always take a guy to make a woman happy? Maybe I just lost a couple of kilos without even trying, or got a credit extension on my Visa Card.' She laughed and leaned confidingly across the table. 'Yeah, it's a guy. A terrific guy. A wonderful guy. The sort I thought I'd never have a hope in hell of meeting.'

Nick could see it was the real thing. He reached over and patted her hand. 'I'm so glad for you, Tess. You deserve to be happy. Work alone's never enough. No matter how high you achieve.'

'I know, Nick. I think I always knew that. I guess I was just looking in all the wrong places.'

Time was running out and they called for the bill. When it arrived, Tess checked the amount and shook her head. 'Do you remember when we could have lived for a month on what this is costing us?'

He nodded. In those days of living on the edge, neither of them would ever have dreamed that they'd come as far as they had. Or that the friendship which had begun so unpromisingly would stand the test of time. Nothing, he thought fervently, would ever be able to break that bond.

The urgent telephone message was waiting when she returned to the office. She returned Chris's call at once.

Her face paled as she listened to what he had to say.

' ... just a small item in this afternoon's columns. Don't even know how I noticed it. *Les Donovan, itinerant* ... Hit and run is how the cops are treating it.' She heard the anger in his voice. 'And sure, Tess, it *could* have been that. But something tells me loud and clear it wasn't.'

'Are you — are you going to contact the police?'

'What's the point?' His bitterness was clear. 'And the irony is that Donovan's death must surely be the ultimate proof that he was speaking the truth.'

'Then we've just lost our prime witness... ' Tess's voice was a whisper of despair.

'How did they get on to him? That's what I want to know. How did those sonsofbitches find out where Donovan was?'

In silent communion, the answer hit both of them simultaneously.

Their lines were tapped.

It took first-class resources to organise something like that ...

Chris understood at once the other implication of Les Donovan's death.

If, as seemed obvious, their conversations had been overheard, then their enemies knew how deeply Tess was involved. And the evidence was inescapable — these people were ruthless. They had killed before, and they would kill again.

As he had feared, Tess's life too was now at risk.

Yet there was one way to keep her safe ...

His stomach gave an agonising lurch. Not yet, he thought. That would be his final option.

Only two days later, Chris realised with sickening certainty that the time to enforce that option had arrived.

It was almost eight when he turned the key in the front door of his apartment. The sight which met his eyes stopped him dead in his tracks.

The place was a shambles. Furniture was overturned; cupboards were hanging off their hinges, pictures, ornaments, books and records were scattered from one end of the living room to the other. Stepping carefully around the mess Chris made his way through the rest of the small apartment. It was the same story in every room. In the spare bedroom he used as an office, his files and papers were a hopeless jumble that would take him days to sort out.

The shredded mattress in the main bedroom proved conclusively however that this was no ordinary break and enter. Whoever had gained access to his apartment was a professional — the lock on the main door was still intact, no windows were broken — and he was searching for something specific.

Chris knew immediately what that was. The tape of Les Donovan's evidence which they had referred to once or twice in their telephone conversations.

The tape that was now safely locked away in a safety deposit vault of a major downtown bank.

Chris knew he had no choice.

Perched on the edge of the ruined mattress, he leaned forward, his head held between his hands. His lips moved in a silent plea.

Oh, God, Tess, I'm sorry, he agonised. *So terribly sorry.*

Dave Arnell felt his whole body stiffen with shock.

Holy Jesus . . .

He read the words again. And again.

It couldn't be . . . It just couldn't be true . . .

But as he made his way through the half-dozen typed pages it all began to make sense. So much fell into place.

Not that this would do much to solve their problem, he thought grimly. He reached for the phone.

'Larry? Get your ass here fast. I got the report.'

Larry Brandt was equally dumbfounded.

'It's crazy! Absolutely unbelievable.' The campaign

manager's hands were unsteady as he turned the pages of the top secret report.

Dave nodded. 'Exactly my reaction. But the whole goddamn story's right there.'

A stunned Larry Brandt shook his head as he finished reading. 'Dynamite... Fuckin' dynamite...' He felt his pulses race as he pushed the confidential report back across the low table.

The two men stared at each other, still struggling to come to terms with the amazing revelations.

At last the campaign manager asked, 'Do you think she knows?'

'Who the fuck can tell?' Dave Arnell seldom swore. But the numbness had begun to wear off and now he was thinking of Adelle. What this would mean to her.

Larry Brandt was speaking. 'We got more than we bargained for, Dave. One helluva lot more. Now we gotta think real hard if there's any way we can use this to our advantage.'

Dave Arnell didn't need anybody to tell him that.

As he drove home from Adelle's Pacific Palisades estate, Dave opened the window and let the cool ocean breeze blow through his hair. They'd had the sort of quiet dinner together he usually enjoyed, but afterwards, when Adelle made it clear she was interested in making love, he'd known it wasn't going to be easy.

Through sheer force of will he'd managed a hard-on, despite the fact that all evening his mind had been preoccupied with the report locked in his office safe.

For weeks now he'd had a team on the top secret job, keeping an eye on her day-to-day movements — the places she went, people she met — and at the same time, tracing back through her past.

It was the latter path that had led to the mind-blowing truth.

Ruth Jordan — the closest friend of the woman who was to become Elizabeth Eden.

Hospital records showed that Ruth Jordan had miscarried at three months.

But a few months later and hundreds of miles away, Ruth Jordan had 'given birth' to a daughter . . .

For Dave Arnell, the discovery that Tess Jordan was in actual fact the only child of Elizabeth Eden had been startling enough.

But nothing like his shock at learning the identity of her father.

CHAPTER

28

'The good news, Mike, is that Jessica is interested and de Niro's agent thinks he'll want to read the script too.'

Tess was keeping her boss up to date at their regular one-on-one informal meeting.

'That's terrific, Tess.' Mike Havelock was as pleased as he sounded. Things were finally starting to happen for WLS. 'Let's mark this one a priority then.'

For the next half-hour they discussed current and anticipated projects and then, the formal business over, Mike stood up and poured them both a drink.

He lifted his glass in a toast. 'To WLS — and all your hard work, Tess. I'm delighted with the way things are going.'

She smiled her thanks and he studied her over the rim of his glass. There was something different about her these days. He couldn't quite put his finger on it. She seemed . . . happier. Perhaps, he thought, she'd come to terms with the dropping of the Elizabeth Eden project. For a while there it had seemed close to becoming an obsession. She'd made no secret of her frustration and anger with his decision to cancel.

But while it had cost big dollars to pull out, he'd thought that was preferable to risking any more bad publicity. Not to mention the danger. To date, the cops had come up with a big fat zero. Whoever had been responsible for the fire and for Jennifer Ross's horrible murder was still at large, a situation that seemed incomprehensible to Mike.

But he wasn't about to raise that sore subject with Tess.

It was later, as she drove home, that Tess's thoughts turned to that exact topic. She was wondering what Mike's reaction would be if she told him what they had discovered about the night Elizabeth Eden had died. Would he believe her if she told him that everything indicated there had been a top-level cover-up? That the President of the United States had been with Elizabeth that night? That they were having an affair? That in all probability he had been her killer?

What had happened on that last night? she pondered. Why had it ended in Elizabeth's death? There were more unanswered questions now than she had ever imagined.

Tess's mouth set in a determined line. That was why she and Chris couldn't let up until they could prove conclusively that Elizabeth's death had involved a cover-up by some of the country's most powerful names and institutions.

She was expecting Chris for dinner that evening, was looking forward to his company. But by nine o'clock when he hadn't arrived, she called his apartment. No reply.

At nine-thirty she rang again with the same result. By eleven when she had received no word she began to worry. It wasn't like Chris not to let her know if he couldn't make it. Had something urgent come up? Something to do with their investigation? Her belly clenched in fear. Could something have happened to him?

She spent a restless night and first thing the next morning, tried Chris's number again.

He answered on the third ring.

'Chris! You're there!'

'Sure I'm here.' His voice sounded strange. Perhaps she'd woken him.

'Chris, what happened last night? I was so worried when you didn't show. I rang all evening, trying to reach you.'

'Last night?' He sounded puzzled.

'We were going to have dinner together. Don't you remember?'

'Guess I forgot, Tess.' No apology. No understanding of how worried she had been.

She let her irritation show. 'Well, don't you think you owe me an apology, Chris? Do you have any idea how worried I was?'

'Tess, listen — I'm a big boy. I don't need anyone to worry about me.' His voice was cold, remote. The voice of a stranger...

Tess felt her breathing start to quicken. 'Chris, what's the matter? You're talking to me as if — Look, I don't understand, don't I have a right to be worried? A right to know what's going on?'

There was a moment's silence from the other end of the line. When he finally spoke, Tess felt her insides turn to water.

'You're right, Tess. There *is* something the matter. I guess it's best that I'm straight with you. I — I feel we're rushing things. Somehow you've read too much into what's happened between us. I'm sorry, but... I'm just not ready for another heavy relationship.'

She felt as if her breath had been choked off. Her heart seemed to be beating at twice its normal rate. 'Chris...' her voice was a dry whisper, 'are you telling me — '

'I'm saying we should cool it, Tess.'

The moment she opened the door, Sara could see her mother-in-law was in a fighting mood.

Sara was prepared. She had been, ever since Adelle had rung two days earlier asking if they could meet. It wasn't hard for Sara to guess at the reason behind this visit.

In the privacy of the sunroom, Adelle wasted no time in coming to the point. 'Sara, I'm sure you're as worried as I am about Robert. He's obviously under a lot of stress and that's why I'm here — to ask you to do everything possible to keep him on track for these last few months. Between us we've got to make sure that nothing distracts him from the goal he's been working towards for so long.' She fixed her daughter-in-law with a determined look. 'I can count on your support, can't I, Sara?'

For Sara Madigan, it was the moment of truth. Of proclaiming where her loyalties lay.

And she had reached her decision after a long, soul-searching conversation with the husband she loved.

When Rob had told her about his outburst to his mother, his anguish had been painful to witness.

'I found myself saying what I suddenly realised was exactly how I felt,' he had explained. 'Only I'd never dared admit it, even to myself before. I'd never had the chance to think what *I* might want to do with my life — it was all planned for me, from the moment my father died. My mother and all the rest of them — they felt cheated: as if what should have been their true destiny had been tragically sidetracked. And so I became the focus for retrieving all they had lost. But no one ever asked *me* if it was what I wanted, Sara. No one!'

He had paced up and down, sweating, agitated, and as she sat in silence, listening to all he had to say, Sara realised that she too was guilty. With her passion for politics and the party, she'd closed her eyes to what was happening to the man who was the focus of all their hopes.

He'd turned to her then, pleading for her understanding. 'Do you see what I mean, Sara? Do you see what they've done to me?'

The pain in his face was more than she could bear. She remembered what had happened to his father. Cut down in his prime. For the Dream. The Cause. The Party. For the ideals to which she too had aspired for so long. The ideals that Rob was going to fight for. Maybe die for.

At that moment Sara knew she couldn't risk that. She loved Rob more than she loved the dream. If anything happened to him she couldn't go on living.

She stood up and gripped his hands in her own. 'Whatever you decide to do now, Rob,' she said quietly, 'I'll back you all the way.'

He put his arms around her and they clung tightly, silently, together.

Now Sara Madigan faced her mother-in-law. 'I'm telling you what I told Rob, Adelle. I'm supporting him whatever his decision; whether he continues the campaign or not.'

For a moment she thought the elegantly dressed woman with the blazing eyes was going to raise a hand and slap her.

'I'm going to stop this once and for all, Dave! It all started with that goddamn newspaper article. That's when Robert started to have doubts.'

Adelle was trembling with rage. 'No one can prove anything about Tom! No matter what they write, they can't prove it! And you know what I'm going to do now, Dave? I'm going to sue that muck-raking broadsheet *and* that smartass reporter! I'm going to cut off all this stinking gossip before it goes any further!'

Dave Arnell had listened to the tirade in silence. Now he knew he had no choice. The time had come to reveal the secret he had kept for over twenty years. 'Adelle, there's no way you can sue.' He held up a hand to cut off her protests. 'If you do that, then something far worse than Tom's affair with Elizabeth Eden will come to light.'

She was staring at him, her nostrils flared, her face still tight with anger.

'What exactly do you mean, Dave? What the hell are you trying to tell me?'

'It's not easy for me, Adelle. For over twenty years I've kept this from you and I only wish to God I didn't have to tell you now. But... the way things are happening, maybe it's almost too dangerous to go on keeping you in the dark.'

Dave Arnell swallowed hard. Adelle was sitting bolt upright, her eyes riveted on his face.

'The — the night Elizabeth Eden was found dead, the Secret Service picked up the police emergency call on its monitors. The Service went into action immediately. Their first step was to issue instructions to the LAPD top brass that the Service was taking complete control.'

Adelle frowned. 'But why? What did Elizabeth Eden's death have to do with the Secret Service?'

Dave Arnell took a deep breath. 'Honey, I never wanted you to know — but Tom's affair with that actress wasn't a brief fling. He was seeing her often, every chance he could, and apart from the Service, who couldn't help but know, of course, there was a small core of us who were especially close to him who also knew what was going on.

'The night Eden died, the President was not only in California — he had been at her home less than an hour before the police received the anonymous call.'

Adelle's blood was thundering in her ears. Her head spun.

A long-time affair... Tom had been with Elizabeth Eden the night she died... Did that mean...?

'Was the suicide anything to do with the — the affair?' Adelle forced herself to ask the question.

Dave shrugged, looked away. 'Could have been. No one ever dared ask Tom about it. Maybe he'd decided to call the whole thing off. Perhaps with the next election on the horizon, he figured it was too dangerous to continue. Who knows? But that night all we were concerned about was covering up the fact that the President had been in Elizabeth Eden's house. If the press had got wind of that, nothing could have kept it out of the headlines.'

He turned back to the woman he loved. 'Do you see now why we can't start making noise about this article? Why we've just gotta sit tight, say nothing, and do our best to keep Rob on track?'

Still dazed, Adelle nodded silently and Dave could see she had accepted his explanation.

A surge of relief washed over him. He'd been dreading having to face any further awkward questions.

Because he thought, *he couldn't — didn't dare — tell her the truth.*

CHAPTER

29

Work was her only relief from the torment of her emotions. With a fierce act of will Tess immersed herself in every detail of the current projects, desperately filling her every waking hour.

But in the lonely hours of the night, those few months of happiness came back to haunt her. Only it was a happiness, she realised now, that had been based on lies and deceit. All that had interested Chris Stanley was achieving his own blatant ambitions. He had used her, used her to gain access to the story that was to make his name. Used her as a means to an end.

In those long hours of sleeplessness, Tess was tormented by the pain and humiliation. She had thought Chris was the one, the only man she'd met in so long who was strong enough to accept her as she was; to love her for herself. She had let him get close, and now she was paying the price.

Anger and shame tore at her as that final telephone conversation played itself over and over in her mind.

'*You're reading too much into what happened . . . You're rushing things . . . I'm just not ready for another heavy relationship . . .* '

Bitter tears stung her eyes. What a fool she'd been! What a crazy, naive fool, to let herself believe, to trust . . .

She thought she was going to go crazy with the pain.

★

On the surface there were few telltale signs.

She lost weight she could ill afford; on a few occasions she snapped, untypically, at people in the office.

Mike sensed a change, noted the strain on her face. He made his own guess as to the reason, but felt it was none of his business to ask questions.

At home, Lola was less reticent. She had taken pleasure in her employer's growing closeness with the good-looking, cheerful reporter. They had seemed so happy together. But now it was three weeks since he had last been to the house and the kind-hearted housekeeper was certain something was wrong.

Finally, her concern obvious, she broached the subject one evening after dinner. 'Mr Stanley, he is not in LA any more?'

It was her alarm at the changes in her employer's mood and weight that gave her the courage to ask the question. Maybe if Ms Tess would talk about it, it would help . . .

'I have no idea where Mr Stanley is,' snapped Tess as she pushed herself up from the table and left the room.

Lola looked after her sadly. She could see there was nothing she could do to help.

Chris rubbed a tired hand across his eyes. He should go to bed, he knew, but that meant facing the demons of the night.

He missed her. God, how he missed her. Not a day went by when he wasn't tempted to pick up the telephone, tell her the truth, beg her to forgive him.

But the horror of what had happened to Carrie always stopped him. The loss, the waste, the guilt . . . Never, he vowed, would he put Tess in that same danger. Better that she hated him than her life be put at risk. The mystery of Elizabeth Eden's death was something he must solve alone.

With a sigh, he pushed his chair back from his desk

and moved through to the bedroom. As he undressed and slipped between the covers, the torment of memory grew sharper.

For almost a month now, Nick had worked back at the office, sometimes three or four nights in a row. It was the only way he could be sure of having the whole place to himself.

'You got some deadline, honey?' Helen had asked that morning when he'd told her he'd be late again.

'Yeah. Just something I've got to get together for Walter.' He avoided his wife's eyes. He hated to lie.

Now, as he sat in front of the computer screen in the deserted office, he studied the next batch of figures with a growing sense of panic. He had gone through enough now to know he wasn't imagining things. Time and time again his suspicions had been confirmed.

It had started months ago, with that first file: the suggestion that perhaps rejected stock might be sold as new if codes and serial numbers were altered. The crash at Big Bear had been the next disquieting factor — and the deafening silence from the two FAA investigators after Walter Conroy had met each of them alone.

Only in recent weeks had Nick had time to resume his investigation; to check if indeed there had been any illegal follow-through on that initial suggestion. It had meant a painstaking search through a huge bank of files, testing codes at random and checking them against orders and supplies all over the globe. Only someone with Nick's expert knowledge would have had the background to even guess where to start.

And finally, slowly, a pattern had begun to emerge. A pattern which suggested that Conroy Aircraft Corporation was involved in a massive scam that included selling both reject and second-hand stock as brand new. From the evidence at hand, it appeared to Nick that parts were being stamped with a new expiry date and their serial numbers fed into inventories of airlines and aircraft operators. He had no doubt there would be forged documents testifying that the stock concerned had been tested to the most stringent standards.

As the evidence mounted, he grew more and more alarmed. If airlines used those parts without testing, the results could be tragic. One faulty bolt, or a single defective electrical connector on a jumbo jet could mean the loss of hundreds of lives.

As he stored his confidential file, Nick wondered where to go next. Did Walter know about this? Was that where he should start now that he had amassed enough convincing evidence?

Yet some instinct told him that a scam as huge as this could not take place without a directive from the top.

As he took the elevator down to the basement car park, he was forced to face the fact that his whole future was on the line. If he threw mud and couldn't make it stick, he'd never work in the aircraft industry again. His professional life would be over.

'How'd she handle it?' Larry Brandt raised a quizzical eyebrow.

Dave Arnell took a sip of his Jack Daniels. It had been a long hard day and he had called in for a nightcap at his campaign manager's home.

He gave a shrug. 'As only Adelle could. It was a shock, I'm sure, but she wasn't about to reveal how she really felt to me.'

Larry Brandt had never been certain about the true nature of the relationship between Dave and the President's widow. He suspected it was more than it appeared on the surface, but even if it was, he figured it was no concern of his.

Now he asked, 'But she never made the obvious connection?'

Dave gave him a sharp look. 'Why should she? As far

as Adelle's concerned, Elizabeth Eden committed suicide.'

For a long moment the two men held each other's gaze.

Later, as he made his way home, Dave found his thoughts returning to that night all those years ago. The details were as crisp and clear as if it had all happened yesterday.

He had been among the entourage on the President's trip west and had just retired to bed in his hotel room when the call came through from Phil Cramer, the head of the Secret Service contingent. Phil knew that Dave, along with Larry Brandt, and maybe one or two of the others, was in on the secret too. He spoke quickly, using the code name for Tom Madigan.

As Dave caught on to what the agent was telling him, he felt the blood drain from his face. 'I'll be there straight away.' He had no need to ask directions; he knew exactly where to go.

He called Larry's room immediately, and without explanation told him to get dressed, they were going out.

The more heads there were to figure this one out the better, he decided fearfully.

As Dave drove, he repeated to the equally shocked campaign manager the essence of Phil Cramer's call.

At the gates of Elizabeth Eden's home, their ID was checked by two grim-faced agents before they were allowed to continue up the drive.

They found a worried-looking Phil Cramer supervising operations in the brightly-lit living room.

'Thank Christ we got here quickly,' the agent declared. 'His goddamn prints are everywhere. And one of those two cops who answered the call found this.' He reached into his pocket and opened his hand to reveal the cuff link with the unmistakable Presidential seal.

'Holy shit . . . ' Larry Brandt stared transfixed.

Dave took a deep breath. 'And the . . . the body. Where . . . ?'

'In the bath. Naked. Both wrists slashed. At first glance it could have passed for suicide. But when we took a closer look there was severe bruising around the neck and one helluva lump on the back of the head. It's a pretty safe bet she's been strangled.'

The three men looked at each other.

Each was sure the others were also wondering whether the President of the United States had just murdered his mistress.

It had been hushed up, of course — with the co-operation of a few at the very top. As Dave and the others had expected, the coroner's report of suicide had been accepted without question by the media, who were all too familiar with Elizabeth Eden's reputation for unstable behaviour and illicit drug use.

The two cops who were first on the scene had been dealt with by various means. One had been happy to accept a 'bonus' to resign from the force. The other, however, had proved more difficult. Les Donovan wanted answers and it was obvious that monetary inducements weren't going to be the solution to shutting his mouth. But in the end he too had been dealt with.

As for the President himself Dave remembered, the name of Elizabeth Eden had never been mentioned again. Whatever had occurred that night between Tom Madigan and his lover, whatever crisis had led to the actress's death, no one would ever know.

As it was, Elizabeth Eden's death had turned a key, closed off a secret compartment. And the Madigan era had continued on its glorious course.

Until, just a few short weeks into Tom Madigan's second term, an assassin's bullet had brought that shining reign to an abrupt and tragic end.

No, Dave promised himself, Adelle must never learn the whole truth about that night.

Nor, he vowed, would she ever be allowed to discover *that it was Tom Madigan who had fathered Elizabeth Eden's secret child.*

CHAPTER

30

Tess woke sweating from a brittle sleep. She rolled over and checked the time on the bedside alarm. Five past four in the morning.

She steadied her breathing and closed her eyes, willing herself to go back to sleep. But already her mind was racing, full of the thoughts she worked so hard to suppress during the day.

Chris ... Elizabeth ...

The humiliation of her affair had been bad enough, but when Chris Stanley had walked out of her life, it had also left her in limbo as far as the investigation went. What now? she wondered. Where did she go from here? Would she be able to carry on alone? She was sure they'd been so close to discovering the truth.

Giving up the battle for sleep, she rose and went down to the kitchen. She poured herself a glass of orange juice, drank it standing up, then went through to the den.

It could have been the hour, or her melancholy, but something made her take the small battered suitcase from its hiding place. Snapping back the locks, she found what she was looking for.

The photo album Ruth had given to her all those years ago.

Tess sat at her desk, turning the pages until she found

the faded black and white shots of the two teenage girls. Arms around each other, happy young faces looking eagerly towards the future. Neither aware of the pain and tragedy that was to come.

Oh, God, why does life have to hurt so much?

With a sob, Tess let the tears flow at last.

Nick knew Helen was annoyed. He couldn't blame her. For weeks he'd been working back at the office, and now he was telling her that Tess wanted to see him that evening.

'I'm sorry, honey, I'll try not to be late. But Tess sounded upset about something. I couldn't let her down.'

He saw the look on his wife's face as she walked away. She was jealous, he realised. A natural enough response. He didn't expect Helen to understand. How could anyone understand who hadn't been there, hadn't shared those desperate days? Those days when survival had counted on fierce friendship and absolute trust.

Now, as he drew up in Tess's driveway, Nick wondered what was troubling her. It wasn't like Tess to lose her cool. Even on the telephone he had sensed her agitation.

She had asked to meet with him as soon as possible. 'I know it's short notice, Nick. But . . . could I see you this evening? At my place? There's something I've just got to talk about with you.'

They kissed hello, and with a frown he noticed at once the change in her. She'd lost weight, her eyes looked hollow and dull. This was a very different woman from the one he'd spoken to on that last occasion.

She led him into the sitting room, fixed them both a drink and took a seat across from him.

'Nick, I've asked you here tonight because I've decided if I don't talk about this I'm going to go crazy. Maybe,' she gave him a desperate look, 'I already am crazy.'

'Tell me what it is, Tess. You know I'll do anything I can to help.'

She saw the concern on his face, heard the note of gentle sympathy in his voice, and knew she was doing the right thing. Nick was the only one who would understand. The only one who might be able to help her.

Quietly, she began. 'When I told you about my past, Nick, about how my — my mother found me again, it wasn't the whole story. You see, a few years after I was reunited with Ruth, I found out that she wasn't my mother at all.'

She saw his eyes open wide in astonishment.

Tess nodded, holding his gaze. 'Yes, Ruth told me the truth on my twenty-first birthday. She told me then who my natural mother was. Nick... I'm the only child of Elizabeth Eden.'

After that, the rest came in a rush: the close friendship between Francie Kovaks and Ruth; their parting and eventual reunion. The birth under a false name and move to a new town. Later, the secret visits.

'When Ruth told me the truth, it was a terrible shock, as you can imagine.' Tess's fingers were knotted tightly together. 'And that was the beginning of my obsession with Elizabeth Eden. There was so much I wanted to find out about the woman I had known only as Aunt Francie. I watched all her movies, read all the books and old fan magazines again and again ... I couldn't get enough.

'But Ruth made clear to me that so much of what had been written about Elizabeth was lies. Her reputation for being temperamental, for drug-taking, her sexual promiscuity — they were all the creation of the studio publicity machine. It was their way of crushing her, of bringing her into line because she fought so hard against the sexually exploitative roles they insisted on lining up for her. Elizabeth was desperate to make it as a real actress; she wanted the respect that came from serious, demanding roles. But in the end, they broke her.' Tess's voice was raw with suppressed anger. 'By the time she died, Hollywood had virtually chewed her up and spat her out.

'Nick, I wanted that movie to be a tribute to my mother, to show what Hollywood had done to her. But you know as well as I the reasons that the project didn't go ahead.' She watched his face as she chose her next words. 'What I've learned since is that more powerful forces than I could ever have imagined were responsible for putting the brakes on that movie. I'm still not sure who, but I sure as hell know why . . . '

Nick was frowning. 'Tess, I don't quite follow. Are you — '

She told him the whole story then. Everything she knew.

'Holy hell . . . ' Nick shook his head in disbelief. It was almost too much to comprehend. 'So you think the Madigan camp is behind this? Because they knew about the affair between Tom Madigan and Eli — your mother?' He ran a hand through his hair. 'But surely . . . surely the President couldn't have been responsible for . . . '

'Murder?' Tess finished for him, her face sombre. 'Who can say, Nick? I've tried to look at it from every angle. Perhaps Elizabeth was threatening him with exposure of the affair. Maybe because he wouldn't leave his wife. Or perhaps he was trying to end the affair with the next election in sight. But even if Tom Madigan wasn't responsible for her death, he was *there* that night. That alone would have caused a scandal of monstrous proportions.'

Nick was still trying to get the facts in order. 'And this Donovan . . . you think his death wasn't an accident?'

'It's just too much of a coincidence. But when we couldn't — '

'We?' Nick looked up expectantly.

Tess felt her cheeks begin to heat. 'There was a guy, a reporter, working on this with me.'

Nick had noted her reaction, the use of the past tense. 'What's happened to him? Is he still involved?'

Tess's eyes darkened. 'No. That's — over.' Hurriedly, she changed the subject. 'Look, Nick, what I want from you is help to decide where to go from here. Do I step back now? Give up when I've come so far — and then hate myself for the rest of my life because I didn't follow through with what I believed in?' Her agitation was obvious. 'It's because of what I found out on my twenty-first birthday that I am what I am today. From that moment on, every step I took was calculated to move myself into a position of influence and power. I knew that's what it would take to ensure that the true story of Elizabeth Eden's suffering could finally be told. I knew I'd be taking on the Hollywood Establishment, the boys who had run their own ugly power games for so long.'

Her breath was coming fast as she swung round to face him. 'Am I wrong to want to see this through, Nick? Tell me. Am I letting this obsession warp me? Should I let the past go?'

He was staring up at her, his blue eyes serious. For a long moment he didn't answer, then he said quietly, 'Tess, you and I grew up being suppressed — for ever at the mercy of those who were richer, more powerful. I don't think either of us is prepared to tolerate that now.'

He rose to his feet, and walked towards her, wrapping her in his arms. 'You'll never rest until you find out the truth of your mother's death. Let me help you do that.'

Before he left he felt he had to ask the question. 'Tess, the reporter you spoke of. Was he the one ... ?'

Her mouth tightened. 'I made a mistake, Nick. Let's leave it at that, OK?'

'Honey, I'm not trying to pry into your private life. I'm only asking because I think maybe I should talk to the guy; see where he intends going on all this. It seems to me we've got a much better chance if we can still work together.'

'No!' Her reply was unequivocal. 'All Chris Stanley's interested in is grabbing the glory for himself. He'll use anyone and do anything to get this story. You're wasting your time if you think he'll cooperate on this.'

Nick could see the raw pain in her eyes and hear the bitterness in her voice. She was hurting like hell, he knew — and his heart went out to her.

But he had taken note of Chris Stanley's name, remembered Tess telling him on that earlier happier occasion that he worked for the *Clarion*. She might be right about his attitude, but it was worth a phone call.

The next morning, he rang the newspaper.

Hiding his curiosity, Chris had agreed to meet in a quiet bar on Melrose. The name Nick Teece meant nothing to him, but he was well aware of the Conroy Aircraft Corporation. There might be a story here, he'd told himself.

Nick Teece was easy to spot. It was early, just on eleven, and he was the only customer in the place.

The two men shook hands and Nick led the way to the privacy of a banquette, although there was little chance of their being overheard.

'Thanks for coming, Mr Stanley.' Nick took in the young man opposite; the tall, lanky, casually dressed reporter was so different from the type he had expected to attract Tess.

'Chris will do fine... What can I do for you, Mr Teece?'

'I'm a friend of Tess Jordan's. A very old friend.'

He saw the expression change on Chris Stanley's face.

'Don't tell me you've come here to talk about Tess?' There was an obvious awkwardness and discomfort in the reporter's manner.

'Certainly not about her private life, if that's what you mean.' Nick made it clear that he was aware of the relationship. 'But last night she filled me in on everything you've both been involved in these last few months.'

Chris Stanley looked warÿ, said nothing, and Nick went on.

'I'm going to tell you something. Tess and I go back a long way; we've been through a lot together. She's a very special person to me, and that's why I'm here. Because I want to find out exactly what's going to happen next.'

'That's something I'm still working on.' Chris's answer was evasive.

'Well, it's important you keep both me and Tess in the picture. You can understand her concern, I'm sure.'

Chris resented the pressure. 'Look,' he answered impatiently, 'this investigation is no picnic. It's one helluva dangerous scene. People have already lost their lives. It's best for someone like Tess Jordan to keep right out of it.'

Something in his tone triggered a switch in Nick's brain. This guy still cared . . . Maybe that was why . . . He leaned across the round table top that separated them. 'Let me explain something to you, Mr Stanley. Tess Jordan's tough; she doesn't scare easily. Just so's you completely understand, I'm going to tell you exactly where she's coming from. You got time to listen?'

A muscle twitched in Chris's jaw. He nodded.

' . . . so someone like Tess who's lived rough on the streets of New York City isn't going to run away when there's something important at stake. Have I made myself clear, Mr Stanley?'

Chris had listened in silent amazement as the man opposite spoke about that other life. A life that he too, it seemed, had shared . . . He was still trying to reconcile the image of the young girl Nick Teece had described with that of the successful, powerful, President of WLS.

'You underestimated Tess if you thought she couldn't cope,' Nick Teece was still speaking. 'She's going to follow through on this, whether you're there to help her or not. So it seems crazy not to pool our resources and work together. I'd like you to think about that.'

He got to his feet, ready to take his leave. He had formed an impression of Chris Stanley. He didn't seem the sort of guy interested in playing dirty games. Tess, he thought, had got it wrong there. And he felt sure the guy would at least think over what he'd said.

Out in the sunshine, the two men shook hands again. Nick gave the reporter a quizzical look. 'Look, it's none of my business what happened between you two, but I think you should know — she's hurting a lot.'

Chris's eyes clouded with emotion. 'Guess that's a two-way street,' he murmured.

CHAPTER

31

He had no way of knowing how she'd respond. All he knew was he had to make the attempt.

It was just after nine pm when he pushed the button on her security entrance gate.

'Who is it?' The sound of her voice, distorted as it was by the intercom, made his stomach turn over.

'Tess . . . it's me.'

There was a long silence and for a fearful moment he thought she'd hung up.

'What do you want?' Cold, unfriendly.

'I want . . . I want your forgiveness, Tess. Please . . . let me explain.'

There was no reply. But next moment, the gate slowly swung open.

She was giving him a chance.

Her eyes were hard as she let him into the house. Without a word she led the way into the living room.

'Tess, I know you have every right to hate me, but please, just hear me out. Let me try to explain.'

'I'm listening,' she answered coolly.

' . . . so can you understand? It was because I loved you that I acted as I did. I didn't want you endangered because of what *I* was getting into. I kept remembering what had happened with Carrie . . . and I couldn't bear to take that same risk with you.'

Chris prayed he could make her understand. 'Then Nick Teece came and spoke with me today. He told me about your past; told me everything. What the two of you had endured, what you'd faced together. He made me understand that you were stronger than I'd even given you credit for. And he made it clear you were determined to see this through whether I was there to help or not.

'Oh, God, Tess,' his tortured eyes pleaded with her, 'I was such a fool to handle things as I did. I've missed you so much. Please, please, will you forgive me?'

Her eyes were bright with tears and without a word she held out her arms. Next moment they were locked together, hungry mouths salving the terrible ache in their hearts.

Later, in bed, their passion burned with an even fiercer intensity. Their bodies entwined in joyous celebration, they proved over and over again that each had come home.

As Chris's lips burned her flesh, as his hands and body possessed her, Tess felt drugged by love and desire.

This time, she vowed in tearful ecstasy, it would never end.

He was curled up close beside her, dozing, when she brought up what was on her mind.

'Chris . . . ' she whispered, 'You said that Nick told you . . . everything?'

He kissed her gently in the darkness. 'Yeah, honey . . . the whole tragic story. You two had it tough, that was for sure.' His voice sounded sleepy.

'He told you all about our time in New York City, you mean?'

'Yeah.'

'So he — he didn't say anything about my mother?'

'Your mother ... ?' Chris sounded puzzled. 'Why should he have mentioned her?'

'Because ... because she's the reason behind everything. You see, Chris, my natural mother was Elizabeth Eden ... '

Suddenly he was wide awake.

No one was more delighted than Nick when he heard how everything had worked out.

Tess had rung to thank him for his role in healing the rift between herself and Chris.

'We're both so grateful, Nick,' she said warmly. 'There were crossed wires on both sides, I guess. Now I understand that Chris was only trying to protect me. But it wasn't till he spoke to you that he realised I fully intended going on with the investigation, even if I had to do it alone. That's when he saw that prolonging the torture for both of us was pointless.'

'I'm delighted you've worked it out, Tess.' Nick's sincerity was obvious. 'Chris Stanley struck me as a good guy — and I'd have had to be blind not to see he was missing you like crazy.'

Before he rang off he asked if they were free to have lunch that Sunday. 'Let me know and I'll check with Helen. If we make it a barbecue here, the kids can amuse themselves in the pool while Helen and I get a chance to know Chris a little better.'

And, he thought, it would prove to his wife that she had nothing to worry about.

But he didn't tell Tess that.

Nick knew he'd made the right move.

He could see how quickly Helen relaxed now that Tess, her husband's oldest and closest friend, was no longer the solo, threatening female.

The four of them got on so well it seemed as if they'd all been friends for years.

The conversation during lunch was light and casual; Nick made it clear that he hadn't discussed the issues at hand with his wife.

Only later, when Helen had coaxed the children inside for a bath, did the talk become more serious.

'The way I see it,' offered Nick, 'everything that happened — the attempt at running Jennifer Ross off the road, her murder, the fire, the death of Donovan — all of it could be the work of the Madigan people. The election of their candidate is at stake. If questions had started to be asked as a result of that movie, not only would Robert Madigan's chance of victory be in serious jeopardy, but a cover-up that had gone undetected for over twenty years, a cover-up of the highest order, might stand to be revealed. They'd be prepared to do anything to stop that happening.'

Tess frowned. 'But the dreadful way Jennifer Ross was killed. Surely they — '

But Nick had thought about that too. 'A deliberate attempt to further cloud the issue. The focus then becomes Jennifer Ross as Elizabeth Eden, not Eden herself, or what happened on the night *she* died.'

Chris looked thoughtful. 'It's difficult to accept, I know, but it's a viable scenario given the circumstances. The Service and those close to Tom Madigan could have been living with this secret for over twenty years. They're feeling safe, sure they've got away with it ... when suddenly they learn about the movie project.' He shook his head. 'All hell must have broken loose.'

'So ... where do we go from here?' asked Nick.

Chris drummed his fingers against his empty glass. 'Don't forget that phone tap — they know we still have that tape of Donovan.'

'But that wouldn't hold up in a court of law,' protested Tess.

'Maybe not, but if that information was leaked, it would certainly be enough to put Robert Madigan's hopes of becoming President in serious jeopardy.'

'But how does that help us put a name to exactly who's behind all this?' She still sounded doubtful.

Chris spoke slowly, his face serious. 'I think maybe the time has come to confront the Madigan camp.'

Two days afterwards, Chris put a call through to Larry Brandt, Madigan's campaign manager.

As he gave his name, Chris felt sure it would be readily recognised by those working for Robert Madigan's election. The feature article alone would have seen to that.

'I'd like the chance to talk with yourself and possibly Dave Arnell or Lou Ledgerson,' he said when Brandt finally came on the line. Both men, he knew, had been part of Tom Madigan's inner circle, and were now senior members of the Madigan election team.

On the other end of the line, Larry Brandt couldn't help but be impressed at the gall of the guy. 'You're researching another article, Mr Stanley?' There was an edge to the campaign manager's voice.

'You could say that,' Chris replied evenly.

As he replaced the receiver, Larry Brandt's eyes narrowed in thought. He had agreed to meet with the smart-ass reporter. He'd surmised quickly it was best to see exactly what was in the wind.

But one thing was certain. Only he and Dave would be at the meeting.

'Oh, God, Chris . . . are you sure this is the way to go?'

He stroked her hair as she lay next to him. He could hear the trepidation in her voice. 'I'll be careful, Tess, I promise you.'

He meant it. There was so much to live for now, so much to look forward to.

'But you can't even be absolutely sure that you'll be talking to the right people.'

'These were the guys at the top when Tom Madigan was President, Tess. It stands to reason that one or all of them could have been implicated in the cover-up. And now when they see we're not going to give up, I'm convinced they'll take action. They can't afford not to.'

He felt her clutch him closer in the darkness. He knew what she was thinking.

Last time they'd tried a similar strategy, Les Donovan had died.

He was shown into a small, nondescript office in the building that housed the Madigan campaign head-quarters.

'Mr Brandt shouldn't be too long,' he was informed by a slim, attractive secretary.

Twenty minutes later, as Chris's impatience grew, two men finally entered the room. He recognised their faces from newspaper photographs.

The shorter of the two, a well-dressed, fit-looking man in his fifties, was Larry Brandt. He had been the campaign adviser responsible for getting Tom Madigan into the White House; now he was doing his best to achieve the same goal for his son. And maybe, Chris thought, he'd stop at nothing to achieve his aim.

Dave Arnell hadn't weathered the years quite as well as his colleague. Since his days as Tom Madigan's Chief of Staff, his body had thickened and his face grown more haggard. He was watching Chris warily from under his trademark bushy brows.

The introductions made, the three men sat down and Dave Arnell asked curtly, 'What can we do for you, Mr Stanley?'

He'd been annoyed when Larry'd told him that he'd agreed to the reporter's request for a meeting.

'What the hell is he after, Larry?'

'That's what we're going to find out,' his colleague had answered smoothly. 'Better we know what he's planning next so that we can all be prepared. I don't want Rob upset at this late stage by any more bombshells from this sonofabitch.'

Now Dave Arnell fixed Chris with a hard-eyed stare as he waited for his reply.

Returning the older man's gaze, Chris began, 'There's something I think you gentlemen should know...'

Larry Brandt gave a snort of derision. 'Are you *serious*? Do you really expect us to believe this crap?'

Dave Arnell leaned forward in his seat. 'I think you'd be better off writing fiction, Mr Stanley. To date, that seems what you're best at.'

Ignoring the taunts, Chris replied evenly, 'So you don't give any credence to what Les Donovan has left on tape?'

'That President Madigan was with Elizabeth Eden the night she died? That the truth has somehow been able to be kept from the public for over twenty years?' Larry Brandt's lips twisted in contempt. 'Come on, buddy... Do you really expect us to accept the ravings of some ex-cop with a grudge against the force?' He shook his head. 'No, I think you'd better go back and check on your source. I'd suggest sometime when he doesn't have a gallon of booze under his belt.'

Chris stared coolly at both men. 'That's pretty impossible now. You see... Les Donovan was killed recently.'

Face expressionless, Dave Arnell rose to his feet. 'I think you've wasted enough of our time. Whatever you profess to have on tape is utterly without substantiation. No newspaper in the country would touch an allegation like that with a barge pole.'

Larry Brandt saw Chris to the door. 'I don't think pursuing something like this would do much for your reputation as a newspaperman, do you, Mr Stanley?'

Later, Chris was certain he hadn't imagined the threat in the man's tone.

Anne Conroy's heart was hammering against her ribs. She felt the breath catch in her throat as she reread the curt paragraphs printed on official notepaper.

Oh God. Her face grew flushed with rapture. *It was a dream come true . . .*

She had been doing her usual search through Walter's briefcase, looking for his soft-backed personal diary, when she'd caught sight of the letter on official Pentagon letterhead.

She might have ignored it if her eye hadn't been caught by the words in Walter's handwriting written in the margin: *Search and destroy all related files.*

It took her a couple of readings, but eventually Anne Conroy understood the meaning of the official correspondence.

She laughed out loud in pure delight.

She knew now that Walter was never going to leave her.

Anne made a copy of the incriminating letter on the machine in Walter's office.

First thing the next morning she caught the early post.

She realised Walter was playing for time and she was determined to cut off that avenue of escape . . .

She had known exactly where to send the letter. LA. To Nick Teece.

On the two occasions Anne had met the West Coast President of CAC there was no mistaking his idealism and dedication. Given the circumstances, Nick Teece could surely be counted on to take prompt and urgent action.

CHAPTER

32

The letter was marked private and confidential and was addressed to the West Coast President of Conroy Aircraft Corporation.

Nick slit open the plain buff envelope and saw the Pentagon letterhead. Conroy Aircraft Corporation had long-established contracts with the military, and the Pentagon was one of their biggest customers.

As he began to read, Nick realised the letter was actually directed to Walter Conroy. Someone, somewhere, had stuffed up and sent it to the LA office instead of to CAC's Dallas headquarters.

Suddenly Nick's blood went cold as the typed words began to sink in.

It was his nightmare come true.

The letter offered further evidence that the scam he had worked so hard to uncover went even further than he imagined. Suspicious CAC supplied hardware had surfaced within the Pentagon itself . . .

The words he was reading made it frighteningly clear that if Walter Conroy didn't ' . . . accelerate his provision of the documentation referring to the claimed discrepancies, the Pentagon would be forced to suspend immediately all CAC contracts pending full and total investigation'.

And there in the margin, in his own handwriting, were Walter's incriminating instructions...

But who, Nick wondered dazedly, had acquired this letter? And who had sent it to *him*? Such puzzling questions were outweighed only by his amazement that Walter had imagined he could get away with supplying second-hand equipment to the military. Surely he, more than anyone, was fully aware that all materials were checked and double-checked before being utilised by personnel.

With trembling fingers, he folded the damning sheet of paper. He knew with certainty now that Conroy and CAC were finished. With his own painstakingly collected data as further proof, the scam had no chance of being covered up. The Pentagon would surely waste no time in indicting the multimillionaire President of Conroy Aircraft Corporation.

Nick knew where his duty lay. Innocent lives were at risk and he couldn't afford to delay. He asked his secretary to place a call through to General Robert Wilson of the Pentagon. It was the name that appeared at the end of the letter.

In a few minutes the woman was back on the line. 'I'm sorry, Mr Teece, General Wilson won't be back until tomorrow lunchtime. Is there anyone else you'd like to talk with?'

'No. I'll call again.'

Nick had no idea who else might know about this and it would do no good to start a panic. He'd wait — and pray — until he could speak to the man who was handling the investigation.

It was after midnight. He lay tossing in bed, unable to sleep, when out of the blue the other stunning ramification of his discovery hit him with a sledgehammer force.

Holy Jesus...!

*

Tess was just about to step into the shower when the ringing of the phone brought her back into the bedroom.

'Tess! I'm sorry to call so early, but this is urgent. I need to talk with you and Chris as soon as possible. Can you reach him and let me know when and where we all can meet?'

Tess heard the tension in Nick's voice; she didn't waste time asking what was wrong. 'Chris is here with me now, Nick.'

'I'll be there as soon as possible,' he said tersely, and hung up.

They sat outside on the shaded part of the terrace.

'I hardly know where to start,' Nick announced, running a hand through his blond hair. 'It's incredible...'

Then, as his coffee grew cold, he started to tell his two stunned listeners the whole story.

Tess held both hands to her cheeks. 'So that means...'

Chris finished the sentence for her '... that Conroy too had a rock-solid motive for wanting that movie stopped.'

Nick leaned forward earnestly. 'You're absolutely right. He can't be discounted. He was in big trouble once the Pentagon began to ask questions and must have been pinning his every hope on his son-in-law becoming President. It was his only chance of escaping the net that was closing around him. I'm absolutely positive that's how he would have looked at it. And if murder and arson were necessary to save the destruction of his empire, then so be it.'

Chris nodded, but at the same time something was niggling at the edge of his consciousness. Something he couldn't quite pin down. Something that didn't make sense...

Tess was still trying to piece it all together. 'But that

still doesn't solve the mystery of my mother's death. Conroy surely can't be implicated in that.'

Nick nodded in grudging acknowledgement. 'You're right, of course. But for me at least, the next step is clear. I've got to present the Pentagon with full details of that faulty stock as soon as possible. Lives are at risk every moment I delay.'

He looked at Chris. 'As to how Conroy might be linked to the fire and the murders — well, I'm beginning to think it's time we went to the FBI with everything we know.'

But what about the earlier cover-up? Chris thought. *How did they know that the FBI hadn't been involved then?*

He kept the disquieting thought to himself as he replied, 'Speak to the Pentagon by all means, Nick. But in my opinion it's too early to call in the Feds. We still don't have any definite proof tying Conroy or anyone on the Madigan side into the rest of this. If we act too hastily now we face the danger of screwing up the whole investigation.'

Nick looked at him with a frown. 'There's something on your mind, Chris. What is it?'

Chris shook his head. 'I can't tell you because I haven't sorted it out myself. But if I haven't managed to pinpoint what's bothering me in forty-eight hours then perhaps you're right. We should go to the FBI.'

But he was determined to break the case before that happened.

Sweat beaded the Idolator's brow.

As always, his everyday persona disappeared as soon as he sat in the darkened room watching the sensual images of the woman he worshipped flickering across the screen.

It seemed so long ago. And it seemed like yesterday. Elizabeth, with her pouting mouth, her full luscious body, her blatant inviting stare. In feverish excitement, he caressed his rigid flesh, saving his final explosive climax for the last lingering shot of that adored face.

Only when the movie finally came to an end did he allow his attention to turn to the album of photographs that lay open by his side. Pages and pages of Elizabeth in the languid sexual poses that made the blood surge through his veins. Photographs pasted in with fastidious care, which had brought him rapturous fulfilment over and over again.

But now Elizabeth's photos had been joined by those of another.

Newspaper clippings of a slim, dark-haired woman.

Tess Jordan.

The Idolator heard the roaring in his head.

Dave Arnell watched his candidate with increasing anxiety.

Something had changed in Rob. The evidence was there to someone who knew him as well as Dave did. The fire, the zeal, the confidence — all had waned, he thought, as he sat in the back of the studio watching and listening to the interview.

Dave Arnell cursed under his breath. It was that article which had started the change. That's when Rob had begun to lose it, had begun to voice his doubts about the path he was taking. And if there was one thing Dave was sure of, it was that you couldn't win a fight like the one in front of them without having the instincts of a killer.

A killer . . .

Dave's face grew grim. It was that slimy smartass reporter sticking his noise in where it wasn't wanted that was the real worry now.

Chris Stanley was dangerous. Dangerous, because it was obvious he meant to see this through to the end.

Dave knew he had to do something. Something quick.

*

Suzie Hawkins felt safer, much safer, in her new abode. She'd even begun to quite enjoy living in Dennison Mobile Home Park. Sixty-odd kilometres from downtown LA, the air was cleaner and the people friendlier.

Not that Suzie was looking to make friends. To start letting people close meant questions, too many questions about a past that had suddenly become dangerous to recall.

She gave an involuntary shudder as she remembered all that had happened. Someone had wanted that movie stopped real bad ...

She shrugged off the thought. All that was behind her now.

Her gaze fell on the framed photograph proudly displayed on the top of her second-hand refrigerator. Her eyes softened behind their heavy make-up. Little Louisa was a healthy eight-year-old now. The operation had been a success. Suzie had taken a chance, spoken of what she knew, and it had paid off.

And now, safe in Dennison, she didn't have to worry any longer.

CHAPTER

33

The call from the Pentagon's senior legal adviser was put through to Walter at his Dallas home.

The owner of Conroy Aircraft Corporation felt his bowels turn to water as the attorney curtly explained the case against him: '... and with further detailed evidence to hand of dates, invoice numbers, and shipment codes, I wish to advise that we will be proceeding with an arraignment immediately.'

A circle of ice seemed to ring Walter's lips. He found it impossible to speak. Somehow, they had found out...

Ashen-faced, he replaced the receiver. There was only one thing to do now.

Chris was just about to leave the office for a job in Santa Barbara when the call was put through from Dave Arnell.

'I think we should meet, Mr Stanley.' The Madigan aide wasted no time in small talk. 'There's something very important I'd like to discuss. Would you be free to come to my office, say at six this evening?'

'Of course.' Chris did his best to hide his surprise.

As he replaced the receiver, he felt a thrill of nervous anticipation. Something told him the hour of reckoning had come.

*

'I'm sorry, Ms Jordan, Chris Stanley is in Santa Barbara for the day. Is there any message in case he calls in?'

Tess ground her teeth with impatience. 'No . . . Wait! Ask him to call his home answering service if you hear from him.' Distractedly, Tess thanked the *Clarion* switchgirl and hung up.

Of all days for Chris to be out of town, she thought in frustration. She looked at her watch. Two hours to go. Six o'clock, Suzie Hawkins had said. She would be driving in from Dennison and would meet Tess at the house.

Elizabeth Eden's house.

Tess had been taken aback at the suggestion. 'At *Elizabeth's*?' She wondered if she had heard right.

But Suzie Hawkins had repeated her instructions. There was something she had to show Tess. Something she had hidden all those years ago, that would have a direct bearing on the mystery of Elizabeth's death.

'I want this whole terrible business cleared up once and for all,' the ex-actress had insisted, a noticeable tremor in her voice.

As she'd replaced the receiver, Tess was assailed by conflicting emotions of confusion and anticipation at this new and unexpected development. What could Suzie Hawkins have to say that she hadn't revealed before? Why was she going to tell them now? And what in the world could she have hidden at the house?

On two or three occasions over the years, Tess had been tempted to visit the place where her mother had lived and died. But each time she had resisted the desire, frightened, perhaps, of her own emotional response.

The house had been uninhabited for years. Boarded up at the time of Elizabeth's death to keep out the ghouls and souvenir hunters, it had later been tenanted and was badly in need of refurbishment. Yet even when it was due to be spruced up for the external shots for the movie, Tess had had no wish to visit the place in person, preferring instead to work from photographs with the designers.

Now, however, there was no resisting Suzie Hawkin's curious invitation.

But she didn't want to go alone. Not when Chris had stressed how careful they both had to be from now on.

She thought quickly. Nick . . . She said a silent prayer he would be in his LA office.

He was. As soon as she told him what had happened, explained that Chris was out of town, Nick assured her he'd accompany her to the meeting with Suzie Hawkins.

'I'll pick you up, OK?' Tess felt tense with anticipation. 'Nick, maybe this is what we've been looking for. It might just be the key to everything.'

Like Tess, Nick could only wonder what in the world Suzie Hawkins might have to reveal.

The house was double-storeyed with arched doorways and peeling, blistered stucco walls. Weeds grew through what had once been an expensively tiled courtyard, and most of the windows were covered with worn and faded shutters.

'Who owns it now?' Nick looked curiously at the house as they walked from the car to the front door.

'The City. I found out all about it long ago. It seems my mother left no will, and everything went to the City of Los Angeles to disperse as the supervisors wished.

'The house was difficult to sell after . . . the death. Then it became the focus of argument between those supervisors who wanted it renovated and opened to the public, and others who preferred it to be sold or put to better use. However before a decision could be reached, the place was found to be built right over one of the main fault lines on the earthquake charts. That made the City too nervous about placing it on the market — they were afraid of legal action in the event of quake in the area.

'In time, it was leased, but the tenants had to sign a document releasing the City from liability for injury or loss of life when the next big one hit.'

'Where did Suzie — ' The question died on Nick's

lips. He looked at Tess as they entered the front porch. The front door was open.

Tess returned his look with a shrug. 'Maybe she had a key. I — I guess we should go inside.'

The house was already shadowy in the twilight. The floorboards creaked as they made their way down the wide hall.

'Suzie! Are you there?' Tess's voice resounded through the empty rooms. In the half-light, Nick saw the tension in her face and reached for her hand. He understood the effect the house must be having on her.

'Suzie!' Tess called out again, but there was no reply.

'Maybe we're a bit early,' Nick suggested. 'Look, why don't you do the rest of this floor and I'll look upstairs?'

Upstairs — where the bedroom and the bathroom were; where Elizabeth's body had been found.

'Thanks,' she whispered, grateful for his sensitivity.

But she knew it would only be a momentary respite. For Tess had made up her mind that she would not leave the house until she had viewed the room where her mother had died.

With a squeeze of her hand, Nick made his way up the dusty staircase, while Tess continued into the kitchen and adjoining sunroom.

She called Suzie's name several times more, peered out through filthy venetians into the overgrown garden beyond, but neither the woman nor her vehicle were to be seen.

Giving herself a further moment to gather her courage, Tess quickly retraced her steps.

Suzie Hawkins, it seemed, had yet to arrive.

At last she could put off the moment no longer . . . Slowly, fearfully, she climbed the curved wooden staircase to the upper floor.

At the top she paused, listening for any sound that would lead her to Nick. She very much wanted him by her side when she took this next traumatic step.

But she heard nothing.

It was darker now and slowly Tess made her way down the long hallway. She would start at one end, she decided, and work her way back. That way she would be sure to find Nick.

One by one, she opened the doors on either side of the hall. Each creaked open to reveal empty, dusty, cobweb-filled rooms. Once a giant cockroach scuttled close to her foot and she pulled back with a shudder. There was still no sign of Nick.

Finally, there were only the two doors left: the one which she knew led to her mother's bedroom, the other to the bathroom beyond. The location of the room where Elizabeth Eden had died was etched in Tess's mind. She had poured over the plan of the house in the old fan magazines which had appeared at the time of Elizabeth's death. She knew exactly how the rooms were laid out.

As she turned the handle on the bedroom door, her mouth was dry.

But the door wouldn't open.

Tess frowned. Maybe the timberwork had warped. She tried again, pushing her weight against it. Without success.

She knew there was another way to get into the room. The bathroom was accessible from the hall, as well as from the bedroom beyond.

This time she had better luck. The bathroom door opened easily. As the grimy room with its old-fashioned fittings was revealed, Tess stood transfixed, her eyes riveted to the large oval bathtub stained with years of rusty water dripping from the tap.

She closed her eyes, felt herself begin to sway. For a moment she thought she was going to faint. The emotion of the moment was so overpowering that she felt herself enveloped by the presence of the dead woman. That beautiful, vital, young woman whose tragically short life had ended in this room.

Tears prickled behind her lids, and she bit her lip hard to hold back her emotions.

'*Yes . . . right there. That's where they found her.*'

Tess screamed. She spun round in shock. The voice had come from somewhere behind her. Then she saw that the door further down the hall, the one she had been unable to move, was now standing open. The sight that met her eyes made the blood freeze in her veins.

The man's face was hidden behind a balaclava and in his gloved right hand he held a long-bladed knife. On the floor at his feet Nick lay unconscious, his mouth taped and his hands and feet roped together. Blood was running in rivulets from an ugly wound on his temple.

'Nick! Oh, God . . . ' White-faced with shock, she made to move.

'Get back! Or your boyfriend won't ever open his eyes again.' The knife was pointed at Nick; the order given in a tone that chilled her blood.

'Who are you? What — what do you want?' Her voice was a croak of terror. She realised with horror that they'd walked into a trap. In some way Suzie Hawkins had been used to lure Tess to the house.

She stared in wide-eyed fear at the man holding the weapon.

'Don't worry . . . I'll tell you exactly what I want.' The man in the balaclava answered her question in a delirium of expectation. His voice was thick with desire.

All Tess's instincts told her she was looking at the killer of Jennifer Ross.

CHAPTER

34

'**I**n here. Slowly.' He gestured to the room behind him.
Dry-mouthed with fear, Tess did as she was told,
her heart tearing in anguish as she moved past Nick's
inert form. She had walked into a trap — and taken Nick
with her.

In the room itself, she got another shock. The rest of
the house had been bare of furniture, but in this room, a
bed stood in the centre of the floor. On one wall, a cheap
chain-store mirror hung over the peeling wallpaper.

The man left Nick slumped in the doorway and
followed her into the room. Still holding the knife in one
hand he used his other to snap back the locks of a small
suitcase that lay on the fringed bedcover. He pulled out a
bag of cosmetics — and a glossy photograph.

'Do your face like that.'

Paralysed, Tess stared at the posed publicity shot of
Elizabeth Eden.

Oh, no ... Oh God, no ...

Then the sharp point of the knife was against her
throat.

'Do it,' he snarled. 'Use the mirror.'

She knew she had no choice.

With trembling fingers, she started to draw a thin line
of dark pencil around her eyes.

'Thicker ... She always wore it thicker.'

He meant Elizabeth. What did this madman know about Elizabeth?

Tess played for time, praying for a miracle. But when at last she'd applied the pancake base and rich coloured lipstick, the man produced something else from the case.

'Now this.'

Tess caught her breath and her heart lurched wildly. It was a wig. A platinum wig.

'Hurry! Put it on.'

She could hear the growing impatience in his tone and did as she was commanded, staring with fascinated horror at her own image.

But he hadn't finished. 'Now this.'

He tossed at her the tight-fitting strapless gown.

Oh, God, she prayed, let me think of some way out of this nightmare. Please, please God ...

As she stripped out of her clothes, tears of humiliation and fear rolled down her cheeks, streaking her newly-applied make-up. When only her panties were left, he gestured for her to remove those too.

At last, with shaking fingers, she drew on the clinging gown that was a copy of the one her mother had made her trademark.

The man was close beside her now. Tess could hear the rasp of his heavy breathing. She shuddered as he trailed his free hand across the bare flesh of her shoulders and chest.

Slowly, he shook his head, and she heard the wonder in his tremulous tone. 'It's incredible. You — you look so much like her now. So much like your mother ... '

Tess gasped, she felt the blood run out of her face.

The man misread her shock. 'You didn't know?' He spoke in a caressing whisper as he continued to stroke her neck, her cheek, the platinum wig. 'Oh, yes,' he purred, 'Elizabeth had a child ... But she gave you away.' His voice took on a harsher note. 'Elizabeth didn't always know what was best for her ... '

Tess felt her mind spinning out of control. How could he know? How had he found out? Ruth had told her that no one but herself and Elizabeth had known the truth. Then how —

Suddenly, as the answer struck her, Tess felt herself turned to stone. *This madman could be her father* . . .

He pointed to the bed. 'Lie down.'

Tess stood frozen to the spot.

The next moment, her captor grasped her arm in a vice-like grip, and threw her roughly onto the cover. For the first time, he released his weapon, dropping the knife beside him on the floor as he quickly unzipped his trousers and lunged towards her.

'No! No!' Tess struggled, twisted, hit out wildly. Free from the threat of the glistening blade, she prayed she might have a chance. But her attacker was stronger than he looked.

Panting heavily, he pinned her arms above her head, his manic eyes staring down at her from the slits in the hood. His hard body straddled hers and then he said the words that made her heart stop beating. 'Don't fight me! Or do you want to die like she did?'

Tess felt the hairs stand up on the back of her neck. She knew then that this was the man who had murdered not only Jennifer Ross, but her mother too . . .

His face was close to hers, and now his voice dropped to a menacing whisper. 'Don't you know how I've dreamed of this moment? Ached for it? I loved her. No one could have loved her like I did . . .'

Tess was choking with fear. He had killed her mother, and now he was going to rape and kill her . . .

His penis was hard against her thigh as he wrenched down the top of the strapless gown and began to fondle and kiss her breasts.

'They're small . . . so much smaller than Elizabeth's.' His voice came thickly. 'She had magnificent breasts . . .'

Tess could almost smell his excitement as he began to drag the gown up her thighs. 'NO!' She writhed wildly even though she knew her struggle was useless.

His palm caught her a stinging blow across the cheek. Through tears of pain, she saw the angry spittle form at the corner of his mouth. 'Think you're too good for me, don't you, bitch? Just like she did!' His anger was instant and terrifying. 'Oh, yes, it was all right for her to sleep with *him*! He was powerful; he was important . . . But she was kidding herself — he'd never have left his wife to marry her. She couldn't see that she was just his slut!'

In that instant Tess knew that despite her terror, her pain, she had to know . . . '*Who? Who* are you talking about?'

To her astonishment a wild laugh burst from his lips. 'You don't know, do you? You really don't know . . . ' Chest heaving, he stared down at her. 'She was screwing him again, baby. Elizabeth Eden and Tom Madigan were lovers, just as they'd been years before. You're the goddamn bastard of the former President of the United States!'

Tess felt as if she'd fallen off the edge of the world . . .

Chris was back in town in plenty of time for his appointment with Dave Arnell and Larry Brandt. All day long he'd been distracted, wondering what lay behind this request for a meeting.

As he drove into the office parking lot at five-thirty, he consoled himself with the thought that in just a short time his curiosity would be relieved.

As soon as he got into his office and saw the note from Tess he rang his answer service.

What the hell? His face creased in a frown. A meeting with Suzie Hawkins? At Elizabeth Eden's house? That was *bizarre*.

He checked his watch. Quarter to six. There was no way he could meet with Tess. If he wanted to keep his appointment with Arnell, he'd have to leave at once.

But as he drove away from the *Clarion* building, Chris felt an uneasiness in the pit of his belly. Something didn't jell here. Something was wrong. But again he couldn't put his finger on it . . .

The car radio was tuned to the news station. Just as he was about to take the freeway exit to the Madigan campaign headquarters, the announcer's words caught his attention.

The blood drained from his face, and in that same shattering instant, Chris finally realised what had been troubling him for so long.

With screeching tyres, he pulled the car back into the stream of traffic.

Oh Jesus, how blind he'd been!

The sweat broke out on his brow. It was five minutes to six. Driving dangerously, he forced his way in and out of the peak hour traffic, praying harder than he'd ever prayed in his life.

The man rubbed his penis up and down her bare thighs as he spoke. The words spilled from his lips, as if, after so many years, some compulsion was forcing him to tell the rest of the story . . .

'He was the only one the bitch had eyes for. Just *him.* She never saw that I would have given her anything! That night I couldn't stand it any longer. He was with her, I knew that. When he left, I took my chance, went back to the house. Of course she let me in. She knew who I was. Yet she could never see how I felt; how precious she was to me; how I adored her.

'That night I was determined to make her understand, make her see how much I needed her, how much I could offer her.' A harshness crept into his tone. 'But she refused to listen, told me to get out. The bitch rejected me before I had a chance . . . She treated me like — like a worthless piece of shit!'

Again his mood changed abruptly as a sob bubbled

from his lips. 'If — if she hadn't done that ... she might still be alive. I didn't mean to kill her ... But when she spoke to me like that, I ... '

Tess felt the drip of his tears on her bare chest. She hardly dared breathe. One part of her was listening in mesmerised horror, yet at the same time her mind was racing, frantically trying to come up with a way of escape.

Her best chance was to stay calm, play for time. Maybe his erratic changes of mood would work in her favour. Maybe.

But he was talking again, once more in control. And this time Tess caught the note of triumph in his tone. 'Afterwards, I didn't panic. I put her in the bath, made it appear as though she'd suicided — even though I knew the ploy wouldn't stand up to scrutiny. But everything was in my favour. The Service knew Madigan had been with her that night; they knew of the affair. The last thing they'd want would be to have the President connected in any way to the death. I know how these people operate. Elizabeth Eden's death would never be investigated ... Not while there was even the remotest chance the President of the United States might be implicated.'

Unexpectedly, he chuckled, and the sound sent shivers down Tess's spine.

'Leaving the cufflink was my bit of extra insurance. He didn't even know he'd lost it. But when I remembered I had it on me, it just seemed too impossible to resist. That, coupled with the fact that his fingerprints would be all over the place — and I knew there was no way the Service would dig any deeper into the death of Elizabeth Eden.'

He's proud of the way he covered up the crime, Tess thought. *He can't resist showing off his cleverness ...*

And now he was telling her because he knew she'd never be able to tell anyone else ...

'How — how did you know Tom Madigan was my father?' Somehow she found the courage to ask the question.

Immediately, Tess realised her mistake.

'*Forget fucking Tom Madigan!* I hate that fucking sonofabitch!'

He took her chin in his fingers and wrenched her face up to look at him. '*I'm* the one you want! *I'm* the only one who can give you everything you need — *can't you see that*?'

He was trembling with rage. With one savage movement, he tore the dress from her thighs and forced his erection between her legs.

Tess screamed and kicked, writhing in a frenzied attempt to thwart the violation. But pinned and helpless, overpowered by his manic strength, she knew the inevitability of her fate. Hot tears filled her eyes. Like Jennifer Ross, like her mother, she too —

'JESUS!'

Her gaze flew towards the door and her heart turned over.

The man too started up in shock — and lunged for his knife with a growl of rage.

'*Chris! Be careful!*' screamed Tess.

But Chris had seen the danger. Arms outstretched, he launched himself across the room and grabbed at the attacker. Both men rolled off the bed and fell heavily onto the wooden floor. The knife glinted in the madman's hand.

Tess leapt to her feet. She had to do something! But there was nothing at hand, nothing to use as a weapon. Then, from the corner of her eye, she caught a movement by the door. Nick! He had regained consciousness!

At once she was by his side, pulling the tape from his mouth, fumbling with the rope that bound his feet.

'Nick! Oh, Nick, we've got to help him!'

At last his feet were free, and she turned to the bonds on his wrists.

'*Tess! Look out!*' Wild-eyed, Nick was staring over her shoulder.

She spun around. Chris lay dazed on the floor. With a growl of rage, the attacker turned his attention to Tess and Nick.

Instantly, Tess scrambled to her feet. Suddenly those instincts that had served her so well on the streets of New York so many years before came back to her.

As the man sprang towards her, the knife flashing in his hand, Tess grabbed for a section of the rope that had bound Nick's legs.

'Bitch!' the madman shrieked. 'You're just like her! A worthless fucking bitch!'

Every nerve on edge, Tess sidestepped quickly as the blade sliced through the air, narrowly missing her.

Just then Chris moaned, momentarily distracting the attacker. Seizing her chance, Tess tried to loop the rope around the masked man's neck. But he swung back just in time, caught her a vicious blow to the side of the head and knocked her to the ground.

As Tess lay winded, Chris resumed his attack.

The knife flashed. Chris was quick, but not quick enough. A line of crimson immediately sprang up along his shirt sleeve. He grunted, staggered, and his opponent saw his chance. He raised the knife high above his head to deliver the fatal blow.

Tess screamed and tried to grab him from behind. Suddenly the man shot from her reach and fell heavily to the floor. It took her a moment to realise what had happened.

Nick had rolled across the floor, his hands still tied. Lashing out with his legs, he had delivered an almighty kick into the small of their attacker's back.

The man lay moaning and writhing on the bare boards, the point of the blade protruding from his ribcage. A pool of blood spread in an ever increasing circle beneath him. He had fallen on to his own weapon.

Chris was by her side, holding her in his arms. 'Are you all right, my darling?' Trembling, unable to speak, she nodded against his chest and he kissed her before bending to release Nick.

Seconds later, as the man's groans grew softer, Chris knelt down beside him and pulled off the balaclava that covered his face.

The three of them stared down at the contorted features of the dying man.

'Oh my God,' breathed Chris.

It was Larry Brandt.

CHAPTER

35

'No! No!, no, no, no!'
Adelle Madigan shrieked out her disbelief. Her eyes were huge and wild with shock as she clutched her son's arm.

'I don't believe you! Tell me it's not true, Robbie. Please, I beg you! *Tell me it's not true!*'

Robert Madigan looked down at his mother, his face expressionless. 'It's true. I can assure you. I'm pulling out.'

'But Robbie! Your dream . . . Your father's dream . . .' She was trembling with emotion.

'*Your* dream, mother. Never mine. And do you really think I'd still have a chance after what happened with Walter?'

The news of Walter Conroy's suicide had come as a terrible shock. But it had given Rob his out. From tragedy, he thought, had come his salvation . . .

'Walter? Who cares about Walter?' Adelle turned away, her eyes blank and unseeing as she tried to cope with the devastation of her future.

Then she swung back to her son, desperate for one last chance to change his mind. 'It won't matter about Walter, Rob. People will be sympathetic, you'll see. You won't lose votes.'

Robert Madigan's mouth twisted in contempt.

'You're living in a dream world, mother. Walter Conroy stands accused of major fraud — fraud which caused the loss of innocent lives. And now there are other whispers too, as you know — to do with the Elizabeth Eden project. Do you really — '

His mother cut across him, her ravaged, tear-stained face straining up into his. 'But he's *dead*, Robbie! It doesn't matter now.'

Her son looked down into the face that suddenly looked its age. She really meant it, he saw. As long as Walter's suicide did nothing to spoil his own chance of making it to the White House, it meant absolutely nothing in his mother's scheme of things.

Robert Madigan wasn't surprised. He had known for long enough now that all Adelle really cared about was her own return to power and glory.

He shook his head, but in place of contempt, he now felt a sort of pity. 'You just don't understand me, do you mother? You never did.' He turned, and without another word, left the room.

It was Sara now who deserved his comfort. Not the woman who had dominated his life for so long.

Anne Conroy hadn't left her bedroom for days. The drapes remained permanently drawn and she sat in the gloom, staring at nothing.

Her eyes were sunken into their sockets and her hair hung lankly around her shattered face. She had never meant it to end like this.

When she had sent that letter to LA she had hoped only to get rid of Eleanor Benson and recapture her own future. A future where Walter would need her and depend on her as much as he had at the beginning.

Anne had felt sure that, faced with the ruin of CAC, Walter would take his punishment — and with first class lawyers that would surely only mean a massive fine — then look at ways of starting again.

And it was then she intended to reveal her secret, tell him about the fortune she had built so astutely over the years. In her mind's eye she had joyfully imagined Walter's amazement, then his relief and immense gratitude as she offered him the capital to make a brand new start.

Tears filled Anne Conroy's eyes. Nothing had worked out as she'd planned. Instead of fighting back as he had so many times before, this time Walter Conroy had given in.

He'd put a pistol to his head in the bathroom of his Century Plaza penthouse.

Anne Conroy had lost everything.

Dave Arnell felt punch drunk after the events of the last few days. He wondered if things might have turned out differently if he'd called that meeting with Chris Stanley twenty-four hours earlier.

It was to be his final, bold-faced gamble to try to keep the lid on the secrets of the past. He had intended to confront Stanley with the news of Tess Jordan's parentage in the hope the reporter would recognise that a continuation of his investigation could only harm the woman he loved.

But Dave had never had that chance, as one after another bombshell had gone off around him.

First there had been Walter Conroy's suicide in the wake of revelations of a huge scam involving CAC.

Then, shortly afterwards, Robert Madigan had made public to a stunned nation his withdrawal from the Presidential race.

Now there was the horror of Larry Brandt . . .

Dave stepped into the elevator and pushed the button to take him down to the street. He had just spent four gruelling hours with senior officers of the FBI. For the first time he learned the truth about what had happened the night Elizabeth Eden died.

Had he known the President was at the house that

night? A deceptively baby-faced agent had led the questioning.

Yes, Dave nodded, he knew.

Had he reason to believe that the President might have been implicated in the actress's death?

Dave nodded again. He'd thought that perhaps the woman was putting pressure on Tom Madigan to leave his wife. And with the next election just a short time away . . . He shrugged his shoulders. People had killed for less.

Larry Brandt, for instance.

Dave had been stunned at the revelation that his campaign manager was the murderer not only of Elizabeth Eden, but also of Jennifer Ross and a woman called Suzie Hawkins. Never once had he had the slightest inkling of the extent of his colleague's obsession with the woman who had been the President's mistress. Told about the locked room in Larry Brandt's home, which bore overwhelming evidence of his obsession, Dave could only shake his head in disbelief. It was there too, that photos of the mutilated body of Jennifer Ross had been found, establishing without a doubt Larry Brandt's role in her death.

Looking back, Dave recalled how he and Larry had discussed the gruesome murder. They had accepted it gratefully as a favour from the gods. A random sex killing had been Larry Brandt's conclusion: by some obsessed fan . . . the curious humour of the criminal mind.

And Suzie Hawkins . . . It was the first time Dave had heard the name. Larry must have picked it up via the wire tap and kept it to himself. Traces of her blood had been found in the trunk of Larry's car . . .

Having been given a lead, the Feds were working overtime. They knew about Tess Jordan, the circumstances of her birth, her father . . . But it was the more recent events they were keen to probe now: Les Donovan . . . the fire at WLS . . . illegal wire tapping . . .

Dave Arnell fielded their questions like the expert he was. After all, how could anything be proved? All they could try to pin on him was the cover-up all those years before.

But his political instinct told him he was safe. Better a dead scapegoat than a live one. A corpse couldn't be questioned about the suspicious death of the ex-cop, nor about the arson attempt at World Link Studios. Larry Brandt would carry the can.

At least, he thought, as he started his car and pulled away from the FBI building, one mystery had been cleared up. He knew now who had been behind the initial threats to Jennifer Ross. For Walter Conroy too, it seemed, there had been a lot at stake...

But the gruesome murder was without doubt the work of the madman Dave had called a colleague for over twenty-five years.

The series of staggering disclosures coming on top of Robert Madigan's surprise resignation had thrown the Party into chaos. But Dave figured that wasn't his problem any longer. His career was finished. He had just one more task to perform for the Madigan family.

He took the exit for the freeway north to Adelle's estate. She was still in a state of shock about her son's resignation, and what Dave had to tell her would do nothing to improve her emotional state. He had hoped she would never have to know, but the least he could do now was tell her before she heard it from some smartass reporters.

His hands tightened around the steering wheel. How would Adelle handle being told that Tess Jordan, the woman she loathed, was her son's half-sister?

The cabin belonged to an old friend of Chris. It was the haven they needed until the immediate uproar in the media began to abate.

America had been rocked by the revelations of love

and murder, of political intrigue and official cover-ups. Reporters from all over the world had converged on LA, hungry for the story of the century. Every evening the nation sat glued to the television news eager for the next sensational detail.

The discovery that Tess Jordan was the secret love child of Elizabeth Eden and Tom Madigan sent the media into a frenzy. Bombarded for interviews, Tess responded with a short dignified statement through the studio's own PR department.

But it was not enough for the frantic hordes of ravenous press. With her daily routine almost impossible to maintain, Tess realised she would have to find somewhere to lie low until the scores of sensational headlines eventually drifted from the front pages of the nation's newspapers.

That's when Chris had come up with the cabin in the Catskills. Suitably disguised, and flying under different names, they had slipped quietly out of LA.

For three weeks they had enjoyed the clear mountain air, the peace and solitude. As the days passed, both had time to ponder and come to terms with the astounding events of the last few months.

For Chris, the task had been to forgive himself for his 'dumbass stupidity' as he'd put it to Tess.

It was a topic he returned to often as they sat on the porch in the evening looking up at the clear starry skies.

'I knew there was something niggling at the back of my mind, but it took me too long to realise what it was,' he said, shaking his head in self-recrimination. 'If I'd thought of it earlier, you might never have had to endure what you did. It wasn't till I heard that news report on my way to the meeting with Dave Arnell, that I finally saw the light.'

Tess knew now what he meant. Driving to his appointment with Arnell, Chris had heard the report on the discovery of a body at the rear of a roadside diner on the outskirts of Dennison. The woman had been strangled. She was identified as Suzie Hawkins.

Chris knew immediately that something was very wrong. And almost simultaneously, as if the news of Suzie Hawkins's death had activated a trigger, he found the answer to what had been nagging at the edges of his mind.

At last he'd remembered the one point that hadn't jelled after his initial meeting with Arnell and Brandt.

'An ex-cop with a grudge against the force . . .' That was how Larry Brandt had referred to Les Donovan. But if there'd been no cover-up, how had the campaign manager known about Donovan and the fact that he carried a grudge? He blamed himself for not picking up the slip earlier.

'No one's to blame, Chris.' Tess did her best to comfort him. 'Brandt's obsession and it's terrible aftermath obviously caused something inside him to snap. Once he and Arnell received the report revealing I was Elizabeth's daughter, Larry Brandt wouldn't have rested until he'd got to me one way or another.'

Eyes hardening, Chris replied, 'Well, they'll never touch Arnell. He'll get off scot-free. I'm certain he was responsible for Donovan's accident, *and* the fire at the studios, but of course there's no way either can be proved.'

'At least Conroy's role is certain,' countered Tess.

Once they had a lead it hadn't taken the police long to trace the two-bit thug Walter Conroy had hired to try to run Jennifer Ross off the road. They were convinced too that he was also responsible for the threatening note delivered in the flowers.

Chris shook his head. 'Arnell and Brandt musn't have been able to believe their luck when Jennifer Ross had that accident . . . someone else doing their dirty work for them.'

He turned to look at Tess. Her face was a shadowy profile in the growing dusk. 'It's obvious they were digging into your past hoping to find something they could use to shut us up. But when they turned up that amazing bombshell the irony was they couldn't use it against you without hurting Robert Madigan himself.'

Robert Madigan... Tess repeated the name silently to herself. Her half-brother.

The phone call had come just hours before she'd left LA. 'I'd like to meet you,' he'd said simply.

But Tess had needed time to think about that... Time was what she and Chris had over the days and nights that followed. They ate, talked, walked, covering miles over the trails, and slowly the healing began. While Chris began to judge himself less harshly, Tess gradually overcame the trauma of her terrifying encounter with Larry Brandt.

And each night they lay entwined in each other's arms, more grateful than ever for what they had come so close to losing.

'I love you Tess. I want you beside me all my life.' Chris whispered the words in her hair as moonbeams filtered across the floor and the scent of cyprus pine filled the bedroom.

She felt her heart swell with joy. 'I've been waiting for you so long, my darling... '

Like the rest of America, Carl Harris had stayed glued to the network news channels for every detail of the unfolding story on the Elizabeth Eden/Madigan conspiracy.

His emotions were mixed.

While suffused with relief that his own secret seemed unlikely to come to light, at the same time he burned with indignant anger at the way he'd been duped.

The facts of the story proved that his cousin had done nothing to deserve the thirty thousand dollars Carl had coughed up. He knew now that the threats, the fire, the murder — none had been Gino's doing. Yet he'd been happy to take the credit and the money.

The actor's face burned beneath his tan, and his lips were set tight.

Fuckin' family. They could never be trusted.

Adelle Madigan could stand it no longer. Everything she had counted on was gone — her son, her future, her reputation and her status. She could no longer bring herself to read the newspapers or watch television.

The cover-up meant nothing to her. What was so mortifying, so totally humiliating, was the fact that all America was talking about her husband's affair with that notorious bitch — and the fact that, years before, the union had produced a child.

No wonder, Adelle thought fiercely, old man Madigan had rushed his son so quickly to the altar with her. A messy affair with some pregnant starlet wouldn't have done much to advance Tom Madigan's political career.

Yet in the end, the whole sordid story had been revealed, and now *she* was the one who would have to live with the innuendo and humiliation till the end of her days.

Well, Adelle had no intention of doing that.

To spare her any further public scrutiny, the formalities were taken care of in the VIP room of LA International Airport.

Then, her face almost hidden behind huge dark glasses, her hair covered by a Hermes scarf, Adelle slipped into the limousine for the short drive across the tarmac to the waiting aircraft. The jet had been provided by one of her resilient and long-time admirers; it would, Adelle hoped, take her to a new, and hopefully less public life in Europe.

Dave held out his hand to assist her up the metal steps and Adelle managed to return his smile. At least, she thought with relief, she still had Dave.

At the aircraft entrance she let him move inside ahead of her. Turning around, Adelle Madigan paused to take a last bitter look at the country she hoped she would never see again.

CHAPTER

36

A wave of excitement swept around the packed auditorium. Across the world, millions of viewers shared in the anticipation of the moment.

On centre stage the well-known actor ripped open the envelope. He took a deep breath, and in the mellifluous tones that had earned him a fortune, announced the Best Actress Award.

'And the winner is ... Suzanne Baird, for *A Woman of Our Time!*'

The vast auditorium exploded in uproar. From a row near the front of the stage, a statuesque brunette in a red, close-fitting gown rose to her feet.

Suzanne Baird felt as if she were floating on air. She had done it! An unknown, picked from the hundreds of hopefuls eager to play the role of Elizabeth Eden in the movie of her amazing life, Suzanne had achieved the highest accolade of her profession.

Eyes brimming with tears, she accepted the Oscar and turned to face her peers. It seemed as if the pandemonium would never end. The movie which had come so close to never being made, had scooped the cream of that years Oscars — Best Director, Best Screenplay, and now, Best Actress. The project born in the face of such enormous odds, and resulting in such staggering revelations, had captured the imagination of all Americans.

The true story of Elizabeth Eden's life had broken all previous box-office records. It had damaged reputations and exposed the guilty, both alive and dead. Yet among the new generation of stars and starmakers there was widespread acclaim for the purging of a system that had destroyed so many promising careers. It was generally agreed that the exposé was long overdue, and there was little sympathy for those tainted by the movie's revelations — those conspicuous that evening, by their absence.

At last the uproar abated, and with confidence and aplomb Suzanne Baird began her speech of thanks. She knew that nothing she achieved in the future would ever compare to this moment.

'... and finally, I would like to pay tribute to the courage, determination, and love of Tess Jordan who was determined to see this important movie made. She is her mother's daughter ... and certainly a woman of our time.'

The applause thundered again as the spotlights picked out Tess among the rows of seats.

Beside her, her husband clutched her hand. Chris's face was shining with pride and love. 'Stand up, darling. Take a bow. You deserve it.'

On her other side, Nick was also urging her to acknowledge the stupendous acclaim of her peers.

And after a moment, she did. Rising to her feet, a tall slim figure in a gold dress, she smiled her thanks to an industry whose capacity for adulation was as powerful and dangerous as its capacity for destruction ...

This is for you Mom ... For all you missed, and suffered, and endured ... Tess whispered the words silently in her heart.

EPILOGUE

The post-awards party was held at the Havelock mansion.

Mike Havelock was grinning from ear to ear as he accepted the effusive congratulations of his guests.

Thanks to *A Woman of Our Time*, WLS was back on top. The box-office receipts were enormous, and it seemed as if everyone in town — agents, stars, writers, directors — was keen to work with WLS.

Mike looked across the room to where Tess was the centre of attention of an admiring group. He had never doubted her abilities when he had appointed her President of WLS — but her knowledge and expertise had far exceeded even his expectations. *A Woman of Our Time* was the big one, but there were numerous other projects she had also steered to success. Tess had been determined to give the movie-going public something more than car chases, violence, and subordinate, manipulated women.

'Movies have such an enormous influence, Mike,' she had so often told him, 'it's important we get our message right.'

Before he turned away, the owner of WLS saw Chris Stanley move to his wife's side. Mike smiled to himself. It was plain for all to see that the guy made Tess very happy. And they were a dynamic team. Chris Stanley's book on the Elizabeth Eden story, released to coincide with the movie, had raced to the top of the best-seller lists.

Just moments later, Mike felt a tap on his arm. It was Tess.

'Can I have a word with you, Mike? In private?'

'Sure, Tess. Come into the library.'

He closed the door, offered her a fresh drink which she refused. But when Mike Havelock heard what she had to say, he felt he needed one himself.

'You're *what*...?' He paled. 'Surely you're not serious?'

But Tess nodded. She had known it would be a shock, but had decided it was best to tell him as soon as possible. From the talk among the guests, WLS was going to be developing some major projects in the near future. She wanted Mike to know exactly where she stood.

'You're getting *out* of the industry? At once?' His tone, his face, revealed his incredulity. 'But — to do *what*, for God's sake, Tess?'

Those direct green eyes looked unwaveringly into his. 'I'm going back into law, Mike. I'm going to do what I always wanted to do — work for those who lack a voice.'

She saw the stunned expression on his face and wondered how much more astonished Mike Havelock would be when he learned that she was starting a law firm with her half-brother, Robert Madigan...

'How did he take it?' Chris was watching for her as she rejoined the party.

'I think he's still trying to understand.'

Her husband looked at her for a long moment, love and respect gleaming in his eyes. Then he put an arm around her waist. 'Nick and Helen are leaving. They've asked us back for a nightcap. Are you ready to go?'

'That sounds wonderful. After talking to Mike I don't really feel as if I belong here any longer.'

They moved outside into the cool night air. Their car

arrived and they climbed inside. As they made their way down the drive Tess could hear the muffled sounds of the party they had left behind. The sounds of the movers and shakers, the talented and the acclaimed, the users and the used ...

When she had determined to make the true story of her mother's life, little had she guessed how much she would uncover. Or how much she would gain, she thought warmly, moving closer to her husband.

'Any regrets?' Chris whispered, stroking her hair.

'No.' Tess answered softly. 'None at all.'

Jennifer Bacia
Angel of Honour

In a world of passion, power and revenge, the price of freedom is sometimes the ultimate sacrifice...

Her mother was a legendary screen goddess. Her father was the President.

Wild, beautiful, passionate, she rebels against her convent upbringing to pursue secret desires and forbidden pleasures.

Rejecting the land of her birth for fame and fortune in Europe, she loses herself in the decadent high society of Paris and London...until a single, shattering event changes her life forever.

Her name is Noella de Bartez.

Angel of Honour is her story – the electrifying tale of her rise to power, of the men who loved her, and the one who betrayed her...